Baggage

Shelia Bolt Rudesill

To Bud, my very own Prince Charming

Acknowledgments

The stories of friends, patients, and my relationships with them made this book possible. The characters, *Carolyn* and *Sarah Without an H* were inspired by one caring NICU RN, Carolyn Hardy, who reminds me of a modern-day Florence Nightingale.

1

In two days, on Christmas Day, Holly Gaynor would turn forty—both an optimistic and hard-earned milestone, much more of a milestone than turning sixteen or even twenty-one. She suspected that this birthday would bring something so incomprehensible that she could hardly stand the anticipation. As optimistic as she felt, she hung in limbo, not certain if she wanted to pass through a portal that could take her God knows where. Holly stretched then shook out her hair before she sprang from her bed. She shrieked when she opened the curtains. The celebration had begun!

Unexpected freezing rain had swept across central North Carolina the night before. Gray clouds began to gather just after sunset, and sleet peacefully tapped against Holly's windows by midnight. The change in weather hadn't interrupted her lighthearted slumber or her blissful anticipation of the events of the next few days. Holly watched as delicate flakes floated from the dusky sky—three, maybe four inches had accumulated already. White crystals covered everything in sight and mounded like beehives on the tops of lamp posts. She welcomed the snow in this southern town of Chapel Hill, North Carolina where she'd grown up. She'd experienced too many spring-like Christmases and her gifts of snow saucers and crocheted beanies with pom-poms had seemed ridiculous. The last time it snowed at Christmas in Chapel Hill had been three years before she was born, and she'd wished and hoped and prayed for a white Christmas ever since.

"My fortieth year. This snow is just the beginning." Holly stood straighter and jutted her chin. She raised an imaginary baton and strutted in front of the window. "I'm ready to march through that snow and into something absolutely outrageous."

"What are you doing, Mama?" Meg, Holly's sleepy eyed seventeen-year-old daughter asked."

Holly began singing, "I'm dreaming of a white Christmas…" She stepped away from the window to give Meg a full view.

"Snow. Oh, my gosh, Mama." Meg raced to the window. "We're going to have a white Christmas for my last Christmas home. Isn't it gorgeous, like living in a world of crystals?"

"How about a walk before breakfast?"

"Let me just pull on some sweats and grab a coat and I'll be right with you."

Holly did the same and the two sat side-by-side on the bottom of the stairs to put on their boots and wool gloves. Holly grabbed her Nikon and followed Meg out the front door. When she switched on the long line of blue lights that outlined the house, Meg stopped on the bottom step, legs separated slightly, arms straight, and raised to the sky as if she were in a trance. Holly snapped a picture of Meg's back against a blanket of snowy crystals that reflected silver and blue in the gray light.

"Listen," Meg said softly. "There's not a sound." She turned around with a look of awe.

Holly snapped another picture.

Meg stepped off the front porch and crunched through the accumulating snow. "Take a picture from here, Mama." Meg pointed toward the front window. "Look at the way the snow

2

is reflecting the Christmas lights. It's your dream come true, Mama—a winter wonderland for your birthday."

While Holly took a collage of the wintry scene, Meg packed a handful of snow into a ball and hurled it through the air, hitting Holly in the temple. Holly secured the camera over her neck and one shoulder and stooped to gather a mound of snow. Meg ran toward the street to dodge an attack but Holly's snowball hit her square in the back. Holly quickly gathered another mound and threw it, but Meg sidestepped it. Before Meg could pack a second handful, Holly rushed up from behind and grabbed Meg for balance. They both hit the ground squealing. Holly scooped a handful of snow and slipped it down the back of Meg's sweatshirt.

"Stop. I give. I'm freezing." Meg squealed. She managed to gather her own handful of slush and stick it down the front of her mother's shirt when Holly didn't get up quickly.

The snow slid down Holly's chest as she pulled away. "You brat." Holly tried to hold the wet shirt away from her skin.

"You started it." Meg struggled to stand and regain her balance in the slippery slush while Holly giggled at her attempt.

They continued their walk as the snow mounded. Meg slipped on her butt and sailed down the sidewalk, but Holly's fingers were so cold and stiff she couldn't push the shutter to capture Meg's embarrassed joy.

Holly thawed her hands under warm water from the kitchen faucet then tuned the radio to a station that played nonstop Christmas music. She had a batch of sugar cookies ready for the oven when Meg entered the kitchen. Holly had set the teakettle on the stove to boil water for hot chocolate. The whistle on the kettle changed from a sizzle to a shrill shriek before Meg removed it from the burner.

"Look out the window, Mama." Meg held the teakettle in

midair. "The snow is really coming down now. Let's build a snowman this afternoon." Her smile was just as radiant as it had been the first time they'd built a snowman, twelve years earlier, when Marcus was alive.

"Good thing we don't have to go anywhere." Holly stood next to Meg and looked out into the backyard. A bluebird uncovered a bright red berry in a snowy branch of the holly tree then flew away with it in his beak. A pair of cardinals lit on an icy branch, heads twitching fervently, feathers ruffling. Holly opened the cupboard moving cans of tuna and tomato soup until she found a bag of sunflower seeds. She pushed open the kitchen window, scaring the scarlet birds into flight then scattered the nuts and seeds as far away as she could throw them. The sudden burst of cold air turned her hands and cheeks ruby-red. She took in an icy breath of crisp air feeling lightheaded and giddy. Almost as soon as she closed the window, the cardinals returned to begin picking breakfast from the deep cushion of snow. "Aren't they beautiful, so bright against the snow?"

"Want me to get your camera?"

"No. I just want to watch them for now." Holly screwed up her lips, blew a sigh, and began biting the tip of her magenta thumbnail without worrying about destroying her fresh manicure.

"I'll be right back." Meg flashed a sly smile, set the kettle back on the stove to simmer then slid around the corner to the living room in her stocking feet. She returned with a large box, gift-wrapped in birthday paper and bows.

"Is this what I think it is?"

Meg smiled. "It's your birthday present, but I think you need it today."

Holly ripped the ribbons and paper off the box. "Yes. Perfect. You, my darling, are the perfect daughter. How did you know I wanted a bird feeder?"

"Because I'm a mind reader?"

4

Holly pulled a copper bird feeder from the box. "Thanks, honey, but we don't have any—"

"Birdseed? Yes, we do." Meg smiled proudly. "Just take a look in the dryer."

"The dryer? The clothes dryer?"

"Where else could I hide a twenty-five-pound bag of sunflower seeds? I knew we wouldn't be doing any laundry until after Christmas."

"Awesome," was all Holly could think to say.

"I thought we could hang it from the oak tree," Meg said pointing to the kitchen window, "so we can watch the birds from the kitchen and the deck."

"Perfect. That's the most beautiful tree in the world, you know. I think that glorious oak, with its shelter and protection, is the main reason I wanted to live in this house."

"Mama. Shelter and protection are synonyms."

"Sorry. Just let me fill this up and get my boots. I want to hang it right now."

"You're going to put a ladder in six inches of snow? You'll kill yourself, for heaven's sake." Meg clapped her hands on her hips. "I'm not going to help you. Why don't you wait for a man to come over?"

"Such a sexist statement from my own daughter." Holly pulled on her wet coat and boots and headed for the garage.

"Don't slip on the steps...there's a layer of ice under the snow...remember?"

Holly spoke slowly, as if each word had six syllables. "I will hold onto the rail, darling." She flashed Meg a defiant grin.

Meg covered her face with her hands and turned to hide the smile she was certain would turn into a screeching laugh the minute her mother tried to skate across the backyard. To Meg's surprising relief, Holly made it to the spot beneath the branch she'd chosen with both the ladder and the bird feeder safely in hand. After Holly stabilized the ladder against a rock,

Meg pulled the neck of her sweatshirt up over her eyes, sneaking a peek every few seconds.

"Hooray," Holly shouted as she hung the feeder securely on a branch.

Meg watched as her mother took slow, steady steps down the ladder. When she reached the bottom step, she turned to Meg and smiled. Then, as she twisted to step to the ground, her feet went out from under her and she fell flat on her face.

Meg pushed the window open. "Make a snow angel while you're down there, why don't you?" she shouted as her mother did just that.

Holly stepped inside wearing a look of triumph. "Bet that's the first prone snow angel you've ever seen."

Meg clicked her tongue. "And you think I need instant gratification."

"It's beautiful, isn't it?"

"The snow angel?"

"No, darling, the feeder in the tree. Look. A cardinal and a goldfinch already. Poor things may have starved to death."

"God, Mama. Am I the mother or the child?"

"Right now, you're the mother, and a pretty darned good one, I must say."

"Well, you're not minding me very well, that's for sure." Meg giggled then kissed her mother on the cheek. "What a wonderful day and we haven't even had breakfast yet."

As soon as Holly dried off again, she and Meg shared a festive breakfast of steaming hot chocolate with gooey marshmallows and fresh from the oven sugar cookies.

After breakfast, Meg set a bowl of chocolate ganache on the counter next to the four layers of dark chocolate cake she'd baked the evening before. She gazed up at Holly. "Too bad your birthday and Christmas are on the same day."

"No, my darling, it's too bad Christmas isn't your birthday."

6

Meg grimaced. "Why?"

"Because you're the best gift anyone ever gave me, that's why."

"What about Daddy?"

Holly pulled a holiday cookie tin close to her heart. "If it wasn't for Daddy, I wouldn't have you."

"But you didn't have Daddy for long and you've had me for seventeen years."

Meg stirred the ganache once more and spread it over the bottom layer of the cake before placing the next layer on top. "Daddy's been dead for ten years. You need a man to take care of you."

"I beg your pardon, missy, I've been taking care of the two of us quite well for the past ten years. I didn't need a man for that."

"Mama, I didn't mean it that way. It's just that, well, what are you going to do when I go off to college in the fall?"

"I'll get a puppy. Honestly, Meg, I'll be just fine."

"Well then, since you're so good at taking care of us, maybe you need a man to take care of as well."

"That's something I definitely don't want. Besides, no man will ever be as great as your father."

"How do you know that? You don't date. You don't even have any male friends."

"I have Brody."

"Brody is Lisa's husband. You can't date your best friend's husband."

"Who says I want to date Brody?"

"Mama." Meg stared at Holly, mouth agape.

"Just calm down." Holly watched Meg spread the last of the ganache on the third cake layer.

"It's just that—"

"It's just that Prince Charming will have to beat my front door down before I'll marry again."

"Quick. Help me," Meg squealed as she lifted the last

7

cake layer. "It's gonna crack."

The buzzing of the doorbell added to the frantic attempt to assemble the cake and keep it from breaking apart like a calving glacier.

"Damn, who could that be? Anybody who wanted to drop in would just walk in, not ring the damn doorbell." Holly held the fragile sides of the flimsy layer and working as one with Meg, guided it to the top of the cake before it crumbled to bits. "Just a minute," she yelled as the ringing stopped and a loud knock echoed into the kitchen.

"I'll get it." Meg licked the ganache from her knuckles and headed for the front door. She returned with a smug smile. "It's for you, Mama. It's Prince Charming."

Holly and Meg had moved into a relatively new subdivision in Chapel Hill at the end of the previous summer. The house and neighborhood were perfect as far as they were concerned. Maple trees lined the streets providing shade for manicured front lawns, while rose vines climbed up white picket fences. Children and dogs played in the shadows of deciduous trees in graceful back yards. Hiking trails meandered through a dense green forest just behind their house. Ferns and delicate lady slipper shared the space with deer and nut gathering squirrels.

The first time Holly walked one of the trails, she half expected to find leprechauns and fairies just around the next bend. On that still summer afternoon, she had recalled a quaint village in England she'd read about when she was a girl, a place where she'd imagined herself intermingling with talking animals dressed in gowns and trouser suits with suspenders.

The house had been on the market for just two days when Barbara Miller from Century 21 called to make an appointment to show it to Holly. Barbara suspected it was the house of Holly's romantic dreams, and when Holly and Meg viewed it, her suspicion proved correct. By the end of the day, the owners had accepted Holly's offer and she and Barbara toasted the deal over a bottle of champagne on Holly's dilapidated back porch on Cameron Court. That house, the one she'd lived in since the day she'd married Marcus, was within walking distance of her job as an administrative assistant at the School of Public Health at the University of North Carolina, just a few blocks from downtown Chapel Hill. Over the years the area had become flooded with students and noise and crime. This new house, in suburbia, would only be a five-minute commute to her office.

Holly reveled in the fact that Meg would spend her last year at home in the new house, allowing her to leave her scent and make memories that Holly could cherish once the empty-nest phase of her life began. Holly would have Meg all to herself for one more year. She'd vowed to make the most of it.

When Holly turned the corner into the hallway and saw a tall attractive man in Levi's and a gray University of Iowa sweatshirt standing on the front porch, the vision struck her broadside. Meg hadn't been joking. She knew he'd seen her surprise by the way he smiled while raising his eyebrows. He looked like a man who could finish eighteen holes of golf without breaking a sweat. The hint of a receding hairline, with slight graying at the temples, told Holly that he had to be about her age. Good thing he was dressed so casually. Had he been wearing a uniform of some kind, she might have peed her pants.

"May I help you?" Holly stammered.

The man smiled like a precocious child. "Please forgive the interruption, but Barbara Miller told me you sell beadwork necklaces."

"I do. I mean, yes, I do beadwork on fabric." Her words twisted in her mouth as tiny beads of sweat formed on her scalp.

"I'm doing my Christmas shopping today...a little late,"

he said with a chuckle that lit up his blue eyes. "Barbara covets your designs. I would like to purchase one for her for Christmas. You do remember Barbara, don't you?"

Holly grabbed at her apron. This man is Barbara's prince, not mine, she thought taking in a breath of the frigid air. "Yes, she helped us buy this house." A rush of snow swept the carpet. "I'm so sorry. Won't you come in? How rude of me to let you stand there in the cold."

The man wiped wet snow from his shoes, stepped inside, and closed the door. "How rude of me to barge in on you. Am I interrupting something?"

"Just baking. Come with me while I check the progress."

When they entered the kitchen, Meg stood up from the barstool. "Tada," she sang as she spread her arms before the cake, which she had completely drenched with the dark chocolate glaze.

"It's gorgeous, honey." Holly applauded then held her palms together, resting her index fingers on her chin. "Ah, Meg," she said, feeling like a teenager introducing a new boyfriend to her parents, "I'd like to introduce you to Mr.—"

"Prince, Charles Prince. You can call me Charlie."

Meg beamed. "See, Mama. I told you."

Holly stood starry-eyed for a moment then turned to Meg with a stern look. "I'm sorry, Mr. Prince—" Holly burst out laughing so hard she couldn't speak. She tried to take in a deep breath but wheezed and choked on her copious saliva. That was new to her—drooling over a man.

Meg couldn't stop laughing, either. She wrapped her arms across her waist and held her sides.

Charlie chuckled, caught up in the hysteria of a joke he didn't understand. He looked down at his blue and gray athletic shoes and then up his body. He touched his chest with both hands. "Is everything okay? Have I come undone or something?"

"Please forgive us." Holly jiggled her head, dislodging a

lock of hair from a loose clasp. "Charlie, this is my wonderful daughter, Meg," she said as she tucked the hair behind her ear.

Meg stretched to her full height, her face bright. She reached out and shook Charlie's hand. Holly was glad that she didn't genuflect.

"Pleased to meet you both." Charlie turned to Holly. "And you are?"

"You don't know my name?"

"No. Barbara wouldn't be so unprofessional as to give it out, even to me. I looked at this house before you did, apparently. You put an offer down first and got it. She just told me once that 'the woman who bought my house' did some incredible beadwork that she really liked."

"That's true," Holly said.

"I've been at a complete loss as to what to get her for Christmas and it just clicked in my head as I drove past. I know it's terribly forward of me to have stopped, but…"

"That's fine. I'm Holly, Holly Gaynor. It's a pleasure to meet you."

"How did you get here?" Meg asked.

Charlie glanced out the window. "You mean the roads?"

"I mean, most people can't drive in snow in North Carolina."

"You're right. Most drive the same as they do in the pouring rain."

Meg giggled. "You mean like they're racing at Le Mans?" Charlie smiled.

"And they spin out of control and land in a ditch or, heaven forbid, crash head-on into another car," Holly said. "I bet the EMTs will have a time of it today."

"I do my best to drive defensively, or at least to try to stay out of everyone's way. Even at that, I slip-slided here."

"Aren't you afraid you'll get stranded somewhere?" Holly asked, half-expecting him to get stranded right there.

Meg looked up from the mixer, her eyes twinkling. "You

could stay here."

"Meg..." Holly tried to stare her down without laughing. Like mother, like daughter, she thought.

"I work for a law firm in Raleigh and live near Pittsboro, so I have to drive in whatever the weather throws at me." Charlie gestured toward the cake in an apparent effort to change the subject. "So, what's this?"

"Tomorrow night we celebrate Christmas." Meg swung her still-damp ponytail over her shoulder and looked into Charlie's eyes through her long bangs. "The next day, on Christmas, we celebrate Mama's birthday. This masterpiece is Mama's birthday cake."

"While you two chat, I'll get the necklaces." Holly washed her hands at the sink and dried them on her apron on the way down the hall. She could hear their conversation from her sewing room.

"Is Holly really your mother?"

Meg squinted at Charlie. "Yes, I'm pretty certain she is, although we haven't had our DNA checked. Why?"

"I thought you looked more like sisters."

"Ha. Mama would love to hear that. We do look alike. We even have the same cat eyes."

"Cat eyes?" He took a step closer.

"Yeah, look." Meg opened her eyes wide, revealing dark-brown irises with streaks of gold and slightly oblong rather than round pupils. "My grandmother, my mom's mother, has the same oddity. We should have astigmatism, but we don't. We're just weird that way."

"Interesting, I'll have to make a side-by-side comparison when your mom gets back."

Holly's stomach flipped like a gymnast before she felt a pang of guilt that made her stop short in front of a framed faded photograph of Marcus that she'd taken on their honeymoon. He stood smiling at the foot of an ancient ruin in

Provence, smiling as though he would live forever. After ten years, his face remained in sharp focus in Holly's mind. She had immortalized him with photographs that decorated just about every room of the house, as well as her desk at work. Because he lived on in her mind, she hadn't given a thought to another man being able to arouse or excite her in the way Charlie, Prince Charming, just had.

What silliness. Prince Charming. She wondered if Barbara had mentioned the prices of the necklaces. If not, Charlie was in for a big surprise. If so, they must be pretty damned serious about each other. She blew air into her cheeks until she looked like a chipmunk then blew it out slowly and huffed.

"Charlie, come into the dining room and I'll show you the necklaces." Holly opened a plastic storage box and unwrapped her handiwork.

"Beautiful. Intricate designs. Much different than I'd imagined."

"And what was that?"

"Beads strung on chain...something like that. Not sewn onto fabric. These are pieces of art. Art to wear."

"Thanks." Holly couldn't remember a finer compliment.

Charlie touched the tiny beads. "Are you a belly dancer?"

"Ah, no. Why do you ask?"

"I'm sorry. I just assumed. Barbara said that you made belly dance belts as well, so I...wondered." Charlie winked then looked back at the necklaces.

Holly felt faint. She tried to speak without hesitation or excitement in her voice wondering if the wink had been flirtatious. "Actually, Barbara saw a set of belly dance belts that I made for a troupe in Cary. Most of my projects aren't that ambitious."

Charlie ran his hand over the necklaces until he stopped on one in violet and purple. "Which one do you think Barbara

13

would like? I know she likes purple."

Holly picked up one in purple and teal. "This one. I remember her trying this one on. She liked the colors. It seems to be everyone's favorite, yet it hasn't sold."

"Because it's the most expensive?" He picked it up and held it at arm's length. "It really is beautiful."

"So, Barbara told you my prices?"

"Just that she couldn't afford them."

"This one is two hundred and seventy-five dollars. I keep lowering the price. It's a good deal."

Charlie closed his eyes a moment then looked at Holly. His blue eyes had turned cloudy gray.

She felt a lump grow in her throat until she thought she might need the Heimlich maneuver.

"What about the purple and violet one?" Charlie looked over the remaining necklaces yet kept hold of the first one he'd picked up.

Holly cleared her throat. "That one is three-fifty."

"What about the blue one?"

"Ah, my favorite and the most expensive."

"How expensive?"

"My asking price is four-fifty, but I could cut you a deal."

"Like what?"

"Well, since you're a friend of Barbara's, I can sell it for half if you mow my lawn for a year." Holly smiled when Charlie cocked his head, feeling so dizzy she had to hold onto a chair.

"Are you serious?"

"Yes, but honestly, the one you won't let go of is the one Barbara would choose."

"Then I guess I'll take it. Do you take credit cards?"

"No, this is just a hobby."

"Will you take a check? Can you wrap it for me?"

"Yes and yes."

"Have a seat. I'll be right back." Holly gathered the

necklaces and left the room. Prince Charming didn't seem that available. She closed her eyes tightly trying to fight back the hurricane she'd suppressed when Marcus died from leukemia just three months after his first symptom. Hadn't she grieved enough? Is that why she was grieving over an impossible relationship with Charlie, someone she didn't even know?

Charlie and Meg were chatting in the kitchen when Holly returned.

"Would you like some coffee or eggnog or a glass of wine while I wrap this?" Holly spoke to Charlie but looked at Meg and sucked air through her teeth.

"Coffee would be great," he said.

"Great." Holly concentrated on wrapping the necklace and avoided looking at Meg. She squelched a joyful expression.

Meg pulled a stool out from under the bar. "You can sit here, Charlie. I'll pour the coffee. Do you take sugar or cream?"

"Neither, thanks. Just coffee. I guess you can say I'm a purist."

"Did you hear that, Mama? He drinks his coffee the same way your father taught you."

Holly smiled without looking up while Meg filled two holiday mugs with fresh coffee—Santa for Holly, Rudolph for Charlie. She set the mugs on the bar in front of them and went back to whisking a bowl of egg whites.

"Smart man, your father," Charlie said, scooting the stool closer to the bar. He watched intently while Holly opened a silver gift bag and wrapped the necklace in white tissue paper covered in silver glitter. With shaking hands, she pushed several sheets of the paper into the bag, leaving the ends sticking out of the top. When she finished, the presentation looked as fabulous as the gift tucked inside.

"Meg tells me she's an only child."

Holly glanced at Meg before meeting Charlie's gaze.

"That's correct."

"I was about to tell Meg that I have two daughters about her age. Jordan is sixteen and a junior at Northwood. Jessica is eighteen and in her first term at the University of Illinois in Champaign."

"Illinois? I have a scholarship to Northwestern in Evanston in the fall." Meg stood proud. "That's just up the road, practically, from Champaign."

"What a small world." Charlie reached out to shake Meg's hand. "Congratulations on the scholarship."

"Thanks. It's for lacrosse." She shook Charlie's hand, leaving it greasy from the butter she'd been spreading on a cookie sheet. She raised her shoulders and giggled. "Sorry about that. Let me get you a wet paper towel."

"Lacrosse, huh?"

"That's right. I haven't decided on a major yet, but I love playing lacrosse."

"You must be all muscle under those baggy sweats." Charlie covered his eyes with one hand. "Excuse me, I wasn't being fresh." He looked at Holly apologetically. "What I meant to say is that lacrosse is a rough, fast-moving game. You'd have to be in good physical condition to play well enough to get a scholarship."

Meg smiled without separating her lips. She pulled up one sleeve, made a fist, and pumped up her biceps. "I know what you were trying to say. Don't worry. No offense taken."

Holly sat back, reveling in the animated conversation between Meg and Charlie. Like most only children, Meg wasn't afraid to converse with adults. The thought of Meg and Charlie's daughter at neighboring universities struck a smile across her befuddled mind.

"Your daughter…Jordan?" Meg squinted.

"Yes, Jordan."

"Does she play sports?"

"No, I'm afraid she's somewhat of a loner. She likes

horses better than she likes most people."

"Why?" Meg leaned back against the kitchen sink.

"That's a long story and a sore subject to boot. She tried out for cheerleading, but she was so awkward that most of the girls laughed at her. Needless to say, she didn't make the squad, so she gave up on cheerleading as well as socializing in general."

"I'm sorry." Meg spoke kindly. "Not that I know much about disappointments. Mom says I'm leading a charmed life, so I'm trying to learn about people who don't have as good a life as I do. Was her sport cheerleading?"

"Not at all. She was trying to carry on a family tradition."

"Was her mother a cheerleader?" Meg asked.

"For about sixteen years. The girls' mother got them into cheerleading about as soon as they could walk. They did cheers and lifts and flips all over the living room."

"Wow. Did you hear that, Mama?"

"Impressive." Holly realized that he'd said, "the girls' mother" not "my wife". She glanced at his naked left hand.

"Jessica cheered all through school. She took cheerleading clinics last fall and will try out for the varsity squad in April. She thinks she's a shoo-in."

"Is she?" Holly asked.

Charlie shrugged. "She thinks she's pretty hot stuff. I don't know. It might do her some good to get knocked down a peg."

Meg laughed. "I know some cheerleaders. They date the football and basketball stars and are always the queen of something."

"That's my Jess. If she's not the queen, she's on the queen's court."

Meg let out a humph. "So was her mom the same?"

"Exactly. She cheered from middle-school through college." Charlie lifted the mug and smiled at the Rudolph on it. "If she wasn't the queen of something, she managed to steal

17

the show."

Holly suddenly felt inferior. She'd never been a queen of anything, but come to think of it, she'd never wanted to be the center of attention, either. Poor Jordan, if she's trying to live up to those legends. Holly changed the subject. "Does Jordan have a horse?"

"No. She's experimenting with riding styles and saddles at a ranch down the road near Siler City. I think she's leaning toward dressage. She wants to ride bareback without a bridle, which surprised me. In cheerleading, she was the one who always cracked her knee on the coffee table or stumbled backward into the wall. Poor kid grew up with an ice bag instead of a teddy bear."

Holly tilted her head. "Oh, that's too bad."

"She got so used to all the bumps and bruises that came with cheerleading that she's fearless on horseback."

"Doesn't she want a horse of her own?" Holly was glad to be talking about the daughter and not the wife.

"Of course she does. A handsome three-year-old gelding bay is waiting for her, but Santa won't deliver him until Christmas Eve. So let's hope this snow clears out by then."

"That's wonderful." Holly's eyes turned moist. "I wish I could be there to see it." As soon as she'd spat those words out, she wished she could retract them. She imagined Barbara having that honor or maybe the girl's mother.

"Yes, I hope it will be wonderful, to use your word." Charlie looked at Holly intently before sipping the coffee. "I hope the horse will help and not hinder. She hasn't learned to trust people yet."

Holly looked up. "Yet?"

"It started long ago and I'm sure my side of it will bore you."

"Maybe not." Holly searched for words, questions that would make him stay a little longer.

Meg picked up the coffee pot. "More coffee? It's still

hot."

"Sure. Top it off. I like my coffee hot." Charlie held out his cup while looking out the window. "It's getting worse. The visibility is about zero."

"Yeah. It's coming down hard now." Holly held her mug out to Meg.

Meg smiled a silly smile when she filled her mother's cup.

"Is this your last stop?" Holly asked. "I mean, do you have more shopping?"

Charlie looked at Holly over the top of the cup. "No, this is it. He looked at the gift bag. "Just a last-minute thing."

"Good. So you're not in a hurry." Holly sank into the barstool. "Maybe we can put you to work baking."

"There's more?"

"We're just getting started. We still have a blintz casserole to put together for Christmas brunch, a New York cheesecake and what else?" Meg looked at a stack of recipes on the bar. "Coffee cakes."

"Cakes?"

"One recipe makes four coffee cakes." Meg smiled proudly.

"Phew. I'm exhausted just listening. Are you cooking for the whole neighborhood?"

"Just Mama's two best friends and the grans. Everybody likes something different so we try to, accommodate." Meg curtsied.

Charlie chuckled. "The grans?"

"Both sets of grandparents." Meg went back to the stack of recipes. "There's one more cake, a special walnut cake." Meg beamed. "It's a tradition. It was my father's favorite so we make it every Christmas to remember him."

"Remember him?"

"Yeah." Meg looked from Charlie to Holly then back to Charlie. "My father died ten years ago."

"I'm sorry." Charlie looked at his watch. "I didn't mean to pry."

"It's okay." Holly smiled. "It was a long time ago."

"The snow's building up. As much as I'd like to continue this conversation, maybe I need go before this turns into a blizzard. Thanks for the coffee. It's been a pleasure meeting both of you." Charlie stood, handed Holly a check then picked up the gift bag. "Thank you for this." He held the bag at chest level. "Have a good Christmas and a happy birthday, Holly." Charlie walked around the bar to shake Meg's hand, but just held it gently for a moment. "You are an absolute delight. Merry Christmas."

For probably the first time in her life, Meg stood dumbfounded.

At the front door, Charlie took Holly's hand and held it tenderly then brought it to his face and brushed his lips across her knuckles. "I can't thank you enough." He looked deeply into her eyes. "You do have the same cat eyes as Meg. Beautiful."

Holly lightly clasped his fingers, watching as his eyes turned a vibrant blue.

"Goodbye then," he said before turning to jog through a half-foot of snow to a silver, all-wheel-drive Ford truck. He opened the passenger door and placed the gift bag on the seat then turned and jogged halfway back to Holly. He held out his hands, palms up, and looked to the sky, smiling.

The snow had abruptly stopped. Streaks of sunlight lit up the ground in golden hues. A bright blue sky replaced the thinning gray clouds. Holly quivered. Prince Charming? Wonderland? Delusion?

"I don't know what to say. This is surreal. I don't want to leave, but, well...I need to." Charlie trudged backward to his truck without breaking his stare. "Merry Christmas, Holly," he said before climbing into the cab.

Holly clung to the doorknob while she watched the truck

move down the street and disappear around the corner.

When Holly returned to the kitchen, Meg had finished washing the bowls and utensils. She stood in front of the sink, gazing out the window. "Did you see the snow stop and the sun come out just like that?" Meg turned toward Holly. "What's wrong, Mama?"

"I don't know, darling." Holly poured herself a small glass of Hennessy before she sat at the bar and just stared.

"It's a sign, isn't it, Mama?" I mean the sun, the way the blizzard just stopped..."

Holly grabbed at her chest.

"He likes you. He likes you a lot."

"What about Barbara? He must like her a lot also."

"His eyes lit up every time he looked at you. They didn't change at all when he talked about Barbara."

"Really?"

"He's your Prince Charming, Mama." Meg sat next to Holly and held her hand. "You said you wouldn't marry again until Prince Charming knocked your door down...and he did."

2

By Christmas Eve morning the roads had been cleared and the sun shone brightly on Holly's little winter wonderland. The grans—Holly and Meg's only relatives, arrived in the early afternoon in time to play in the snow with Meg and trudge through the subdivision to view the neighbor's holiday decorations while reminiscing about Christmases past. Holly tried not to think about the next Christmases when the possibility of Meg running off to Colorado or Europe with friends might seem more exciting than spending an old-fashioned Christmas with her mother at home. She'd raised Meg to be independent, but she wondered if she was ready for her to take to the skies. Holly took a vow that night not to clip her wings. She wanted Meg to soar, even if that meant Meg might leave her behind.

Holly and Meg called Holly's parents Grandma and Grandpa while they called Marcus' parents Nana and Bug. No one intended to call Grandfather Gaynor Bug, but he'd been holding Meg when she pointed to his bushy eyebrows and spoke her first word, Bug. The name stuck and from that day forward everyone called him Bug, even his golf buddies.

The grans hadn't always liked each other. Holly's parents didn't expect her to marry out of the church. Being staunch

Roman Catholics, they couldn't accept that she'd chosen a Protestant over all the available good Catholic boys. It took Marcus' illness to finally bring them together and his death to unite them.

Holly's best friends, Lisa and Brody Adams, joined the celebration with their usual charm and wit, but for the first time in twenty years, without their only son, Jason, who had married and moved to Seattle for med school last August. Like his father, Jason hoped to become an internist. Holly's heart went out to Lisa, especially. Even though Lisa matriculated into the empty-nest school a few years back, Jason had always made it home for the holidays, even for just one or two nights. Holly felt Lisa's loneliness but tried not to dwell on it. She couldn't imagine a Christmas without Meg.

The Christmas Eve feast, Christmas morning brunch, and Holly's birthday party on Christmas night had become a tradition at Holly's house the year she married Marcus. The menu on Christmas Eve hadn't changed in over twenty years—succulent roast beef with sausages, roasted potatoes, Brussels sprouts, and the crowning glory that brings the whole meal together—puffy Yorkshire pudding and rich brown gravy. Although this English fare began in Marcus' family, Holly carried on the tradition not only to honor them but because it had become her favorite meal. She usually didn't allow herself so many carbs but Christmas and her birthday were a justified excuse to indulge.

After the grand meal on Christmas Eve, when all the gifts were exchanged, when the adults were a bit tipsy from wine and champagne, Meg served coffee and the frosty walnut cake. The cake Marcus' mother and then Holly baked for him every Christmas for thirty years. In a way, it was everyone's celebration of a good man who died too young—a son, a son-in-law, a husband, a father, and a best friend. Holly silently saluted Marcus even though she couldn't get Charlie out of her mind.

While Holly and Lisa collected plates and cups and saucers from the living room, the grans gathered around Meg.

"There's one more gift for you, Meg. It's a little something from all of us," Bug said.

Holly's mother pulled a little stocking from her bag and handed it to Meg. "Here darling, we thought this might come in handy when you go to college."

Meg took the stocking and looked inside. "You didn't." She pulled out a set of car keys. "A car? Wow, thank you, thank you. Where is it?"

"Right out in the alley," Grandpa said as he led the other proud grandparents and their sniffling, precious granddaughter out the back door.

There in the glow of the streetlight sat a brand new, bright red Versa hatchback with a huge green bow on the hood. "It's awesome. It's perfect for all my sports stuff." Meg ran to the car, careful to stay on the path Brody salted earlier and climbed into the driver's seat. She turned on the ignition, rolled the window down, and squealed in delight. "Come on, everybody. Let's take her for a spin."

The grans piled into the car leaving Lisa, Brody, and Holly to watch from the backdoor. Meg honked the horn to the rhythm of Jingle Bells as she drove off.

"Must be nice to be the only grandchild, huh?" Brody said.

"Unfortunately, yes." Holly invited them back inside. "I can't believe they did that behind my back."

"You didn't know?" Lisa arched a brow.

Holly folded her arms across her chest and tapped her toe on the wood floor. "The plan, and they all knew it, was to help Meg buy a car, a good used one, not a brand new one free and clear. How is she going to learn to take care of herself if they keep spoiling her like this?"

Brody chuckled. "Meg will be fine. She's got a good head on her shoulders, thanks to you."

Baggage

"Thanks, Brody. I hope you're right." Holly wrinkled her nose. "A car just seems like Meg is one step closer to fleeing the nest."

"Your life will definitely change," Brody said. "Just like ours has."

Lisa grabbed Holly's arm. "We have some news." She shared a smile with Brody. "We're going to be grandparents. Jason called this morning."

Holly's brooding frown turned into a broad smile. "Congratulations. When?"

"First week of June. Can you believe it?" The muscles in Lisa's face tightened. "I'm happy for them, but they're so young."

"I was a father at twenty," Brody said, looking rather proud, "and a junior in college with a full-time job, but, unfortunately, without a car."

"Like father, like son...except for the car part. Hey, you're going to be forty-year-old grandparents." Holly hugged them each knowing that this bit of news was getting Lisa through her first Christmas without her son.

"I'm so happy for you, but I hope this doesn't mean you'll be moving to Seattle."

"She would if she could," Brody said. "But, I imagine they'll be back on the East Coast for Jason's residency. All the aunts, uncles, and cousins are within a hundred miles of here, including both sets of grandparents."

"Well, you're the sexiest grandparents I've ever seen." Holly laughed. "It's just so difficult to imagine."

~*~

Holly and Brody had dated rather awkwardly their junior year of high school until Lisa came along and stole his affections or as Holly liked to tease, saved her from corruption. Holly's strict Roman Catholic parents instilled the

25

fear that Holly would surely go to hell if she had sex before marriage. The relationship with Brody included heavy petting that Holly enjoyed, but guilt overwhelmed the pleasure and she didn't have a clue how to stop it before God dammed her to hell. Luckily, Lisa appeared just in time to save her from the wrath of God. Holly spent the next couple of years in a state of confusion. She was certain that all the boys were the same and feared her raging hormones would get her into trouble. Unlike Lisa, who enjoyed the pleasure she shared with not only Brody but a few other boys as well, Holly believed she should save her pleasure for the marriage bed. After all, she reasoned, her relationship with Brody had simply been friendship gone overboard, like children who took off their underpants and played 'doctor' in a secluded garden shed. Holly wanted the same thing her parents wanted for her—true love.

For graduation from high school, Brody bought Lisa an engagement ring. It wasn't until Holly's second year of college that she met Marcus—the soul mate she'd been waiting for. After their second date, Holly introduced him to Lisa and Brody. The four started a friendship that would last forever.

~*~

Meg drove up the front drive and honked the horn once more to the beat of *Jingle Bells*.

Holly stepped out onto the front porch. "How does it drive?"

Great, Mama, "Guess we're going to have to clean out the garage so both cars will fit." She turned off the ignition and looked to her grandparents. "This is so great. Thank you all so much."

"We knew you'd need something dependable when you go off to the university," Grandpa said.

Baggage

Holly held the back door open and helped Nana out. "What a great surprise for Meg, but—"

"But nothing," Nana said. "We just wanted to take the burden off you. The four of us wanted to do something special for our only granddaughter."

"We all wanted Meg to have something new," Bug said. "We didn't want her to breakdown in some godforsaken wilderness."

Holly let out a long sigh. "She's going to Illinois, not the jungle. Besides, it's major highways all the way."

"She can use the money she's been saving for a car to get a GPS," Grandpa said. "You never know what can happen to a young pretty girl if she gets off the beaten track."

"We just want her to be…safe," Grandma chimed in. "We want to keep her around for a long time."

Holly bit her bottom lip. "I know. It's just that, well, you all knew the plan." She smiled then. "I guess I'll do the same for my grandchildren someday."

"That's the spirit," Bug said.

"Don't worry guys. I'll get a GPS right away and a Bluetooth too so everyone can call me every five minutes while I'm on the road. Okay?"

They headed into the house together, laughing.

"This has been my best Christmas." Meg smiled as she closed the door behind them. "Thank you so much. I love all of you."

"Well, it's off to bed for us old folks," Bug said, taking off his coat. "Guess we'll see you at the crack of dawn."

"Bug, we need to help Holly clean up." Nana flashed a frown.

"Brody and I will help. Go, on and get some rest while you can. You've already had a long drive from Salter Path," Lisa said with a wink.

"Well then, we'll head back to Raleigh, honey, since your

mama doesn't need any help." Grandma hugged Meg and kissed her cheek. "And we'll see you in time for brunch."

"Good night everybody. Thanks again for the car and all the other stuff." Meg smiled as the grans went their separate ways.

"Mama, can I drive my new car over to Aubrey's?"

Holly squinted. "You can't wait until tomorrow?"

"Please, Mama? She'll never speak to me again if I don't show it to her tonight. I'll be back in less than an hour. Promise." Meg put on her best pout.

"Get out of here you little spoiled brat."

"I love you too, Mama." Meg held the car keys to her chest as she dashed out the door.

Lisa donned an apron over her black crepe party dress. She ran her fingers through her cropped blond hair and looked squarely into Holly's eyes. "You're not yourself. What is it?"

"It's a silly thing that happened yesterday." Holly tried not to show her feelings about what she considered a childish crush.

"What?"

"While Meg and I were working on my birthday cake, she began bugging me to go out on dates."

"That's nothing new," Brody said, stretching to his full height of six feet two inches. He stared at her with gray eyes that matched his full head of prematurely gray hair.

"But, she's more insistent now knowing she's going out-of-state to school in the fall. She wants to make sure I'm taken care of."

"And that upset you?" Lisa scraped the leftovers off the plates and placed them into the dishwasher.

"Not really. It's just that we were joking around and I said something about not looking for a man, but waiting for Prince Charming to knock my door down. As soon as those words came out of my mouth, someone rang the bell and then banged on the door. And there he stood." Holly escaped, for a moment, into a dream.

"Prince Charming?" Lisa asked.

Holly let out a heavy sigh and leaned against the counter to steady herself. "He could have been."

"So, who was he? Tell me." Lisa took hold of Holly's shoulders.

"Charles Prince."

Brody chuckled. "Not Prince Charles?"

"No. Just Charlie. He's a friend, or probably the significant other of the real estate agent who helped me buy this house."

"Why did he come here?" Lisa asked.

"To buy one of my beaded necklaces."

Lisa swung around. "Why? How did he know you made them?"

"I'd shown them to Barbara, the agent, and she fell in love with one of them but didn't want to put out the bucks for it. She'd mentioned them to Charlie and on a whim, he stopped to buy one for her."

"So, she told him about the necklaces and where you live?" Lisa turned to Brody. "Isn't that a little too much information?"

Brody nodded. "Sounds unprofessional to me."

"No, she didn't give him my name. She'd showed him this house the day before I looked at it. They became friends and at some point, she apparently mentioned my necklaces. He needed a Christmas gift for her and remembered that she liked my work."

"Did he look like he was casing the joint?"

"Oh, Brody, don't scare me. No, he wasn't casing. He's much too prosperous looking. He drove a new Ford 4x4 F-150 XL that must have cost thirty-five grand and he says he's a lawyer...well, he said he worked for a law firm. Besides, he's handsome and kind and soft-spoken. He's not a serial killer. He has two daughters. He mentioned a wife, but it didn't sound as though they're together. He didn't wear a wedding ring." Holly sighed louder than before. "He's the first man to stir my passion since Marcus died. I never thought I'd meet someone to match Marcus or take his place. Then in one second, Marcus starts to fade from my mind and Charlie is filling it up. I was perfectly content until Charlie invaded my mind. Damn. I feel like a kid in middle school."

"Maybe he and Barbara aren't serious. Maybe they're just friends or maybe she's his sister." Lisa gritted her teeth. "Well, maybe."

"Or he could be a lonely widower." Brody shrugged. "Well, he could be."

The snow that fell before Christmas Eve still covered the ground Christmas night—all eight inches of it, which seemed a miracle. The sky remained crisp and clear, day and night with sun and moon battling for the greater applause. Meg got her snowman and got into a rip-roaring snowball fight with her girlfriends. When they came in at dusk for hot chocolate Meg took Holly aside. "You haven't taken one picture today. Are you lovesick, Mama?"

Holly blinked as if waking up from a deep sleep. "I don't want my birthday party without—"

"Prince Charming."

"I guess."

"Then make the right wish when you blow out your candles."

"Get back to your friends, honey. I'm okay."

But Holly wasn't okay. On Christmas night, surrounded by family and friends, she felt lonely. When she blew out the candles, she held a vision of Charlie and her childhood belief that because she'd blown them all out her wish would come true. She'd tried to push Charlie out of her mind, deny her feelings, but as she watched the last candle flicker she felt a surge of excitement as if she were teetering on the edge of a high diving board. She closed her eyes, held her breath, and dove straight into her fortieth year. Life is what it is.

3

By the first week in January, the temperature soared to sixty-five, muggy degrees. Holly donned a pair of summer shorts and a cotton shirt. She sat perfectly still on her back deck watching a bright red cardinal nervously pick seeds from the bird feeder. Two black and gray chickadees and a male goldfinch flitted from tree branch to fence awaiting a turn at the feast of seeds, but the cardinal kept them at bay until he had his fill.

Holly longed for a huge snowstorm as an excuse to sequester herself from the world. So far, this new wonderland proved to be pretty boring except for the influx of birds which brightened the otherwise dull horizon. The day after New Year's she hung bricks of suet, bags of nyjer seed, and a tray with dried mealworms. So many birds visited Holly's feeding station that Meg named it The Tweet-n-Go. More likely than not, in the early morning or just before dusk, Holly snapped photos of the birds with her telephoto lens. To Holly, the birds and her photography were just the distraction she needed from a barrage of mixed emotions.

She thought about Charlie—the way his eyes changed color with the light or his mood. She wondered if she'd imagined the colors of his eyes or simply imagined him. She reminded herself to count her blessings not dwell on something that didn't belong to her. She imagined Meg in her lacrosse uniform, the way her mouth and faceguard made her look as though she should be underwater. She saw her ponytail flying as she ran down the field as swift and lithe as a cheetah.

Holly and Meg had always been close. Holly couldn't remember either of them keeping secrets from the other until last summer, just after they moved to the new house. Meg met a boy at the hospital where she volunteered during school breaks and Saturday afternoons. On New Year's Eve, she'd announced that she was in love with this boy named Mike, but when Holly questioned her about this budding romance Meg became elusive. Holly marked it up to puppy love and didn't pursue the issue. Since this boyfriend hadn't bothered to visit or ask Meg out, how serious could the relationship be? Holly guessed that Mike had to be a volunteer as well, since the only time Meg seemed to have contact with him was at the hospital. Maybe she loved him, but if he loved her, he had a funny way of showing it. It seemed to Holly that neither she nor Meg was making progress in the romance category.

When Holly got home from work the first day after Christmas break, she found a message on home phone voice mail.

"Hello, Holly, this is Barbara Miller. Do you remember me?" Barbara spoke with a refined southern drawl. Long, lazy vowels poured from her mouth like honey. "I was your real estate agent, but that is *not* why I am calling. I just wanted to thank you for the absolutely *gorgeous* necklace. It is exactly the one I wanted. Can we get together one evening this week? Please call me."

Holly clicked off the message. She stood motionless feeling as if her heart was pumping iced tea.

Meg promenaded out of her bedroom and down the hall. "Are you okay, Mama?"

Holly sat at the kitchen bar with her head in her hands for a second then raised her head and forced a smile. "Of course, sweetheart."

"Are you going to call her back?"

"Why?"

"To find out about Charlie. I told you that there's no way he can be interested in Barbara, not by the way he looked at you."

"I don't think I can just come out and ask about him."

"Mom..." Meg sat on the barstool next to her mother.

"I'm sorry. Yes, I'm afraid to call because I don't know what her relationship is with our Mr. Prince Charming."

Meg shrugged. "I guess I know what you mean but you're carrying a touch for him."

"Whatever is, is." Holly looked at Meg. "I'll call Barbara after dinner."

"No, Mama, call her now."

Holly frowned at Meg, picked up the phone, pushed the callback button.

"Barbara? Hello. This is Holly. What a surprise hearing from you." Holly stared blankly at Meg and tipped the phone away from her ear so Meg could hear.

"Holly, I just cannot tell you how overwhelmed I was to receive one of your necklaces for Christmas. I just *adore* it."

"I'm so glad you like it."

"It has to be the one I tried on last summer. I just cannot imagine that Charlie remembered me talking about it. He is one resourceful man."

Holly tapped her nail on the granite countertop.

"I would love to see what you've done with your home. I wasn't calling just to thank you, but to see you again. Do you think we could get together soon?"

"Is tomorrow night too soon? You can join us for supper."

"I would love that, honey. I have some exciting news to share."

"Something you can't share now?"

"No way, no, no, no. Not over the phone. I have to show

it to you. In person."

"Okay then. See you at about seven? Does that work for you?"

"Yes ma'am, it certainly does. I will bring a bottle of fine wine."

Holly hung up the phone and growled. "Wonder what she wants to show me? A diamond?"

"Mama..."

"She said Charlie was, what was it...resourceful? I wonder what she meant by that?"

"Maybe that's all she has to say about him. She could have said, Charlie is such a sweetheart." Meg looked up with a frown. "If I wanted to say something about Mike, the first word out of my mouth wouldn't be resourceful."

"What would it be?"

"Something more like hot or incredible."

"Is he?"

Meg grabbed a dishtowel and slapped it against her thigh. "I can't talk about him."

"Meg..." Holly looked at her with curiosity and a little concern. "I'm your best friend forever, remember? You've never kept anything from me? What is it?"

"I don't want to talk about it. There's nothing to say." A red rim formed around Meg's eyes.

"Do you see him at school?"

"No."

"Where do you see him? At the hospital? Is he friends with your friends?"

"I told you, I don't want to talk about him." Meg stomped off to her room. When the door closed Holly heard loud sobs then uncontrolled weeping.

Who could this boy be that could change Meg from a well-adjusted young woman to a moody teenager? Where in hell does he go to school? He must be a decent kid if he volunteers at the hospital. Why doesn't he call her? Why doesn't she call him? Why hasn't he visited or asked her out?

Panic smacked at Holly as a scenario of possible explanations raced through her head. Maybe this kid isn't a kid. Maybe he's a doctor or an intern or a janitor. Maybe he's a mental patient. Of course. Meg always wants to help people. Did she meet him when she delivered something to the psych ward? Did he threaten her? Hurt her in some way. Oh, my God.

When Meg's weeping ceased, Holly knocked lightly on her bedroom door. When Meg didn't answer, she felt a chill. She sauntered to the living room and switched on the gas logs in the fireplace.

On Holly's way home the next afternoon, she couldn't get either Meg's relationship or Barbara's exciting news, whatever that was, out of her mind. She tried to be positive, but couldn't stop obsessing over what she would do when Barbara announced her engagement to Charlie or Meg dragged herself home after a negative confrontation with Mike. As soon as she got home, she mixed a martini and tried to convince herself that the alcohol would dull her senses enough to be able to share Barbara's news as well as Meg's mood with grace.

Meg wasn't home from school yet which seemed odd. Holly knew she'd want to be right in the middle of things with Barbara. She hoped Meg wasn't off somewhere with Mike. She let out a long breath, sipped her drink, and tried to think about dinner. She'd decided to serve *salade niçoise* because she wasn't in the mood to cook a five-course meal. The dish was simple to prepare—a plate of fancy lettuce, fresh spinach, green beans, small boiled potatoes, a mixture of olives, pickles, canned artichoke hearts, miniature corn-on-the-cob, and a baked tuna fillet on top.

Baggage

When the doorbell rang, Holly took a gulp of the martini, set it on the counter then dragged herself to the door.

"Hey, Holly, it is so good to see you." Barbara looked radiant in a vintage brown faux fur jacket, short red dress, and black leather high heeled boots.

"Won't you come in?" Holly said as the two embraced.

Barbara handed Holly a bottle of cabernet and took a quick look around. "I *love* what you have done with this place. It is gorgeous."

"Well, thanks. Here let me take your jacket. I'll show you around. We acquired a few antiques after my parents visited Istanbul and decided to trade their Victorian decor for the Ottoman Empire." Holly rolled her eyes and shrugged. "So, Meg and I completely redecorated to accommodate their castoffs. We also had the deck enlarged and planted some ornamental trees. You'll have to come back in the summer when the trees and flowers are in bloom." Holly knew she was rambling nervously. She didn't want to hear the inevitable.

"I would love to." Barbara adjusted the black lace scarf that draped her shoulders.

"Speaking of gorgeous, just look at you." Barbara looked slimmer, not that she needed to lose weight. The simple dress showed off her curves and allowed her thick brown hair to caress her neck. Holly glanced at Barbara's left hand and there it was—a gigantic diamond ring.

A broad smile spread across Barbara's face. "I. Am. In. Love. And because of it, I have lost twelve pounds."

"Congratulations." Holly's chest suddenly felt tight. She forced a smile. Prince Charming wasn't her fairytale after all. She didn't want to hear the part about living happily ever after. She bit the inside of her cheek as hard as she could to fight off a flood of tears. "I'm having a martini. Would you like to join me?"

"I will be happy to join you." Barbara sat on a barstool just as the back door opened.

"Meg, honey, I was hoping you'd be here to have dinner with us." Barbara stood up. "Come here and let me hug your neck."

Meg smiled slightly as she hugged Barbara. Holly could tell that she'd seen the diamond.

"Hello, darling. How was your day?" Holly asked.

"Fine. Is it okay to ask Aubrey over?"

"Of course." Holly was glad that she'd bought four tuna fillets, but that wasn't what made her smile. She knew what confidants Meg and Aubrey were. Surely, Aubrey knew about Mike and something was bound to slip out, something that Meg wouldn't be able to deny.

Holly poured a martini for Barbara and after a quick toast to the New Year, gave her the grand tour of the house.

Barbara examined the furnishings, running her hand along the antique sideboard, the backs of the dining room chairs, the carved walnut beds and dressers. She looked at every vase, picture and frame, lamp, and chandelier, all the while flashing her diamond. "It is just amazing that you turned a modern house into old European elegance. You could be an interior decorator."

"Thanks. Meg and I like the dark wood and the cozy feel to it all." Holly smiled with pride. "What we didn't inherit, we got at yard sales and the antique shops in Hillsborough. We want to work on the kitchen next but haven't come up with any ideas that aren't tacky."

Barbara took a turn around the kitchen, shaking her head, making humming sounds. "If I may make a suggestion?"

"Of course."

"Textured walls…for a start." She cocked her head. "You could replace the wrought iron bookshelves with wooden ones that match the dining room. And some kind of window treatment, maybe something in stained or beveled glass."

Holly stared at the window. "Beveled glass would be nice. I want to be able to see out. I actually think I've seen some old doors with beveled glass inserts. You're a genius, Barbara."

When Meg returned in jeans and a baby pink sweater, Holly and Barbara were enjoying a second round of martinis.

"Are we celebrating something?" Meg grinned.

"Well." Barbara sat up straight, held out her left hand to show off the diamond. "We are celebrating our reunion and I guess you could say that we are celebrating my engagement."

Meg paled. "To Prince Charming?"

Holly stiffened but refused the urge to gulp her drink again. She already felt a bit tipsy.

"Well, I guess he is my Prince Charming. His name is Harve. Harve Johnson. I would invite you to the wedding, but it will be in Tahoe next week. That's where he lives. We met at a convention in Memphis. It was love at first sight. Yes, it was. I'm going to move my business to Lake Tahoe."

"Great. We were so afraid that you were engaged to Charlie." Meg blurted.

"My goodness gracious, no. Charlie is a good friend, that is all." Barbara squinted. "Prince Charming? Tell me more."

The doorbell rang and Meg ran to answer it.

"There's nothing to tell." Holly fought back a flood of happy tears.

"I'll tell you." Meg bounced back into the room with Aubrey right behind.

"Hello, everyone." Aubrey stepped out of her clogs and sat across the bar from Barbara. She wore jeans and an identical pink sweater to Meg's. Her strawberry blond curls were windblown and she brushed her fingers through them, fluffing them into place.

After the introductions, Meg sat next to Aubrey and proceeded to tell Barbara the story of Charlie coming to buy the necklace.

"That's another reason I wanted to see you tonight, Holly." Barbara leaned back. "That Charlie is a clever man.

He saw this house the day before you did but could not make up his mind. So, he went home to think about it. About four or five days after your offer was accepted, he called to view it again. He was pretty upset that someone had beaten him to a contract. He was a mess, that man. Let me tell you."

Holly sipped her drink and felt a pain ease in her chest. "A mess because he didn't get this house?"

"Not exactly. He actually found a place that better suited his needs down in Pittsboro." Barbara twirled the martini glass between her thumb and diamonded finger. "No, his wife just up and asked for a divorce and gave him two weeks to vacate. She told him to take their daughters and all their stuff. Said she was tired of taking care of all of them. That was about a month before I met him at the office. We starting meeting, not dating, just meeting for coffee or a drink. He needed to talk, and well, I am a good listener. He is a looker, that man. Yes, he is. Just not my type." Barbara took a sip of her drink. "I met my Harve in September. The first time he came to visit me in Chapel Hill I introduced him to Charlie. They got along so well that we invited Charlie to dinner a couple of times, but once his older girl went off to college he couldn't leave that younger one home alone. We talked on the phone a lot after that. Still do. I certainly did not expect that he would come here and buy the very necklace I coveted. He's okay now. I mean he's dealing with his impending divorce and being a single dad. The necklace was the only way he knew to thank me for listening when he needed to talk."

When Barbara finished her marathon of words, Meg grinned at Holly as if to say, "See, I told you so." Holly served the meal and felt all tingly for the rest of the evening. No one mentioned Mike. Meg and Aubrey giggled often and shared their thoughts through eye contact and facial expressions. It seemed that everything was supercalifragilistic.

When Barbara left, Holly couldn't wait to talk to Lisa

about the new twist in her saga. She reached for her phone but it rang before she could pick it up.

"This is Charlie Prince. Do you remember me barging in on you just before Christmas?"

"Yes, I remember. You're Barbara's friend."

"That I am. She just called to give me your number. She...encouraged me to call."

Holly felt glad that Charlie couldn't see her smiling, excited face. "I won't embarrass both of us by asking what she had to say."

Charlie chuckled. "She said you'd be happy to hear from me. I'm hoping she's right, because, if not, I'm going to feel like a foolish teenager with a crush on the most popular girl in school and my best friend has just announced it over the school PA system."

"Actually, I am happy to hear from you."

"Phew. If you're free on Saturday night, I'd like to take you to dinner."

Holly thought about playing it cool, but after all the expectations as well as the worry and suspense since they'd met she thought better of it. Besides, he'd just laid his heart on the table in front of her. "Saturday would be fine."

"There's a new restaurant in Raleigh, Anastasia's. Have you been there?"

"No. I don't get to Raleigh very often. Is it Greek?"

"I'm not sure about that. My secretary told me that it has a romantic ambiance, a good place for a first date."

"I'm certain Barbara told you that you didn't have to impress me."

"She did, but I want to anyway. Pick you up at seven?"

"Sure. I'm looking forward to it."

Holly sat up in bed holding the phone against her heart. Not only did he want to see her, but he also wanted to romance her, impress her—as if he hadn't done that already. Three days until Saturday. She felt a longing, an arousal that needed to be kindled. She wondered if she could wait that long to feel his gentle touch, to be wrapped up in his arms, to have her senses aroused and then satiated. She looked at the phone before gently setting it on the nightstand. She was too excited to sleep or even wake Meg to tell her the good news, so she turned out the light, curled up under a down comforter, and just smiled.

Late Saturday afternoon, Meg sauntered up the sidewalk after her morning at the hospital with the Junior Volunteers. Once inside, she flew into Holly's arms and wept so wrenchingly that she couldn't speak.

"What is it, sweetheart?" Holly's thoughts raced from Meg's friends to her new car to an insult, to angry words. She could see that Meg wasn't bleeding or didn't appear to have a physical injury, but she trembled so violently that it reminded Holly of the moments after Marcus had slipped away. She tried to shake that memory and concentrate on Meg. "What's happened? You're shaking."

They sat on the sofa clinging together while Meg cried and gasped and blew her nose. Finally, she found her voice. "It's Mike," she said and the wrenching tears grew horrific.

Holly paled. She knew, but she didn't want to believe what her heart was telling her. "What happened?"

"Something terrible. Something, mean and unbelievable." Meg coughed, blew her nose again, took in a deep breath while pulling away to look at Holly straight on. She spoke softly. "I'm sorry, Mama. I was afraid to tell you. I was afraid you'd hate him…and me."

"Megan Marie Gaynor, there's nothing you could ever do to make me hate you. Nothing. Do you understand?" Holly felt her temples pulse out in pain. She tried to swallow, but couldn't.

"I do, but you haven't heard my story."

"Tell me, Meg. I promise not to be angry."

Meg wiped her eyes with the backs of her fingers. Holly handed her a tissue and she dabbed at her puffy, bleary eyes.

"I think we're going to need a lot of these before I get done." Meg stood and removed her coat.

"Just tell me. We have plenty of tissues."

Meg hesitated a moment while she pulled off her boots and stashed them at the end of the sofa. "I met Mike last summer," she said before sitting back down next to Holly.

"At the hospital?"

"Yeah."

"Was he a volunteer?"

"Mom, let me tell this. Please." Meg plopped onto the sofa.

"Sorry, darling. Go on."

"Mike was a patient…in a private room. I delivered him some mail. He was so handsome. When I asked him what school he went to, he laughed. He laughed because he was twenty-two. He graduated from Florida State last spring and worked for Glenn-Bio, a company in Research Triangle Park that helps people with metabolic diseases. I didn't know all that right away, I mean about where he worked. He had the same kind of leukemia as Daddy and that made me, well, feel close to him."

"Oh, Meg." Holly had a sinking feeling.

"Anyway, we just hit it off, and he invited me to visit him again, and I did. Lots of times. Then he got discharged. I didn't know his phone number or where he lived. After a while, he got sick again and stayed in the hospital for a couple of weeks. We started kissing and I liked it. Soon after we started making out."

"Making out?" Holly didn't want to hear more.

"He made me feel…beautiful and I, well, I thought I was giving him a reason to live."

"Maybe you were." Holly identified with Meg's feelings. She remembered comforting Marcus and the intimacy they'd shared especially in his last days. She recalled his anger and pain and finally his acceptance. They'd wept the most over Meg. Marcus grieved that he wouldn't get to see her grow up, wouldn't be able to give her away at her wedding. She remembered Marcus kissing them both goodbye every time he fell asleep just in case he didn't wake up.

"There's more and it's not very pretty." Meg held her breath for a long moment. "He's married."

"Married? Meg?"

"That's exactly why I didn't want to tell you. I only found out the day Barbara called and I got so upset when you asked me about him. Remember?"

"Yes, I do. I wish you could've told me about it then."

"Me too. That's why I invited Aubrey over the night Barbara came to dinner. She knew about Mike and, well, I needed to tell someone about his wife." Meg took a deep breath, played with the waded up tissue in her hand. "I was mad at Mike, mad at his wife, mostly mad at myself. I didn't want you mad at me too. Besides, I still wanted more affection, sex, I guess."

"And, was there more—"

"Yes, but we justified it because his wife was mad at him for being sick. She was so angry that she picked up a boyfriend. After I went to Aubrey's on Christmas Eve, I went to be with Mike."

Holly made herself listen. She tried to keep her emotions in check. After all, she'd promised not to be angry.

"When I visited him I honestly just wanted to tell him Merry Christmas and give him a little gift. I found him crying when I got there and I didn't know why. He told me later, that his wife had gone to Key West with her boyfriend for the holidays. Anyway, I wanted to comfort him. I kissed him and he kissed me back like there was no tomorrow. He asked me to snuggle next to him and I did. Then we just kissed. I let him unfasten my bra…touch me…while we kissed."

Holly sat still, but her mind raced. "Touch? Is that all?"

"Yes. I know what you're thinking. We didn't go all the way. Mike's chemo left him weak or else we probably would have." Meg looked to her feet. "I wanted it. Mike kept telling me that he was sorry he couldn't do it. But, that night, I just wanted to kiss him and feel him touch me."

"Your heart must have really hurt."

"When we stopped kissing, he just held me so tightly. We cried together. I didn't want to go home. I just wanted to stay with him forever." Meg burst into tears again and the violent eruptions came like an aftershock.

"So, what has you so upset today?" Again, Holly didn't want to hear more, but she knew she had to listen.

Meg sat silent and breathed deeply. She licked her lips then covered her face with her hands. "Mike died this afternoon."

"Megan, no. I'm so sorry." Holly pulled Meg into a hug. When she felt Meg's body tremble against her own it seemed like déjà vu and she couldn't hold back her tears for Meg or for herself.

"I stood outside his room, listened to his wife scream and sob, and tell him how much she loved him and how sorry she was. She apologized for being mad at him and leaving him. Other people were there too. I don't know who they were. They all cried and told him goodbye. I wanted, so much, to hold him and tell him how much I loved him, but I couldn't let them see me. If they saw me, they'd hate him for loving me. So, I ran away.

"Hold me, Mama. Hold me. I'm so sad and ashamed that I kept this from you."

"I love you so much, sweetheart. Thank you for sharing it all with me now." Holly knew she should say more, something like, 'When you found out he was twenty-two or when you found out he was married you should have stopped seeing him but she couldn't scold her now. Now that it was over. She

45

knew they'd have plenty of time later, after Meg had time to grieve, to talk about what she should have done.

"How can I tell him goodbye? I can't go to the funeral. He loved me, Mama, he really did love me."

Holly clung to Meg while trying to think with her head, not her heart. She wondered how this man could have cheated on his wife and hurt Meg so badly? Tonight wasn't the time to be angry. Tonight Meg needed comfort. "Do you have a picture of him?"

"Yeah, he gave me one of his graduation pictures."

"Maybe you could get a small diary and write down everything you remember about him. You could put his picture in it and on the last page you could write a poem or a letter telling him goodbye." Holly wrapped her arms around Meg and let her mind go blank.

The two sat together in silence for a long while. Holly smoothed back Meg's bangs and kissed her forehead.

"That's a good idea. Thanks for thinking of it." Meg stood. "I think I'll get a glass of water and then go take a nap."

"I'll be here if you need me. Okay?" The weight on Holly's chest kept her trapped on the sofa. She watched Meg amble down the hall with her boots and coat and glass of water. Holly took her cell phone from the coffee table and turned it over and over in her pale, cold hands until she was sure Meg was asleep. Then she called Charlie.

"Holly." Charlie's voice chimed.

"Hello, Charlie," she said, her voice fragile. "I'm so sorry. I don't want to say what I have to say."

"Is everything alright? You sound upset."

"It's Meg. Her boyfriend, her friend, died today and well, it's just that I can't leave her tonight. I'm sorry to spoil our plans."

"Died?"

"Yes. I just can't talk about it right now."

"No problem. I understand. Is there anything I can do?"

"Give me a rain check?"

"You can count on that."

When she said goodbye she clung to the phone. She wanted to call Lisa. She wanted to call her mother, but she just sat until the sun set, and then she made herself a martini.

Meg stayed out of school to grieve the next week. Aubrey came over every afternoon to comfort Meg and share her tears. The other girls came sporadically and soon it was evident to Holly that other than Aubrey, Meg's friends were immature and inept at handling the depth of Meg's grief. Holly stayed home Monday and Tuesday but worked the rest of the week. She thought Meg needed time alone to sort things out and mend her broken heart. Aubrey brought a diary and Meg wrote in it for hours every night. She slept with it in her arms.

Charlie called Holly on Monday and again on Thursday to inquire about Meg and offer himself as Holly's sounding board. He called again on Saturday morning to ask if it would be appropriate and convenient to drop by to offer Meg his condolences.

When Charlie drove up, Meg opened the door even before he stepped out of his car.

"Hi, Charlie. I'm so glad to see you," she said with a raspy voice. "I thought you drove a truck."

"The truck is a utility vehicle. This," Charlie said turning toward the silver Porsche convertible, "is for pleasure."

Meg forced a smile that soon turned blank. "Thanks for dropping by. I'm glad to see you. It's just that I'm so tired. Come on in. Mom's in the kitchen."

Charlie handed Meg a bouquet of miniature pink carnations. "These are for you. I'm sorry about Mike and what you've been through this week. I just wanted you to know that I've been thinking about you."

Meg looked at the flowers then at Charlie through tear-flooded eyes. He kissed her knotted disheveled hair.

"Thanks, Charlie. Mama says, what is, is. I'm sorry about Mama breaking her date with you. Mike's timing was a little off." Meg shrugged. "She'll be happy to see you as well, but you're going to get a once over."

"From your mom?"

"No." Meg forced a smile. "You'll see."

Charlie followed Meg into the kitchen where Holly and Lisa were making peanut butter and marshmallow fluff sandwiches. "Look, what Charlie brought me," Meg said, sniffling, still blank and pale. She looked up at Charlie, tried to smile, but burst into tears. He pulled her to him.

Holly took the flowers, brought them to her face, and inhaled. "Let me put them in water." While she opened a cupboard to find a vase she said, "Charlie, this is my best friend, Lisa Adams. Lisa, Charlie Prince."

Charlie took Lisa's hand in his and squeezed gently. "Nice to meet you, Lisa. Holly's told me a little about you."

"And me about you as well." Lisa smiled then picked up her empty coffee cup. "Can I get you a coffee? Holly just brewed a fresh pot."

Charlie stood close to Meg with his arm still draped around her shoulders. "No, thanks. I just wanted to stop by and check on this little lady."

Holly arranged the flowers in the vase and handed them back to Meg. "Do you want to put them in your room?"

Meg leaned her head against Charlie's chest. "Sure. Thank you so much for this. Maybe someday you'll take me for a spin in the Porsche." She looked up at Charlie and smiled without breaking down, then walked to her room.

"See ya, kiddo." Charlie put his hands in his pockets and watched Meg stroll down the hall.

Lisa refilled her cup. "Are you sure you don't want a cup of coffee?"

"Yes. I have a trunk full of groceries and I promised to

take my daughter to a horse show in Greensboro this afternoon, but thanks."

"I'll walk you to the door," Holly said. "Excuse me for a minute, Lisa."

"Good to meet you." Lisa sat back at the bar and considered Charlie through the steam rising from her coffee.

Charlie winked before he turned to leave.

"That was so sweet of you to think of Meg." Holly opened the door a crack.

"Poor kid. I hate seeing her so upset." Charlie's eyes seemed to share a genuine concern for Meg and his demeanor made Holly want to comfort him.

"I wasn't making an excuse not to go out with you."

"That's not what I thought at all. I'll call you tomorrow. Maybe we can make plans for next weekend."

"I'd like that." Holly blushed when Charlie gave her a peck on the cheek.

He smiled and winked before turning and walking to his car. She watched until he closed the car door and started the engine.

When Holly returned to the kitchen Lisa beamed. "Oh. My. God. He is Prince Charming."

4

When Charlie called on Sunday, he and Holly decided to go to dinner the following Saturday—the last Saturday of January. Thirty-two days from the day they'd met.

Meg began smiling more than crying and seemed to enjoy being with her friends. Her progress pleased Holly and every night at dinner or just before going to bed the two of them talked at length the way they had before Mike came into Meg's life. Only now they talked about love in a different light. Meg began to realize that she should have nicked her relationship with Mike in the bud but she wasn't going to stop loving him and remembering the way he 'loved' her.

The next Saturday, Holly tried on a few outfits before choosing the dress Lisa gave her for Christmas. She hadn't had a date since before she and Marcus were married and she'd only had a few first dates in her life. She turned from front to back before the mirror fidgeting with the standup ruffle around the neck.

"You look terrific." Meg gazed wide-eyed at her mother's reflection in the mirror.

"You don't think I'm too old for this outfit, do you?"

"No way. You're going to have Charlie groveling at your feet."

"I'm not so sure I want groveling."

The deep red silky baby doll dress hung loose to the knees

from a small ruffle around the neck. She wore black leggings and black suede boots with three-inch heels. None of her bras worked, even the strapless ones due to the larger than normal armholes in the dress, so she decided to go braless. She wondered if she looked fashion chic or just plain cheap.

Holly turned away from the mirror and placed her hands on both sides of Meg's face. "Are you okay with me going out on a date?"

"Why wouldn't I be?"

"I know what Mike meant to you. I didn't want to upset you by going out with someone who means so much to me."

Meg sat on the edge of the bed. "Just because I have a broken heart doesn't mean you can't go out on a date."

"I don't want your heart to hurt more because of Charlie and me."

"That's crazy, Mama. Remember, I'm the one who wanted you to get a boyfriend before I go off to college."

"I just want to be certain." Holly turned back to the mirror and played with different hairstyles.

"Is he still taking you to Anastasia's?"

"Yes."

"I looked that place up online. It's expensive. He must have money." Meg giggled.

"Well, if it's true what they say about lawyers—" Holly's phone interrupted them. She flashed Meg a worried look before she said hello.

"I hate to call so late, Holly, but I'm afraid I'm going to have to break our date."

Holly plopped on the bed next to Meg. "Is everything alright?"

"No. I'm afraid that it's not."

"Is there anything I can do?"

"Thanks for asking. It's Troubadour, Jordan's horse. He's feverish and, well, I don't know much about horses, but his coat is foaming with sweat. You can imagine the state

Jordan's in."

Holly flashed a frown at Meg. "Yes. I'm afraid I can."

"I'll make it up to you, Holly. There's just nothing I can do except be here for her."

"I understand completely."

"I was hoping you'd say that you were just a little disappointed."

"To be honest Charlie, I am. We can get together some other time unless you're trying to get rid of me."

"Never. I'd rather be with you than anyone tonight. The vet just drove up to the stable. I've got to go. I'll call you when I can."

"I hope everything works out."

"You and me both."

Holly turned the phone off and tossed it onto the bed.

"Now what's happened, Mama?"

"Remember the horse Jordan got for Christmas?"

"Yeah."

"Well, he's pretty sick, I take it. The vet is there. Jordan is quite upset."

"That's sad. Does Charlie think the horse is going to die?"

"I don't know."

I'm glad he didn't stand you up." Meg snuggled next to her mother. "First me, now Jordan. I'm sorry, Mama."

"Life goes on Meg. Remember my motto."

"What is, is."

Charlie kept Holly posted on Troubadour's slow recovery and Jordan's frail state of mind over the next couple of weeks. They'd talked about meeting for lunch during the week, but Holly worked in Chapel Hill and Charlie worked in Raleigh— an hour's drive away. The majority of their conversations took place on Charlie's morning and afternoon commutes.

By the middle of February, the stallion rallied, so Holly and Charlie set the second Friday in February for another try at their first date. They'd decided to try Anastasia's again, thinking that the third time would be a charm. That morning Meg came into Holly's room and slid under the covers with her.

"Good morning, sunshine." Holly snuggled against her daughter's clammy body. You're in a cold sweat."

"I know. I don't feel so well."

"What's wrong?"

"I'm not sure. I threw up a couple of times during the night and I still feel nauseated." Meg put her hands over her eyes. "I just feel weird."

"What do you mean by weird?"

"No energy. Dizzy, like I'm going to faint."

"Let me take your temperature." Holly got the thermometer from her bathroom and put it under Meg's tongue. When it beeped, Meg looked at it and handed it to Holly.

"Normal," Holly said and sat on the bed to think.

"Maybe I'll stay in bed today." Meg rolled over and pulled the covers up over her head.

"Well, you're not going to school today. Let me run this by Brody and see what he thinks." Holly picked up her phone and dialed. The receptionist put her on hold and Holly listened to Enya until she wanted to throw the phone out the window.

When Brody finally picked up, he listened patiently. "It doesn't sound good, Holly. There's a new strain of swine flu going around. She's probably dehydrated. You'd better get her over here right away."

"You don't think it's anything serious, do you?"

"Holly, you know that I can't make a diagnosis over the phone."

"Sorry. Should I make an appointment?"

"No, just bring her straight over. I'll fit her in."

"Thanks, it's nice to have a doctor as a best friend."

Although an inch of snow covered the ground, Holly heard thunder. The branches of the bare trees looked like black silhouettes against the murky sky. Before she pulled out of the driveway, she checked the road for ice. Her worst winter driving fear was hydroplaning and she didn't want to end up in a ditch or the emergency room or worse.

When they arrived at Brody's office, the receptionist led them directly to an exam room. Brody examined Meg thoroughly all the while maintaining a professional demeanor. "Meg, I'm going to ask the technician to draw some blood. We'll need a urine sample too. I'm not going to jump to any conclusions. The results of the lab work will tell me all sorts of things. Then we'll go from there. Is that alright?"

"Sure."

"You're dehydrated, so I'd like to give you some IV fluids while we wait for the lab results."

Meg looked to Holly. "An IV?"

"Honey, you know Brody wouldn't do anything that wasn't going to help you."

"Sorry, Brody." Meg held her arm out straight. "Go for it." She grimaced.

"I'll send my nurse in. She's much better at IVs than I am." Brody rested his elbow on his belt touching his fist to his chin. He stared at Meg as if he were dissecting pages of medical books.

Just as Brody's nurse entered the room, Meg jumped from the exam table and vomited bile into the sink.

"Looks like I got here just in time." The young nurse set a tray of supplies on the counter and handed Meg a wet washcloth. "My name is Sara, without an H." She smiled as she assisted Meg back onto the table.

Meg folded the washcloth and placed it on her forehead. "Thanks," she said while she watched the nurse assemble her equipment. "Can I ask you a personal question?"

"Go ahead."

"Is your name Sara Without an H, or just plain Sara—S-A-R-A?"

Sara looked at Meg with a deadpan expression for a moment before she burst out laughing.

Once the blood samples were obtained and the IV in place, Meg fell asleep while Holly flipped through half a dozen magazines and finally concentrated on the vision chart that hung on the back of the door.

When Brody returned, the look of concern on his face frightened Holly. Meg opened her eyes when he touched her foot.

"I'd like to get an ultrasound."

"Why?" Meg looked from Brody to Holly.

Brody took a deep breath. "I think you may be pregnant."

Holly had a vision of a monstrous snake, uncoiling slowly and hissing so loudly that her ears rang.

"I can't be pregnant. Mike was sterile. He told me so."

Holly felt suddenly light headed. "Megan, is there something you haven't told me?"

Brody excused himself. "Just open the door when you're ready."

Tears dripped down Meg's cheeks into a wide circle on the white paper that covered the pillow. Meg covered her face with her palms while Holly waited until she regained control.

"When I first met Mike he wasn't so sick. After I visited him a few times, and after we'd started making out, he got stronger. I helped him take a short walk one day and when we got back to his room he closed the door and kissed me. I think it was the first and only time we kissed standing up...and our first full body hug. He led me into the bathroom and shut the door."

"Meg?"

"We just...kissed and well, he pulled up my shirt and kissed..." Meg brushed her hand across her breasts. "Then he kissed me all over...all the way down, you know..."

"He just kissed you?"

"Honest, Mama. We didn't…do it."

"Do what?"

"Intercourse. He rubbed…you know…against me, but he didn't, penetrate."

"Did he have an orgasm?"

"At first, he couldn't get an, you know…"

"An erection?"

"Yeah. He kept apologizing because he…couldn't get one. I didn't care because I didn't want to go all the way, but I didn't try to stop him. It seemed so important to him. Then he got a little hard…and, tried to get inside me, but he could only get the tip inside. I can't be pregnant."

"But he had a climax then?"

"Yes. He wiped me off with a towel. He told me that I was still a virgin. There wasn't any blood. Don't girls bleed the first time?"

Holly nodded.

"I didn't exactly lie to you. We only touched. I did things to make him feel good, and he did things that made me… I didn't tell you more because I didn't want to lie to you." Meg covered her eyes with her hands.

"You didn't have to tell me more. I believe you."

"After that, Mike was so happy. We stood there for a while and just kissed. He said that he couldn't make it happen with his wife which was the real reason she left." Meg let out a deep sigh through pursed lips. "I was glad that he was happy, that I made him happy when his wife couldn't. But it never happened again. Honest. He tried to make it happen again, but it never worked after that."

Holly thought her knees might buckle under her. What a manipulator this jerk was. She tried to control her anger.

"Will you ask Brody to come in? I need to ask him how I could possibly be pregnant."

When Brody returned, Meg told him what she'd told

Holly. She asked, "Can't you examine me and tell whether or not I'm still a virgin? I mean, don't girls bleed the first time? Isn't there something…?"

"I can tell if your hymen is intact," Brody said. "It's still possible to get pregnant without being entered—without intercourse. If he ejaculated into you, there is a very real chance, if he wasn't sterile, that he could have impregnated you."

"Please check me, Brody. I need to know that I'm still a virgin."

"If it would make you feel better, I can take a look."

"Yes, it will make me feel better."

Sara helped Meg scoot to the end of the exam table, covered her with the paper sheet, and instructed her to let her knees fall to the sides. Holly cradled Meg's head while she squeezed her eyes tight and whimpered.

Brody inserted the speculum and took a quick look. "It's intact. Do you want a mirror to see it," he asked. "It looks like a little crescent moon."

"No." Meg began to sob.

After the ordeal, Brody suggested an ultrasound to verify the pregnancy. He left Holly and Meg alone to decide what to do next. Meg wiped her eyes with the paper sheet. "I'm so ashamed that I asked Brody to do that, but I'm glad you know that I'm still a virgin. I can't be pregnant, Mama. I just can't be."

Holly passed Meg a box of tissues. "I guess there's only one way to find out."

"Then open the door and let's get it over with."

Holly could barely walk. Her legs felt as numb as her brain, but she made it to the door and opened it.

Brody came in followed by Sara pushing the ultrasound machine. Holly moved to the opposite side and took a tight hold of Meg's hand. Meg winced when Sara squirted the conducting gel in a circle on Meg's flat abdomen. Everyone watched the images on the screen as Sara moved the probe from right to left in search of a fetus.

"There it is. Look right here." Brody pointed to the screen. That fluttering is the baby's heart beating."

"That's the head," Sara said. "Wow, this is a big baby. You must be into your second trimester."

Silence surrounded them like an empty tunnel until Meg screamed, "No," and then the tunnel echoed the hiss of the snake.

"No. It can't be a baby. Brody just told me I'm a virgin. I've had periods. Mama?" Meg sat up and searched the faces in the room. "It's a mistake. I am *not* pregnant. Even though we did what we did, Mike had leukemia. He had chemo. He was sterile."

"Honey, he manipulated you. He used you," Holly said frankly.

"No! He didn't manipulate me. Mike loved me. I mean he really cared about me. If he thought he could make babies he wouldn't have touched me."

"Meg, the hymen isn't solid. Anytime sperm is in the vagina there's a possibility that the sperm can seep through." Brody looked kindly at Meg.

"What about him being sterile?" Meg's lips screwed into a grimace.

"Did he tell you his diagnosis?" Brody asked.

"Yes. He had Acute Myelocytic Leukemia, just like Daddy." Meg covered her face again and sobbed into her hands. Holly held her close.

"So, the boyfriend who died is the father?"

"If I'm pregnant, he is."

Holly looked at Sara. "Meg's friend, Mike, died last month and she's been sad for a long time."

"I'm sorry, Meg." Sara placed her hand on Meg's shoulder.

"Lie back, Meg," Brody said. "I want to take a closer look."

"What did you see?" Holly flashed an inquisitive expression then turned back to the image on the screen.

"Meg, you said that you've had periods." Brody spoke straightforward. "Quite a few women experience bleeding or what we call spotting throughout their pregnancies. Sometimes it's nothing, but look here." Brody pointed to the screen. "Your placenta is low and it partially covers your cervix. It's called placenta previa. Bleeding from a placenta previa happens when the cervix begins to thin out or dilate, even a little, and disrupts the blood vessels in that area. If your bleeding gets severe, we'll have to deliver your baby right away, even if it's premature or you and the baby both could bleed to death."

Holly held tight to Meg's hand as if she might save her from this precarious predicament. What else could possibly go wrong in Meg's and her once perfect world? Losing Meg would be like losing her heart. There would be nothing left in her wonderland. If Meg died, Holly would just have to die along with her.

Meg didn't seem to grasp the enormity of Brody's statement. "Sara Without an H said that the...fetus looks big."

"It does. We'll measure the femur length and compare that to the date of your last period before this episode with Mike. That will tell us just how far along you are."

"Great." Meg frowned. "Look at me? Does my belly look pregnant? Aren't pregnant people supposed to look like they've swallowed a basketball?"

"Every once in a while a woman comes in complaining of sudden, severe back pain. The pain is labor, but they all swear they didn't know they were pregnant. Some don't believe it until they pop out a full-term baby. One woman was actually trying to get pregnant, so she wasn't in denial." Sara rambled.

Meg looked away.

"While we're looking, do you want to know the sex of the baby?" Sara moved the transducer higher on Meg's abdomen.

Meg swung her head around, away from the screen. "No. I don't ever want to know that. I just want it to go away."

Sara turned the machine off and cleaned the transmitting gel off Meg's belly while Brody spoke. "Because of your previa, a vaginal exam could cause massive bleeding. So, you'll be followed by ultrasounds instead. I'm also going to put you on pelvic rest, which means you need to take it easy, avoid activities that might provoke bleeding, like strenuous workouts or heavy lifting. No vacuuming. No running. No lacrosse. And, of course, no intercourse for the rest of your pregnancy."

"You don't have to worry about me having sex. I'm done with that until I'm at least thirty." Meg attempted a smile, but it turned to a frown quickly. "No more running or lacrosse?"

"Sorry." Brody flashed a look at Holly.

Meg covered her face again. "No more scholarship. Fuck Mike!"

"Megan Marie!"

"I can't help it, Mama." Meg looked up. "I'm sorry Brody. Sorry, Sara Without an H."

"It's alright, Meg." Brody rubbed Meg's knee. "It's good to get your anger out."

Meg grimaced. "Will you tell me when I'm...when to expect it? And don't tell Lisa, okay. I mean I want to be the one to tell her."

"Meg, if I told anyone that you were pregnant, even my wife, I could lose my license to practice medicine."

"Really?" Meg opened her eyes wide.

"Really. It's a breach of patient confidentiality." Brody picked up Meg's chart and tapped it on the end of the examining table.

"I'll tell her tonight, or tomorrow morning. Hey, what time is it?" Meg looked at her watch. "Mama, it's almost five o'clock, you have a date with Charlie tonight. You're gonna be late."

"I'd better call him. I'll be right back."

While Holly went outside to make the call, Sara removed the IV from Meg's hand.

"Nobody's gonna believe that I got pregnant this way."

"I believe you." Brody put his hand back on Meg's knee. "But, you're probably right. It's highly likely that the leukemia itself killed Mike's sperm before any treatment began. Many of the drugs he might have been on lower the sperm count to zilch. Since we know the truth, he must have had enough sperm to impregnate you. Why, it's almost a miracle you got pregnant."

"You mean like Saint Mary's Immaculate Conception?" Meg frowned. "Well, I don't think this baby is the second coming of Christ. And I don't think it's a miracle."

"If I can do anything to help you sort things out, I will." Sara smiled as she pushed the machine out the door and down the hall.

"If you feel up to it, we should let this young man's physicians know about your pregnancy. I think they might find it very interesting."

"Why?"

"It could aid in the research of the disease and the chemo drugs." Brody thought a moment. "They'll probably want proof of paternity."

"But they can't check the baby's DNA with Mike's without permission because of what you called, patient confidentially, right?"

"That's right." Brody nodded. "They'd need permission from the family."

"It's complicated, but I can't let his family know about this." Meg hesitated. "He had a…wife, an unfaithful one, but still…I'd like him and his memory to rest in peace. Know what I mean?"

"You have time to think about it."

Meg shrugged. "I don't know what to do."

"You're a strong, independent young lady. I've known you since you were born. I know you'll make a decision you can live with. When you're dressed, meet me in my office at the end of the hall."

Meg didn't blink or move until Holly returned. "Brody said I can go home." Stating that, she didn't make any attempt to get up. "He also said I might want to tell Mike's doctors because this...fetus is some sort of a freak of nature. I don't think I should tell them. What if it got back to his wife or parents?"

"You may be right. But, on the other hand, it's his baby as well. Maybe the grandparents would like to know that they have a grandchild on the way."

"I can't, Mama. I just can't think about it right now." Meg covered her face with both hands.

"Are you ready to get dressed?"

"I'm ready to run away and die."

Holly felt a chill and grabbed at her shirt.

Meg pulled the scrunchy from her ponytail letting her hair fall around her shoulders.

"You used to do that when you were little." Holly smiled.

"Do what?"

"Every time you were sad you'd wrap your hair around your shoulders."

"I'm sad now. Sadder than I've ever been. Even when Daddy died."

"It's okay to be sad."

"But, Mama, don't you see? I'm not just sad, I'm sorry that I, we, Mike and I, did what we did. I mean, I'm sad he's gone. I'm not sad that we did what we did. I'm sad that we didn't use protection. But why would we? We...never expected...this."

Holly couldn't hold back the tears. She stood and

embraced Meg. "It's done. Look at it this way. Right or wrong, Mike left you a beautiful gift. Now, you just need to decide what to do with it."

"I don't deserve a mother like you. I never thought of this as a gift. Maybe a gag gift or the booby prize. I don't think Mike made a practice of fooling around with underage girls. If he was still alive someone could put him in jail for having sex with me."

The two clung together. "Honey, we're both surprised and upset right now. I don't know what Mike was thinking." Holly squinted. "Men need to have intercourse to prove their manhood and to show their love. Let's just hope that he loved you in all the ways he could and that he wasn't taking advantage of you."

"I guess we'll never know. Thing is, I didn't want my first time to be standing up against a cold tile wall."

"Oh, honey…"

Meg pulled away. "It wasn't even my first time, but it could have been. I mean if Mike had been stronger I know I would've let him take my virginity. At that moment…I wanted him to…'prove his love' as you say. At least my body wanted it. Man, I'm so confused."

"Do you want to be alone?"

"Yeah. I'll meet you in Brody's office."

While Holly sat alone in Brody's office, she wondered about her words. A gift. A dying, married boy's parting gift. Wonderful.

Meg entered the office and interrupted Holly's nightmare.

"Sara Without an H, is real nice."

"Did you two have a talk?"

"She said she'd be there for me. She didn't treat me like I did something bad."

"She seems like a sweet young lady."

Brody entered the office and settled himself behind his large desk. He looked at Meg then Holly over the top of his tortoiseshell reading spectacles. "I'm going to refer you to an obstetrician. Dr. Gilbert at UNC OB/GYN. She's an excellent attending physician. Since you're high risk, because of the previa and Mike's medical history, I think UNC is the way to go. You can look up her bio online and see if you agree. Do you have any questions?"

Meg wrapped her arms around herself. "I'm trying to think that everything will work out for the best like you said, but I can't see how right now."

"Be patient. Your mom has as much faith as I do that you'll be able to turn this into something positive."

Sara knocked on the door and Brody invited her in. "According to my little pregnancy dial it looks like you're due date is the Fourth of July. You're twenty weeks and two days pregnant. The baby's measurements show that it's twenty weeks and six days along. You're over halfway there."

Meg stood. "Halfway and I didn't even know it existed?" She ran her hands over her belly. "Look at me. How can there be a baby in here. I haven't even gained weight."

On the way home Meg commented again on how well everyone had treated her. But, Holly feared what Meg thought about herself. She'd been proud to win the scholarship to Northwestern, a school that both Holly and Meg knew they couldn't afford otherwise. How could she manage an education with a baby? Would she ever be able to play lacrosse again? Could she win another scholarship next year? How will her friends react to this? How will Meg react to the stigma?

Massive snowflakes smacked and froze on the windshield and the roads turned to black ice. The car slid and skidded a few times, but Holly corrected it. Meg sat silent as if she didn't notice the building snow. Any other time she'd be excited like she was the morning Charlie came into their lives. Holly remembered that morning and their snow-slush fight and all the glorious pictures she'd taken of Meg. She hoped this pregnancy wouldn't rob Meg of what little childhood she had left.

When they got home, Meg headed to her bedroom. "You can tell Lisa everything. I don't have the strength. And tell Charlie hello for me."

"Honey. I canceled with Charlie."

Meg turned around. "You canceled? You can't cancel."

"I want to be here with you, tonight."

"Why? Because you think I'll take a coat hanger and jam it up my vagina and then go running and let this thing fall out so all of this will be over?"

"Megan, no."

"If I did, we could start over and I can stop hurting you. I've ruined everything. I'm going to lose my scholarship and I'm just one big roadblock between you and Charlie."

"You're my daughter—my first responsibility. I just thought you might need a shoulder to cry on tonight."

"Please don't be angry, Mama. I just want you to love me. Please don't stop loving me because I'm pregnant."

Holly followed Meg into her bedroom. They sat on the side of Meg's bed. "Nothing could make me stop loving you. What is, is. Remember?"

"I'm trying to." Meg removed her boots and socks. "What did Charlie think of my latest news flash?"

"I didn't tell him. I told him you weren't feeling well and that it was serious."

"Please, Mama. Don't let me ruin any more of your life." The deluge of tears returned and Holly held tight to her precious daughter.

"If Charlie is the Prince Charming we want him to be, he'll wait."

"Maybe he won't. Please call him back. I'm going to be pregnant for nineteen more weeks. You can't babysit me for the rest of my life."

"I just need to be with you tonight. I'm meeting Charlie for brunch tomorrow. Okay?"

"That's good, Mama. I'm so happy you didn't cancel forever. I think I can sleep now."

Holly stood and watched Meg settle herself under the covers then tip-toed out of the room.

Deep down, Holly felt as if her mothering, her nurturing had been full of rotting, infected splinters. She thought about calling Lisa, but couldn't conjure up the strength. How she wished Charlie could just hold her. Charlie. She laughed to herself. She hadn't wished for someone other than Marcus to come to her in a crisis in years, for heaven's sake. She'd just seen the man twice. Their relationship was over the phone and it wasn't even phone sex, not that she wanted it to be. How she longed to touch his face and feel his thumping heart against hers. How she needed to see a new, brightly feathered songbird at the bird feeder.

Just breathe, she thought. Just breathe.

Holly knew that she'd had it easy with Meg. She really was the perfect daughter. They'd always been able to share everything and they truly were best friends forever. She bragged at how easy it was to raise Meg alone. Meg had always asked for her advice and listened to what she had to say, even if they didn't agree. Meg wasn't what Holly would call popular at school, but she had plenty of friends and didn't get into trouble. She made straight A's, took gymnastics until she grew too tall then switched to lacrosse. She joined service clubs and did volunteer work. Holly's body stiffened. God. The volunteer work had precipitated this mess in the first place.

So now, her precious child was pregnant. Holly wondered just how this pregnancy and baby would affect Meg's future. Her future. Damn. She thought. Damn.

She recalled the terror in Meg's eyes when she saw the

beating heart on the ultrasound. And she remembered the pain in Charlie's voice when he'd called to tell her about Troubadour's illness and Jordan's anxiety. She needed to be with Meg and Charlie. But, how? She and Meg and Charlie and Jordan. She held back the tears as long as she could then ran down the hall to her bedroom, slammed the door as hard as she could, and wept the way she had when Marcus died.

After a few minutes, Meg tapped on Holly's door. "I'm sorry, Mama. I'm such a failure and disappointment to you. I never wanted to hurt you. Please, can I come in?"

"Of course you can." Holly blew her nose, sat up, and leaned against the headboard.

Meg stood at the foot of the bed. Holly thought she looked ten years old with her remorseful tearstained cheeks and mussed hair.

"I guess everything just caught up with me," Holly said as she patted the mattress beside her. "Come on, climb in bed with me. We'll be able to think straight tomorrow."

"Thanks, but I need to be in my own bed right now. I just need a nap."

"That's fine, sweetheart. When you wake up we'll fix some chicken soup." When Meg closed the door behind her, Holly blew air softly through pursed lips and tried to imagine Prince Charming lifting her onto his white stallion.

5

The next morning, Holly opened her closet to look for something appropriate to wear to brunch. The weather remained blustery but had warmed up enough to melt the ice on the roads. She decided to wear the same outfit she'd chosen for her last date with Charlie. Red would certainly brighten the dreary day. She decided that going without a bra made sense and added a seductive touch as well. Finally, she and Charlie could spend a few hours together. A smile broadened her lips. She sucked in her stomach and stood tall with her chin held high like a professional dancer. Nothing could stop them now. Already, she felt free and wanted to float, to dance, to run to Charlie.

Meg hadn't awakened by ten. Her breathing sounded raspy. Holly wondered if she'd lain awake and wept into the night. She didn't know whether to stay or go, but Meg's face appeared as serene as a cat curled up in a sunbeam. Holly jotted a quick note and left it folded on Meg's dresser. She grabbed her coat and danced off to meet her prince.

Gusty winds practically blew Holly through the restaurant's front door. She removed her gloves and shook out her hair. When she looked up, she began to cry.

There he stood, Mr. Charles Prince, a little thinner maybe, but with that same glorious smile. He wore a dark gray wool suit, a crisp white shirt with cufflinks, an almost magenta tie, and polished black dress shoes. He pulled a handkerchief from his chest pocket and offered it to Holly. While she pressed the handkerchief against her tears he brought a bouquet from behind his back—pink, yellow, and coral sweetheart roses wrapped in florist's tissue and a forest green bow. That only brought more tears, followed by a hug then spirited laughter.

"I feel like a damsel in distress." Holly grinned and smelled the roses. "This is…. You are—"

"I'd like to be Sir Charles—an English Lord at your service." Charlie bowed.

Holly tilted her head, questioning.

"I'm sorry. Barbara told me about Prince Charming knocking your door down."

Crimson streaks climbed Holly's neck. "So, there's no secret, huh?"

"None."

"These roses are beautiful. I'm, ah, just overwhelmed."

"We met on December twenty-third. I don't want you to think I'm presumptuous, but I thought by Valentine's Day, which passed three days ago, that we'd be a duo."

"Charlie, we are a duo of sorts." Holly spoke as if she needed to say all that was in her heart before the next catastrophe tried to pull them apart. "I think of you every minute of every day. I long to be—"

"Your table, sir." The maître d' interrupted. "Please, follow me."

When they took their seats at a small table next to an open fireplace, Holly placed the bouquet of roses in the center of the linen covered table. "What I meant to say is that I have a special fondness for you and want to apologize for all you've put up with since we met."

"But you've had to put up with me and my daughter as well." Charlie straightened his tie and leaned slightly toward Holly. "By the way, how is Meg today?"

Holly feared to talk about Meg's pregnancy, embarrassed by it as if her daughter was in the category of a loose woman or a whore even. The sudden realization that Meg would be an unwed mother with a marred reputation caused her to reflux gastric acid into Charlie's fine white handkerchief. "It's sad. I'm not sure I can talk about it yet. I haven't even told Lisa." Holly looked at the roses.

"I have all day. So, tell me."

Before Holly could speak, the waiter brought a bottle of champagne with two flutes and invited them to visit the buffet at their leisure.

"Champagne?" Holly opened her eyes wide.

"It's for a late Valentine's Day, so let's toast our future." Charlie filled the glasses and raised his. "To the damsel in distress and her Prince Charming, may they live happily ever after."

"Sir Charles," Holly mumbled, barely able to speak. She bowed her head before clinking glasses and taking a sip then sat back to let the bubbles burst in her mouth before swallowing. Charlie had said, *may they live happily ever after.* Had wonderland finally arrived? She wanted to say the right words. Everything seemed so perfect. She didn't want to scare Charlie away. She lifted the champagne from the ice bucket and read the label—*Veuve Clicquot La Grande Dame Champagne Brut.* "This is fine champagne, isn't it?"

"It's fit for my *Grande Dame.* Very fine is my valentine and mine, very fine very mine and mine is my valentine."

Holly giggled. "Excuse me?"

"It's just something Gertrude Stein said once. I've waited years to say it to a beautiful lady."

"You're lonely aren't you?"

"Yes. I guess you could say that. It's nothing new, though. I've been lonely since my honeymoon ended."

"You didn't tell me that."

"I didn't want sympathy. It wasn't anything I wanted to

say over the phone."

"Sorry to talk about you behind your back, but Barbara told me that your wife just left you last summer. Why did you stay married for so long?"

"We were in love. We were the happiest couple alive on our wedding day. Jill was four months pregnant and I looked forward to being a father. As soon as the honeymoon ended Jill detached from me emotionally. Later I found out that she only married me because of her pregnancy and wanted to save face. I tried to make it work. After Jessica was born things got better, but Jill wasn't much of a mother. Jessica got in her way. Jill started seeing other men. Then along came Jordan. She's my daughter, but I'm certain I'm not her father."

"What?"

"After Jessica was born, Jill and I didn't have sex until one night she came home late and seduced me. Six months later Jordan was born. Seven pounds. I never had the desire to determine our genetics. I fell in love with her the same way I'd fallen in love with Jessica. When Jill left, I felt released, but the girls haven't gotten over it. Jessica wears a false happy face and Jordan is drowning in her sorrow."

"Why didn't Jill leave earlier?"

"Money, family, prestige. Her parents are part of the old money society. She at least, had the decency not to ruin the family name with a divorce, but she's no saint—there's more to it than that."

"But she did finally leave."

"She waited for her parents to die. She was the last heir. Had she divorced before they both died she would have been disowned and disinherited. So, she was stuck with me."

"I'm so sorry."

"Please don't be. I've actually been a single father for almost twenty years." Charlie emptied his glass. "Shall we dine?"

"Of course." Holly couldn't remember when she last

ate—it must have been dinner the night before last.

When they faced the elegant array of delicacies Holly promptly lost her appetite. She filled her plate with a spoonful of fresh peaches, a strawberry, and a smoked salmon omelet. Charlie went for the prime rib and a huge salad. He eyed the desserts and smiled at Holly.

"Think we'll have room for that chocolate cake? It looks like the one Meg baked for your birthday."

Holly smiled remembering how happy and carefree they were the day Charlie walked into their lives.

When they returned to their seats, Charlie, again, asked about Meg.

"It's difficult to tell you this." Holly put her fork down and folded her hands on her lap. She wanted to trust this man. She felt as if they were playing a game of truth or dare. "Meg's pregnant. Mike is apparently the father."

Charlie placed his thumb on his top lip and closed his eyes. "No, not Meg."

Holly blotted her eyes with Charlie's handkerchief.

Charlie took a deep breath and looked at Holly with sympathy. "My worst fear. My older daughter, Jessica, has been sexually active since she was thirteen. She doesn't know that I know about it. If anyone should be pregnant it should be her. You're one-hundred percent certain?"

"I saw the fetus on an ultrasound. She's twenty weeks already. She doesn't look or act pregnant. I honestly believe that the fetus surprised her as much as it did me."

"And Mike...I'm sorry. That's none of my business."

"It's okay to ask. I want you to know. Because of Mike's illness he couldn't get enough of an erection to penetrate her. But he still somehow did without breaking her hymen. Besides that, he thought he was sterile because of the illness and chemo."

"What an astonishing story." Charlie reached out for Holly's hand. "Too bad for Meg. I'm sorry, Holly. If there's anything I can do to help…"

"Listen when I need to rant?"

Charlie half-smiled. "You've got it."

"She's taking on a huge guilt trip. She's angry at herself for going too far with a married man, for not realizing she wasn't having safe sex, for…everything."

"Married?"

Holly flushed. "A rocky one, but yes. Married."

"And how old was this guy?"

"Twenty-two. When they met Meg thought he was a teenager. She realizes now that she should have stopped seeing him when she found out how old he was and that he was married."

"I'm sorry." Charlie caressed Holly's hand. "I'm at a total loss for words, which isn't good for a lawyer, except to say that you could file for statutory rape."

"Meg doesn't want to go there. She wants his family to remember him in a good way, especially since he died the same way her father died."

"Of course she does, poor kid. Damn." Charlie let go of Holly's hand, pushed away his plate. "And her scholarship?"

"Gone."

"Please forgive me for bringing that up. Will you?"

"Of course. I know that you're fond of Meg and have her best interests at heart. She appreciates your concern."

"You're one hell of a mother. And Meg is fortunate to have you."

"Thanks. Until lately, Meg hasn't had a problem in the world. This is our first crisis."

"If any woman can handle this, you can. I could see right away what a good relationship you have, and that will help. Besides, you know you can blow off steam in my direction. I'm trying to be here for you."

"You are Prince Charming."

Charlie laughed. "Is that who your friend, Lisa, thinks I

am as well?"

"She's been trying to push me into relationships since Marcus died. She was there the day you called and asked to stop by to see Meg. She glued her bottom to the barstool. There was no way she was going to miss an opportunity to check you out."

"Did I pass inspection?"

Holly grinned. "With flying colors."

"I like you so very much. I'll try hard to live up to both Lisa's and your expectations."

Brunch lasted until four-thirty but didn't include the chocolate cake or a trip back to the buffet. When Holly realized the time, panic struck. She picked up her cell, turned it on, and was surprised to see that Meg hadn't called. "I really must be going. Today has been wonderful."

"Yes, it has." Charlie reached across the table and put his hand on Holly's. "Did you hear anything that put you off?"

She turned her hand and interlaced her fingers with his. "No."

"Then I say it was a perfect first date."

Holly shrugged and smiled as she reached for her bag. "So, Meg's pregnancy hasn't scared you away?"

"Just the opposite. Jill was just a couple years older than Meg when we got pregnant out of wedlock. Of course, we had different choices, easier ones, I think, than Meg has without the father of the baby to comfort her. I'll be here for you and Meg, and I know you'll be here," he touched his heart, "for me and my girls."

"You, Sir Charles, are a rare breed."

They walked in silence to Holly's car. "Next date I'll pick you up, okay?"

Before she could say anything, Charlie pulled her to him and kissed her gently. She smiled coyly. He kissed her again, and the kiss lasted for minutes it seemed. She felt her whole body and soul slip into him. The kiss had aroused her and she could tell it had done the same to him. Still, they stood in the open in the cold parking lot pressing their bodies together with mouths searching like crazed, horny teenagers. Holly's groin ached and her breasts tingled. Charlie backed away slightly and brought his hands to the sides of her breasts. She was glad she hadn't worn a bra. She breathed deeply while Charlie nestled his face in her neck and left a moist spot behind her ear from his kiss. He kissed her mouth again, but less intense. Her wanting and needing turned to loving and caring. Charlie backed away without speaking then walked to his car.

Holly watched him walk away but felt him walk into her heart simultaneously as if the first kiss had sealed a royal decree. She felt a twinge of guilt. Could she do this? Could she love someone without betraying Marcus? Charlie turned and waved. Holly slipped into her car and wept.

On her way home, Holly stopped at Lisa's. She had to share some things with her that she couldn't share with Meg.

Lisa met her at the door. "Wow. Don't you look ravishing? Well, except for your bloodshot eyes. I hope that's from happy tears. Come in and tell me all about it."

Holly removed her boots and hung her coat on an armoire in the foyer. She followed Lisa into the family room and sat on the end of a modern white sectional. Lisa sat in a recliner and tucked her legs under her.

"He's Prince Charming alright. We had a glorious time, a perfect time, but..."

"But what?"

"Marcus."

"Holly. You vowed to love Marcus until death and you fulfilled that obligation."

"I know. I feel something special with Charlie, but when I watched him walk away I felt guilty."

"Marcus was probably up there smiling. You know he

wanted you to be happy. He didn't want you to stop living."

"You're right. I'm trying. For the first time since he died I'm honestly trying. Why do I feel guilty about it and will Meg feel the same guilt when she meets her next Mr. Right?"

"I wouldn't worry about Meg. She had a little romance, a first love. She'll get over him by the time she gets to college."

Holly readjusted the pillow at her back. "That's why I'm here. I think she's lost her scholarship."

"What?"

"Take a deep breath, Lisa. There's something I need to tell you."

"What happened? How could she lose her scholarship? Isn't she still making goals and straight A's?"

"She can't play lacrosse. She's pregnant." Holly stared at Lisa while Lisa sat frozen, staring into Holly's eyes.

"Pregnant?"

Holly couldn't speak. She stared back and the two sat like rock statues for a long while until Lisa came to Holly and put her arms around her. They held each other and wept like they'd been left behind by the last lifeboat from the Titanic.

"So, is that why Meg invited us to dinner tonight? To tell us?"

Holly looked confused. "Dinner? I don't know anything about it."

Holly's smile had returned by the time she left Lisa's. Lisa had always been there for her and she didn't disappoint this time. Holly thought Lisa knew more about her than she knew about herself. At least she understood her heart better than anyone. She was more logical than romantic and able to see the real world rather than Holly's idealized one. They would both be grandmothers and Lisa assured her that she would be as happy with her grandchild as Lisa would be with hers.

When Holly returned home, Meg looked up from her laptop at the bar and smiled. "You look angelic. Did he take you to a hotel after brunch? You have that look about you."

"Come here my little munchkin." Holly held Meg tightly while they waltzed around the living room laughing.

"Nothing happened except a kiss."

"I can see it now—a very long, passionate kiss."

"How did you know?"

"It shows, Mama." Meg's face clouded, she flopped onto the sofa.

"Isn't that what you were hoping for?" Holly sat next to Meg.

"It's exactly what I wanted, but that was before this." Meg put her hand on her belly.

"Meg, we need time to let this sink in."

"Time is what I don't have. I looked up pregnancy on the net. A baby is considered full term at thirty-seven weeks. I could be having a baby in sixteen weeks. It also said that some people with placenta previa need to have a C-section. I don't want major surgery to get this kicking frog out."

"Meg? Can you feel the baby move?"

"I think so. I've felt it for a while. I thought it was my stomach growling." Meg lifted her sweatshirt. Put your hand right here." Meg pointed to one side of her belly. "There. Did you feel that?"

Holly pressed her hand more firmly. When the baby moved, Holly shrieked. "Yes. It's really active. How wonderful, a little life in there."

"Hardly wonderful. I don't want it to be in there. How can I go to college with a baby?"

"You've been thinking."

"Remember the time you asked me if I wanted a kitten or a puppy? I didn't. I don't particularly enjoy animals. I don't particularly enjoy little kids either and I've never even held a baby or wanted to. I never wanted dolls, I never played with the ones you and Grandma and Nana forced on me. I never considered babysitting as a way to make money. Maybe, when I get married, I might want a baby, if my husband wants one too. But, babies aren't something I've dreamed of having one day, and now this."

"Oh, honey, I—"

"I don't feel anything like love. My baby moved you, didn't it?"

Holly couldn't speak. She nodded.

"I don't feel anything except emptiness." Meg pulled her shirt down.

"What do you think we should do?"

"Well to start, I planned a little dinner party for tonight. You don't have to do anything but eat and you'll have to do that anyway. Besides, I have to do this tonight, before school on Monday."

Holly smiled. "You're the chef."

"Thanks. I invited Aubrey, Tia, and Vanessa, as well as Lisa and Brody. The girls are going to spend the night. I want to tell all our best friends at once and then have enough time to talk about it. I'm sure my friends won't offer brainless advice with Brody here."

"I stopped at Lisa's on my way home."

"So, Lisa already knows?"

"She does."

"Well, that's good. Now she and Brody can talk about me all they want."

Holly kissed Meg on the cheek. "Lots of changes around here, huh?"

"Didn't you realize what a dull life we've been living? My God Mama, we needed some excitement, and man, did we get it."

Later that evening when everyone had finished a pot of chili and warm slices of cornbread, Meg made the announcement. She stood, made the sign of the cross, and said, "Father forgive me, for I have sinned." Then shrugged. "I just wanted to get that off my chest because a lot of people, especially the kids at school are going to call me names like slut and ho. Some of the boys will think I'm an easy lay."

Meg kept smiling but her voice cracked and the tears trickled. She didn't try to brush them away. "I met a boy who needed me and we fell in love. We shared our love and we accidentally made a baby. Before we knew about the baby, the boy died the same way my father did. So, yesterday I found out that I'm almost twenty-one weeks pregnant. I'm not sure what to do next. That's why I wanted all of you here tonight. I guess I just need to hear what you have to say because I'm a little confused right now and Mom is in shock. I'm not going to apologize because…if I had it all to do over, I'd do the same stupid thing. Please don't scold me. Mama says, what is, is. So, who wants Cherry Garcia ice cream?"

Immediately Aubrey stood up and embraced Meg. Holly thought that Aubrey probably knew more about Meg and Mike than anyone and she had most likely helped write Meg's speech. Vanessa and Tia remained seated with a look of shock on their faces. Brody pursed his lips. Lisa reached over to grasp Holly's hand.

"Well, who's for Cherry Garcia?" Meg asked again. "Honestly you'd think I'd dropped a bomb or something."

When the ice cream cartons were empty, the girls cleaned the kitchen while Holly, Lisa, and Brody went over the details. Near midnight, they had discussed every aspect of Meg's *bomb*, noting that it had been the first one in her seventeen years.

Before going to bed, Holly checked in on the girls. The four of them were asleep on the floor, wrapped in quilts and comforters. Music blared from an iPod. They looked like a collection of American Girl Dolls—Meg, a third-generation

American with her silky dark mane, Vanessa, the daughter of a Viking with her long blond braid, Tia, an African princess with her black cornrows that fanned into ringlets, and Aubrey, a fair Irish lass with strawberry curls. Even though they were seniors in high school, they seemed so young and innocent. Holly hoped they would stick by Meg and that she would allow them to comfort her and support her. Going to school pregnant wasn't going to be easy and Meg had no experience being the brunt of malicious chatter.

On Sunday morning at breakfast, Tia told Holly that some of the girls at school had gotten pregnant to gain attention and to get out of playing sports. Their friends catered to them protected them due to their delicate condition, and the boys smothered them with affection because if they did it once, they'd do it again. There seemed to be some secret society of boys who liked to make it with a pregnant girl. Holly hoped things would be better for Meg.

Holly dragged herself to work Monday morning. She did what she had to do but no more. Visions of Meg's apprehensive face and swollen eyes as she left for school that morning went in and out of focus obliterating any thought of Charlie and their lovely afternoon together. She knew better than to bring her problems to work so she kept busy and avoided the usual office chatter. As the day crawled on, Holly's concern for Meg increased until she couldn't stand being cooped up. She left an hour early to wander the campus in search of solace, hoping that her phone would ring and bring Charlie's heart to hers. She longed to hear the comfort in his voice, but she knew that if she heard his voice she'd break down. She didn't want to show him her weakness.

Holly put Visine in her red eyes and refreshed her makeup in the car before leaving the campus. When she came in from work, she could hear Meg talking to someone on the phone.

"Okay, thanks. I'll see you later." She snapped her cell phone shut and walked into the kitchen.

"Hey, honey. How was school?"

"Okay, I guess."

"You guess? That doesn't sound positive."

"Vanessa caused a big scene in the cafeteria."

"Vanessa? Why?" Holly turned on the coffee machine before sitting at the bar across from Meg. "What happened?"

"I finally got up the nerve to tell her and Tia that Mike was married. She started screaming at me. She doesn't want to be seen with me anymore. She called me all sorts of names and shook her hands at me like she was shaking off slime."

"I'm sorry, honey."

Meg looked at her belly. "I don't sleep around. That's slime. Mike and I loved each other. She doesn't get that. I'm pretty sure that she's made it with a couple of guys. She just won't admit it. I wanted to shout out that, unlike her, I'd never actually fucked a guy, but that's irrelevant."

"Try and remember where she's coming from. Her father left her mother for a younger woman a few years back. It upset her for quite a while, remember?"

"Yeah, right. She's the slut, but she created a scene that makes me look like…shit."

Holly reached to hold Meg's hand. "You're handling this so well. I know it's not easy for you. Grandma told me once that when she was young, girls who got pregnant went to visit an ailing aunt until after their babies were born and adopted. Then they came home like nothing happened."

"I don't have an ailing aunt and I don't want to go away. I earned my scholarship. Fuck it all."

"Meg, watch your language. I know how difficult—"

"I don't care, Mama. Fuck Vanessa, fuck Mike, fuck college. Fuck handling everything. Fuck. Fuck. Fuck." Meg stomped off to her room, shut the door, and locked it behind her.

Just breathe, Holly told herself. Just breathe. She took her coffee and sat on the sofa until well after dark. She thought about Charlie. How could she let herself be so happy while her only child suffered? She recalled their kisses, their conversation. She remembered the champagne. Remembered something she wanted to say but didn't. Thought of Charlie's girls and their pain…all caused by a mother who didn't care one bit about them and Charlie was left to put the pieces back together. She wasn't going to be that kind of mother. But, she would be a good lover to this wonderful man who needed someone just like her. Maybe this time next year there wouldn't be so much baggage.

When her phone rang, Holly stumbled in the dark to find her purse. "Hello."

"Holly. I miss you—"

"Charlie…."

"I think we started something yesterday."

"We did. I'm so glad you called. Work today was…impossible…and Meg…. Her day was worse. Just the sound of your voice is so calming."

"Holly, if it were possible I'd run right over, but please understand that I need to be home for Jordan. She's almost seventeen, but she's more like twelve. She's not ready to hear about…us. She thinks her mom wants us to go back home. And, I can't lie to her. I can't spend time with you and then make up a story about where I was."

"She's lucky to have you." Holly tried not to sound jealous or disappointed.

"My ex found a riding club that's having a weekend camp the weekend after next. I know it's twelve days away, but I thought a weekend in the country might do us both some good."

"My immediate reaction is yes, of course. I'd love to. But, I do have Meg to think about. She's so fragile right now, or maybe it's me who's fragile."

"All the more reason to get your mind off it for a couple of days."

"You're probably right." Holly felt a stitch of pain in her heart and didn't know if it was due to Meg or Charlie. "Surely Meg will be fine. She's pushing us together, you know."

"I get the feeling. Enjoy it. She's pushing you and my daughters are pulling me." Charlie blew air through his teeth loud enough for Holly to hear. "I know this lovely little ranch in Pittsboro. Besides, it's time for you to see what I had to settle for when you swept the house of my dreams away."

Holly laughed. "You're not fooling me, Sir Charles. You settled for an estate—I can reach out my window and touch the house next door."

"I wouldn't exactly call four acres of untamed land an estate, but when you see it you can decide."

"Are you certain Jordan will be alright at the camp?"

"She seems excited to go. I'm not sure if she really wants to, or if she just wants to please her mother. Anyway, it's all set. I'll take Jordan and haul the horse there Friday afternoon. So, looks like I'll be free until Sunday afternoon. You can think about it."

"Sir Charles, I don't need to think about it. I would love to spend the whole weekend with you." Holly paused as a hundred visions swirled through her mind.

"I'm pulling into my drive so I need to hang up. Holly, Saturday was—"

"Perfect." Holly felt that she'd been picked up and dropped back into wonderland.

"I'll call later, my beautiful damsel. I miss you too much."

"I miss you too, Sir Charles."

Holly wrapped her arms across her chest and reveled in a moment of harmony and delight. This thing with Charlie had to be real.

Meg came into the living room without Holly realizing it and switched on a light. "Sir Charles, huh? Sounds like things are progressing."

Holly gasped. "You startled me."

"Sorry, Mama. I didn't mean to scare you. I'm sorry about using the F word." Meg stood beside the light switch next to the alcove that separated the living room from the dining room.

"Sometimes that's the only word that will do. It's just that I'm not used to it coming out of your mouth. It's difficult for you—you're frustrated and emotionally challenged right now. Don't hold back on the F word or anything else that helps you cope."

"You're such a cool mom."

"I try."

"So, what about you and Charlie?"

"Progressing nicely."

"Want to get something to eat and tell me all about it?"

Holly giggled. "Sure. How about grilled cheese and tomato sandwiches?"

After dinner, Meg took a pint of *Ben and Jerry's New York Super Fudge Chunk* ice cream from the freezer and stuck two spoons in it. Holly drained the last of the coffee from the pot while Meg motioned for her to come into the living room.

They sat side-by-side on the sofa and each took a spoonful of the chocolate decadence.

"I thought of something earlier," Meg said.

Holly turned the spoon upside down in her mouth and pulled it out slowly. "What's that?"

"Remember earlier when you told me about what pregnant girls did in Grandma's day?"

Holly smacked her forehead. "The grans."

"They need to know. I forgot all about them. They're going to disown me."

84

6

The day Meg was born the whole of Holly and Marcus' small families were there. Holly gave each one an assignment to keep order, but chaos ensued despite a lengthy birth plan. Meg's head crowned as soon as Holly's bottom hit the labor bed. Emergency calls were placed to both Holly's doctor and the ER doctor while several nurses flung open bedside cabinets, uncovered trays of instruments, started an IV, and removed the bottom half of the bed.

"This baby is coming now." One nurse shouted as she and a second nurse donned sterile gowns and gloves. "Try not to push, Holly. Try to wait for the doctor."

Holly couldn't wait, took in a big breath, and then proceeded to push Meg into the hands of the first nurse. "It's a girl," she said. Holly could hear Meg squalling. Before Marcus could cut the umbilical cord, it shred splattering blood from hell to breakfast. Bug vomited on the shiny floor where it splashed on the shoes and scrub pants of the two nurses who were working on Meg and the bleeding cord. A nurse threw a bath blanket over the vomit before Holly's father passed out. He leaned his back against the wall and slipped to the floor. Holly's mother went to the aid of both men while Marcus' mother completed her job of videotaping the blessed event.

Before Marcus could blink twice the first nurse cut Meg free of the bleeding cord and thrust her onto Holly's chest. Another nurse edged in close to the head of the bed to access

Meg and congratulate Holly. The ER doc, breathing heavily, delivered the placenta after running up five flights of stairs. When the OB doctor arrived Meg was nursing and grasping Marcus' little finger in her pink fist, the room had been cleaned up, and the grans were huddled on the tiny sofa bed proudly watching the playback of the birth of their first grandchild.

Holly knew that Meg's pregnancy wasn't going to be met with that same joy or pride by the grans. Meg's fear echoed in Holly's head—they just might disown her. Probably not Nana and Bug, but Holly's staunchly Catholic parents.

"Holy slush, Meg. I don't have a clue how any of the grans will react." Holly paused. "But it's better if they know sooner rather than later."

"Will you call and see if we can see them this weekend? If I call they'll hear my voice and know something's wrong."

"You're right. I'll call my folks first then Daddy's."

"So much for my eighteenth birthday next week. I guess I won't be celebrating with any of them."

"Maybe you will. You can play the angle that you're giving them a great-grandchild while they're still in their sixties—young enough to enjoy one."

"If it lives and if I keep it. Remember, Brody said its chromosomes might be mixed up even though it looks okay on the ultrasound."

Holly startled.

Meg shrugged. "What if it's not normal? What if it's born...dead?"

"What if it's healthy?"

"You know that Grandma and Grandpa will think I'm dammed to hell."

"I can't disagree." Holly moaned without taking her eyes off Meg. "How do you want to tell them?"

Meg held the spoon filled with ice cream mid-way

between the carton and her mouth then turned the spoon over and watched the ice cream plop back into the carton. "I don't want to tell them at all."

"Better to tell them before they pop in here unexpected and find out for themselves." Holly took one last mouthful of the ice cream and set the carton on the coffee table. "This coming weekend would be a good time to visit. I can take Friday off unless you want to go alone."

"I'd like to tell Grandma and Grandpa first...get it over with. Daddy's parents will be easier. I'll get the worst over with in Raleigh before we head to the beach."

"Sounds good. We can spend Thursday and Friday at Grandma and Grandpa's and the rest of the weekend with Daddy's folks."

"I feel like I'm going to throw up." Meg picked up the carton and took it into the kitchen.

Holly followed and sat at the bar.

"Don't waste a day off for this. Let's just spend Friday night at Grandma's then head to Salter Path on Saturday. None of them are going to take this news like soldiers, are they?"

"They love you. Besides you've never done any wrong in their eyes. I'm not sure how they'll react."

Meg put the back of her hand on her forehead and quoted Shakespeare. "Farewell. A long farewell to all my greatness."

Holly burst out laughing.

On the way to Holly's parents' house in Raleigh, Meg role played what she had to say. But when she and Holly walked into the house, Meg blurted the news. "We came to tell you that I'm pregnant. I'm not happy about it. I'm not proud of it. I don't know what I'm going to do about it. The father is dead. I lost my scholarship—that's all there is."

Grandma knocked two embroidered silk pillows from the divan and plopped down. "How could you have sex while you're still a child? Was it rape? Oh my stars. Was it?" Holly could see red splotches rising above her mother's collar.

"I'm not a child. I'll be eighteen on Thursday. I wasn't raped. I wanted it."

"Wanted sex without a marriage vow?" Grandma made the sign of the cross without waiting for an answer. "No, blessed Mother of God, blessed Mary, no. This can't be."

"It just happened, Grandma. Please don't be mad. Just listen."

Grandpa sat next to his wife and put his hand on her arm. His face ashen and drawn. "Come over here and sit with us, Meg. Tell us everything."

Meg stepped hesitantly over the pillows then sat next to her grandfather. She picked up one of the pillows and held it over her belly.

Holly sat on a deep red Ottoman close to Meg and held her breath. She hoped Meg wouldn't bring up the Immaculate Conception.

After being prompted to tell even the tiniest detail by Grandma, Meg leaned back into a surfeit of oriental pillows.

Grandma wiped her tears on her sleeve. "I just can't believe a decent married man would take advantage of you that way. How are you going to raise a baby without a man? How are you going to get an education? Megan, this is terrible news. Not only are you pregnant out of wedlock, but you've committed adultery. We'll pray for you."

"Thanks. I've already prayed about it. I made a mistake. I guess I should go to confession. I'm taking it one day at a time." Meg looked from her grandmother to her grandfather. "I'm trying to do what's right. I don't want to make any more mistakes."

Grandpa didn't say a word. He took out his handkerchief to wipe his face. When Meg told him goodbye the next morning, he held her close and kissed her hair.

"I'm sorry I disappointed you, Grandpa."

"We all make mistakes. How we deal with our mistakes is

a measure of how strong we are. You're going to do fine, honey."

That was the first time that Holly saw her father cry.

Meg wasn't quite as forthright when they got to Nana's and Bug's. She put on her bubbly personality and suggested a stroll on the beach before lunch.

Holly sat on the balcony overlooking the long empty stretch of beach wishing the sun would shine through the dark clouds. White seagulls stood out like flitting beams as they sailed over the steel gray ocean. When the threesome started out they walked arm-in-arm with Meg in the middle. They walked that way for several minutes then suddenly stopped, dropped arms. Meg turned around, and stomped, as much as one can in wet sand, toward the condo. Meg's grandmother sank to her knees and cried out toward the sky while Bug stooped next to her for a second then quickly tore out after Meg. The perfect daughter of their perfect son was obviously flawed. Holly felt a pain similar to the one she'd felt the day Marcus died. She turned away and began setting the table for lunch, not knowing if anyone would want to eat.

Meg burst through the door with Bug on her heels. "Let's get out of here, Mama. I can't do this anymore."

Before Holly got the chance to speak Bug caught up to Meg and grabbed her arm. "Hold on a minute. Nana didn't mean what she said. She's upset, she'll get over it."

Meg wiggled out of Bug's grip and faced him with her hands planted firmly on her hips. "Mike was dying just like Daddy and I loved him. I didn't get pregnant because I wanted to or because I wanted to make you mad. I was just trying to love him like Mama loved Daddy."

Nana came in covered in sand. She glared at Meg. "Just give us some time to let this sink in."

"I'm not a harlot, Nana." Meg shrieked and gulped her tears. "And I didn't ruin my life. Can't you put yourself in my shoes and feel my pain? It just happened and if I could change things I would."

Nana and Bug held each other's stare. Neither spoke.

"Mama, let's go home."

"Please stay." Bug pleaded. "We're old now. We've forgotten what it means to be young."

"I'm sorry I yelled at you, Nana, but I thought you'd be the first to have a little sympathy for me." Meg went to Holly and threw her arms around her.

Nana sequestered herself in the bedroom while Bug did his best to entertain Holly and Meg for the rest of the afternoon and evening. He took them to Meg's favorite ocean-view restaurant, but no one wanted to eat. Bug didn't defend or try to excuse his wife. He acted as if nothing had happened until after nine when he said, "Tomorrow's another day. Let's all just sleep on Megan's situation and maybe we can talk about it tomorrow."

Holly awoke before sunrise to find Meg's bed empty. She dressed quickly, tiptoed down the stairs and through the living room and kitchen. She slid open the glass door to the balcony and spotted two silhouettes against the misty gray cloudless sky. She fumbled in the half-light to make a pot of coffee, grabbed an afghan from the futon, and sat on the balcony ledge to inhale the salt air and watch the sun begin to peek between the ocean and sky. Before the coffee brewed the sun had turned into a bright yellow ball but the sky and the sea still mingled together in a blue haze. Laughter accompanied the sunrise, overpowering the sound of the squawking gulls rushing waves.

"Mama," Meg called from the shore. "Come walk with Bug and me."

Holly hurried out the door and down the back steps. "My goodness, you two were up early."

"We've been up since four-thirty. We couldn't sleep," Meg said.

"And you've been walking since then."

"Yup." Bug smiled and put his arm around Meg's shoulders. "This here is one of the best and brightest young women in the world. She's gonna be alright. She's gonna decide what's best and stick to it and I, for one, will be there every step of the way. Are you ready for breakfast? I see a light on down at the donut shop."

When Holly and Meg returned to Chapel Hill, Meg went to shower and Holly took it as a chance to call Charlie.

"Good afternoon. Did everybody survive?" Charlie asked.

"Is this a good time to talk?"

"Perfect. Jordan's out walking Troubadour. How did it go?"

Holly sighed. "We knew it was going to be emotional but we didn't expect what we got."

"Like what?"

"All my father could do was cry and my mom wanted to take Meg to confession. I'm sure she went straight to church and lit all the candles she could as soon as we left."

"How did Meg handle it?"

"With a brilliant offense. She protected herself as best she could, but Mom had to give advice and express her outrage at poor dead Mike before she offered forgiveness and support."

"I'm sure it was a shock to them."

"Yeah. We had a long, teary drive to the Crystal Coast."

"Poor Meg." Charlie sounded sincere. "It sounds like they're taking it in their stride."

"We got an unexpected shock out of Marcus' mother, but Bug seemed more upset that Meg had lost her scholarship than her virginity."

Charlie laughed. "What happened?"

"Nana called Meg a harlot and then shut herself in her

bedroom and we never saw her again."

"She didn't…"

"You heard me. It devastated all of us. None of us knows what to make of it, but three out of four ain't bad as they say."

"I want to hear all the details, but I have to go. Jordan's heading for the house. I love you, love you, love you, Holly. Kiss Meg for me and give her a great big hug."

"Thanks, Charlie. I love you too."

"Love?" Meg walked into the living room in a bathrobe with a towel wrapped around her head and a brush in her hand. "Mama, did Charlie tell you he loved you?"

"Three times." Holly smiled. "And he said to give you a kiss and a great big hug, so come here."

"I needed to hear that. It's one of the best birthday presents I've ever gotten." Meg threw her arms around Holly.

"Speaking of your birthday—how do you want to celebrate?"

Meg shrugged. "It seems so insignificant after the big celebration of my pregnancy."

"Eighteen is a pretty significant milestone," Holly said. "Come here and let me brush your hair."

"Yeah. I can vote and have sex with adults." Meg handed Holly the brush before sitting on the floor in front of her. "My sweet sixteen birthday was my right-of-passage into the world of being a driver and not a passenger. I went from being a child to a young lady, but I guess I came of age when—you know, I'm sick of talking about it."

Holly nodded.

"Guess what I found in my jeans back pocket?"

"Let's see. A note?"

"Yeah, but not the kind you're thinking about. A brand new, crisp one hundred dollar bill."

"From whom?"

"Grandpa, I'd imagine. He's the only one who still pats my butt. But then Bug was acting like nothing happened, so maybe it's from him as an apology for Nana."

"Well," Holly bit her bottom lip. "Since your dad died we've all been going around acting like we're all these perfect people in this little glass world that your father made for us. Maybe Nana realized that you were human after all."

"And that cracked her glass house?"

"I guess."

"Well, she cracked mine as well."

"I know she did." Holly kept brushing Meg's hair. She knew she'd miss their intimate moments like this when Meg went off to college—her breath caught. College. She made a mental note to discuss that with Meg, but not today. Not now. "So, back to my question. How do you want to celebrate your birthday?"

"I say, let's blow this hundred dollar bill on junk food and have movie night like we did when Daddy was alive—only this birthday it could be you, Charlie, and me." Meg swung around and smiled. "That's what I want to do. Do you think Charlie could get away? Do you think he would even want to come?"

"All we can do is ask. If he can get away, we'll have to do it on his schedule."

"Will you ask him? It doesn't have to be on my birthday. It can be any day."

While Holly brushed Meg's hair she wondered at how easily Meg could substitute Charlie for Marcus. Or maybe Meg was living in the present while Holly still had one foot stuck in the past. It could be fun, just the three of them laughing and teasing one another. Meg certainly needed to laugh. Holly couldn't remember the last time Meg had let out a joy-filled belly laugh. It must have been the day they'd met Charlie.

When Charlie called the next day, Holly relayed Meg's birthday wish.

"Jesus. I wish I could just say, yes, but I can't see how. I need to tell Jordan what's going on. This is ridiculous sneaking around behind her back. I'm sorry, Holly. Jordan's moodiness has me worried. Am I babying her? Is she playing me for the fool?"

"You know what she can handle, I don't."

"Maybe I should just find out what she can handle. I can't believe a sixteen-year-old can hold so much power over me."

Holly didn't know what to say so she didn't say anything.

"You've been so patient. I can't tell you what that means to me. Can I get back to you? It's past time to broach the subject with Jordan."

"Slowly, Charlie. Don't do anything you'll regret."

Two days passed and Holly didn't hear from Charlie. She tried not to take that as a bad omen. Meg's birthday on Thursday seemed insipid even though Lisa brought over a homemade coconut cake with the kind of sweet, gooey icing Meg loved. Aubrey and Tia pooled their money and brought Meg the latest Ariana Grande download for her iPod. Both sets of grandparents called and Holly's parents sent a card with a check, which upset Meg since it was her first birthday without them at her side. Even though they had vowed to support her, their absence both surprised and disappointed Holly. She feared they had fueled Meg's teetering self-esteem. Holly felt so sorry for Meg that she broke down and bought her the iPhone she'd wished for, but even having that, nothing seemed good enough without Charlie.

Early Monday morning Meg's new phone jingled out *Greenback Boogie*, a ring tone Holly had downloaded for a joke. Meg fumbled to answer. "Charlie!"

"Hey, happy belated birthday, kiddo. I heard you want to have a junk food movie night."

"Can you come over? Please say, yes."

"Well, it looks like I'll be free the day after tomorrow, but only until about nine-thirty. Will that work for you?"

"Yes, yes, yes. Will you be bringing Jordan?"

"Jordan has decided to visit her mother on Wednesday."

"Do you want to talk to Mom? I'm sure it's okay with her—and you have to bring the funniest movie you've ever seen. We're not going to cry over sad movies."

"Gotcha."

"Thanks, Charlie. Hold on, I'll get Mom." Holly had just stepped out of the shower when Meg burst into the bathroom. "Mama, it's Charlie. He can come over on Wednesday."

When Holly took the phone from Meg she wanted to cry with joy. Meg's eyes sparkled like stars reflecting on an ocean of black. "Charlie? How are you? How's Jordan? Did you tell her? How'd it go?"

Charlie laughed. "Let's see—fine, okay, sort of, and, well, it didn't go well, but it wasn't a disaster."

"I'm sorry, I was just so worried and now I'm so excited."

"I can hear it. It's nice having someone worrying about me and getting excited. I like that. I'm imagining it."

"Charlie." Holly giggled. "Tell me what happened."

"I just casually asked what she'd think if I wanted to ask a woman out. She went ballistic. She still thinks her mother will change her mind and let us come home for good. So, her mom is going to take her shopping and out to dinner after school on Wednesday and try to explain things. I made her promise not to bring Jordan home even a minute before ten. Jordan's birthday is this coming Friday, so I told Jill that sending Jordan to the camp for her birthday didn't mean she could get out of celebrating with her in person."

"I remember that Jill paid for the camp, but I didn't know it was a birthday gift. My, God. Our daughter's birthdays are just eight days apart. Incredible."

"You're incredible and I have to go. I'll see you Wednesday evening."

"Thank you so much for this. It means the world to Meg."

On Meg's way home from school that Wednesday, she stopped at Food Lion and bought all the makings for nachos and lemonade, plus an assortment of movie theater type snacks—microwave popcorn, *Milk Duds, M&M's, Gummy Bears,* and *GooGoo Clusters.*

Holly could see Meg's excitement when she brought her grocery bags in through the garage door and set them on the kitchen table, but she heard her excitement when she walked into an explosion of green, purple, yellow, and red decorations in the living room. Fifty helium-filled balloons with long, dangling curling ribbons drifted across the ceiling and clung to accordion crepe paper streamers. Confetti covered the furniture and carpets, and a festive red dragon *piñata* hung from the ceiling fan.

"Mama, did you do this by yourself? It's gorgeous. I love it."

"I didn't have a thing to do with it. Lisa did it for you. She must have worked on it all day."

"It's perfect." Meg turned around and Holly snapped a picture of her wide-eyed grin. At the moment the flash fired, a balloon popped and both Holly and Meg jumped and broke out in screeches and giggles. "This is so great. I hope Lisa doesn't feel left out."

"She's excited for us. I'm sure she'd like to be a bug on the wall."

"Don't worry. I'll call her later, after Charlie leaves, to thank her for the decorations…then I'll let her interrogate me."

Holly grinned. "You'd better get changed. Charlie will be here in half an hour. I'll start browning the meat."

Meg called out to Holly from the bedroom. "You'd better come in here."

There were two white, Mexican fiesta blouses and two Pica skirts hanging from the ceiling fan, a basket filled with paper flowers, and a man's brightly colored poncho-shirt on the bed.

"I get the purple skirt," Meg squealed and grabbed it up. "Look, the flowers have hair clips. I'm going to braid my hair and clip some flowers to the braids."

Holly reached for a gold flower and clipped it over her ear. She picked up the poncho. "This must be for Charlie."

"You must have told Lisa we were having nachos." Meg laughed as she slipped out of her khaki pants, fleece hoodie, and donned the skirt and blouse.

Holly changed into the red skirt and pulled the elastic neckline of the blouse to caress her shoulders. She swayed in front of the mirror.

"You look like dynamite, but you'd better take that bra off."

"I don't think I want to go braless tonight. Maybe I'll wear my bikini top under the blouse."

"Wrong color." Meg opened a drawer and pulled out an orange cami. "Here," she said. Wear this."

When Charlie arrived, Holly and Meg opened the door before he could ring the bell. *Hola, señor Charlie. Recepción,*" Meg said.

"Hola a usted. Feliz, ah something, I'm sorry, I can't remember how to say happy birthday in Spanish."

"Come in." Charlie followed Meg while Holly closed the door.

"Will you look at this? Fabulous." Charlie set a gift bag on the floor beside the sofa. "I hope I don't have to clean up all this confetti." He laughed. "And look at you two *muchachas.*" Charlie kissed Meg on the cheek and then Holly.

"This is for you, from Lisa." Meg handed the poncho to Charlie. "You have to wear it."

Charlie removed his jacket, tie, and dress shirt and placed them on the back of the recliner. Holly gasped to see his hard body in a white muscle shirt. She exchanged glances with Meg who looked as if she were about to say something that would surely embarrass everyone, but she kept her mouth shut for a change. When he had the poncho over his head, Meg helped to pull it down over his chest.

The evening passed too quickly. They laughed through, *A Princess Bride* and quoted Inigo Montoya's most memorable line, "Hello. My name is Inigo Montoya. You killed my father. Prepare to die," over and over again until Charlie had to leave.

"Before I go I have something for you." Charlie stood, picked up the gift bag, and handed it to Meg.

"I just wanted you to be here." Meg held the bag close. "You didn't have to get me anything."

"But I wanted to." Charlie winked. "Open it…go on."

Meg sat on the sofa and took a small silver box from the mounds of tissue paper inside the bag. She opened the box and removed a delicate silver bracelet with tiny multicolored gemstones and pearls. "It's beautiful. Thank you," she said without looking up. A round charm hung from the chain with her name engraved on the front. She turned the charm over and read aloud, "If you believe...you can fly." She threw her hand over her mouth and looked to Charlie through watery eyes. "This is…so, great. I love it. Thank you so much." She stood and leaned her head on Charlie's chest while holding the bracelet up with both hands. "Look, Mama. Isn't it marvelous?"

"This is so sweet of you, Charlie." Holly refrained from throwing her arms around his neck. "You didn't have to."

"No, I didn't have to, but I wanted to." Charlie plucked the orange silk flower from Holly's hair. "May I have this?"

Meg looked at Charlie through squinted eyes. "Of course. Why?"

"To remember tonight. To remember the three of us

standing here, loving that we're standing here." Charlie looked at the flower in his hand and rocked from one foot to the other. "I want to remember how happy I am right now. I haven't felt like this since I was a kid."

"Just like in the movie you want us all to ride off on white horses, right?" Meg asked.

Charlie placed his hands on Meg's shoulders. "As you wish."

Before Holly fell asleep that night she wondered what Charlie meant when he said he hadn't been that happy since he'd been a kid. Even Barbara had commented on his daughter's neediness. She wondered if Jordan had some sort of handicap or insecurity due to her mother's lack of affection. Holly sat straight up in bed. No, she thought, Charlie can't like our family better than his own. She ran the words, "our family" over her tongue. He didn't seem needy, but there was something she couldn't put a finger on. She needed to meet this Jordan and figure out what Charlie wasn't telling her. "Dear God," she prayed, "Charlie gave Meg a perfect day— just like Marcus would have. Is Charlie hiding something from us?" Maybe she could get him to talk about Jordan the next weekend. The last thing she wanted for Meg was the loss of another man. She slept fretfully and awakened several times in a panic and a cold sweat.

The next morning Holly accompanied Meg to her first appointment with Dr. Gilbert, the doctor Brody had suggested. The doctor ordered an ultrasound first. Since Meg still didn't want to know the sex of the baby, the technician told her when to close her eyes so she wouldn't find out by accident. This ultrasound machine was more sophisticated than Brody's and the technician took pictures of the baby's face and hands and gave them to Meg.

"Hey, Froggy, you still don't look like any baby I've ever

seen." Meg giggled and handed the pictures, one at a time, to Holly.

The technician smiled as she handed Meg a warm, wet washcloth to clean the gel off her belly. "Your baby has grown according to the measurements from Dr. Adam's office. I can see the previa, but I'll let Dr. Gilbert take a look and discuss it with you." She took the washcloth from Meg and pulled the paper sheet up over Meg's abdomen. "It looks like a healthy little frog to me. The doctor will be in to examine you in just a minute."

When the tech closed the door behind her, Meg groaned. "I can't believe something that looks like a frog has caused so much havoc." She held tight to the paper blanket with one hand and took hold of Holly's hand with the other. "Do you want to be a grandmother?"

"I think I just fell in love with the little frog." Holly looked at the pictures again. "Look at that face and those tiny hands. I'll be Frog's grandmother if that's what you want." Holly wanted to add, "Is it?" but decided to let Meg tell her when she was ready.

"After the doctor examines me, I'd like to speak with her alone. Is that okay?"

"Certainly." Holly smiled, but couldn't help feeling excluded. Meg had matured beyond her years in the months since she'd met Mike. She'd always known she'd have to let go of Meg one day but now seemed too soon.

"Megan Gaynor?" Dr. Gilbert asked when she entered the room. She reached out to shake Meg's hand but didn't smile. "I'm Dr. Gilbert." Mousy brown hair hung haphazardly around the doctor's deadpan face. Her scrubs looked one size too small for her stocky frame and she looked as if she'd just been rescued from a burning building in the middle of the night.

"This is my mom," Meg said, "Holly Gaynor."

"It's a pleasure." Holly extended her hand but the doctor glanced at her foot to head before turning her attention to Meg.

"Your ultrasound looks better than I expected. The previa has moved away from your cervix but I want you to remain on pelvic rest with absolutely no intercourse. Do you understand?"

Meg's face paled and she turned to Holly. "I understand."

"Intercourse could kill both you and the baby, so it's imperative that—"

Holly stood and walked around the examining table so she could look at the doctor face-to-face. "I'm sure that if you look closely at Dr. Adams' notes you'll see my daughter's hymen is intact and the boy who accidentally impregnated her is dead. She understands pelvic rest completely."

"It's just that intercourse would be life-threatening for both Meg and the baby." The doctor looked at Meg. "Your weight is actually two pounds less than it was in Dr. Adam's report. Despite that, your baby has grown." The doctor leafed through Meg's chart. "Make sure Megan is eating healthy foods and drinking only nutritious beverages including lots of water. No junk or fast foods. Juice instead of soft drinks. Do you understand?"

Holly felt like whacking the doctor with the stethoscope that hung from her flabby neck. She bit her lip and nodded instead.

"Good. I want to see you in four weeks. You can make an appointment on your way out." The doctor turned toward the door.

"Excuse me," Meg said. Could I speak with you alone...for just a minute, that is, if you have...time."

The doctor glanced at her watch, raised her eyebrows. "Of course."

Holly closed the door behind her and stomped to the waiting area afraid she might kick anything in her way. What an unprofessional, uncaring, excuse for a God dammed doctor. Holly wondered if she was always a bitch or just prejudiced against single teenage moms.

Holly felt too nervous to sit so she leaned against the wall and pulled the pictures of Frog from her purse. She tried to get the doctor and Meg's private conversation out of her mind. Seeing the pictures of the baby brought more fear than joy. Yes, she wanted to be a grandmother. Yes, she already loved that little bundle. Yes, she would support Meg emotionally and financially until she could find her own way. So, what frightened her? Things could certainly be worse. The father of the baby could be alive and be a creep who might ruin Meg's life. She didn't want to see Meg hurt or put into an unhealthy situation. If Meg gave the baby up, would she someday regret it so much that it would ruin her life?

She wondered about Mike. What kind of man was he? Did he love Meg the way Meg thought he had, or did he simply use her to get back at his wife? If he were somehow still alive would he fess up to being the father? And if he went into remission and lived, what would he do with Meg and his wife? Holly tucked her hair behind her ear wondering why poor dead Mike worried her.

She visualized Meg in a maze without an exit. Or was she the one caught in the maze? She realized that she still hadn't come to terms with this baby but she couldn't take the blame for that. It was up to Meg to decide if this baby would be a friend or foe. Holly had to stand ready to catch whatever pitch Meg decided to throw.

Late Friday afternoon while Holly packed for her next adventure with Sir Charles her phone rang. She smiled when she saw his name on the screen.

"Holly, you're not going to believe this."

"What is it?" she asked, her smile fading.

"I'm afraid I'm going to have to cancel out on you again."

Holly sank onto the sofa. "I'm sorry. What's happened?"

"It's Troubadour. He's in bad shape. His back legs are weak. He can barely stand. The vet's on the way and Jordan is out of control. I'll call you as soon as I can. I'm sorry, Holly. I was looking forward to having you all to myself this weekend."

"You have to do what you have to do and I understand completely. You're a great dad."

"I'll make it up to you. I promise, once again. I have to go now."

"I'll be thinking about you, Charlie. You know you can call me anytime—whenever you need to talk."

Holly turned her phone off and stared at the black screen. "No." she cried. She took a deep breath and looked around the room still laden with confetti and crepe paper. The balloons had lost most of their helium and hovered inches off the floor. Neither she nor Meg could clean the room fearing that the magical spell cast on Wednesday evening would shatter.

Meg's perfect day seemed to have healed some wounds, thanks to Lisa and Charlie. She giggled more and the sparkle in her eyes returned. Holly decided not to tell her about Troubadour and Charlie just yet. She'd already left for Aubrey's for the weekend, so she decided to allow her two more days of elation.

Holly sifted through a stack of novels until she found one that looked as if it might have a happy ending. She wrapped an afghan around her shoulders and snuggled up on the sofa to read about someone else's romances.

The phone awoke Holly a few minutes after six the next morning. She'd fallen asleep on the sofa and now felt disoriented. When she realized where she was, she turned on the lamp and fumbled for the phone.

"Charlie. It must be bad news at this hour."

"Yeah. What a long night. Troubadour's legs got so weak

that he couldn't stand. By about three this morning his hindquarters were completely paralyzed. The vet thinks it's an abscess on his spine. He's probably had it for a while. The vet thinks that the antibiotics he got the last time only masked the infection which never really went away."

"Did he survive?"

"He didn't." Charlie sounded tired and stressed. "The vet had to put him down."

"Oh no. How's Jordan?"

"Distraught. She refused to leave his side, so I spent the night in the stable with her. The scene was heartbreaking. She petted him and encouraged him all night. She buried her face in his mane and sobbed. The vet wanted to put him down earlier but I think he was holding out for a miracle—for Jordan's sake."

"I just can't imagine. It would've been bad enough if Troubadour had died without intervention."

"He nearly did. Close to the end, he developed a fever. The vet gave him fluids, antibiotics, and cool baths but he went into an uncontrollable seizure. The vet shot anticonvulsants into him, which didn't faze him. He told us it was time to put him out of his misery. Jordan screamed in protest and held onto Troubadour while the vet gave the lethal injection."

"The poor child."

"The drug worked quickly. Troubadour is at peace, but it's just the beginning of Jordan's anguish." Charlie paused. "Holly, I'm worried about her. She's always been emotional but this went way overboard. I thought she was going to kill the vet with her bare hands. She was completely out of control—screaming and kicking. I've never seen her like this. I held her until she couldn't fight anymore. She called Jill but didn't get the sympathy she'd hoped for. I didn't hear the conversation, but Jill basically told her to stop crying over a silly horse and grow up. That just started the violent behavior all over again."

"What are you going to do? I don't know what to say."

"You don't have to say anything. Jordan finally cried herself to sleep. I need to nod off as well. She didn't have a very happy birthday."

"Thanks for calling—"

"I just needed to hear your voice, Holly. I'm sorry I woke you. Go back to sleep and I'll call again as soon as I can."

"Don't worry about waking me, anytime. I mean that. Is there anything I can do?"

"That's the response I was hoping to hear from Jill, but she could care less. She has no sensitivity at all. Couldn't she hear the pain in Jordan's voice? What a bitch she is."

"Charlie, like I keep telling Meg, what is, is. Maybe you and Jordan can figure out a way to make something good come of this."

"Thanks, Holly. I love you and I'm sorry I dumped all this on you."

The phone went dead and Holly let out a loud moan. "I love you too, Charlie. I wish I could show you how much."

Holly and Charlie continued their phone conversations over the next couple of weeks. Holly hadn't realized that Jordan had been depressed and seeing a psychologist since Jill ejaculated her way out of the family. Maybe Charlie wasn't keeping a secret after all. Maybe he just didn't want to load her with his problems while she had to deal with Meg's. Maybe there hadn't been that much to tell. Jordan's emotional state had plummeted since Troubadour's unfortunate death. Now her doctor felt she needed to be under a watchful eye twenty-four hours a day. When he suggested hospitalization, Charlie wouldn't hear of it. Jill had abandoned Jordan and he wasn't going to follow suit.

7

Meg took a length of the birthday crepe paper to hang over the mirror on her vanity. She set the *piñata* in the center so it reflected in the mirror. With some of the confetti, crepe paper, and a deflated balloon she made a thank you card for Charlie and added a picture Holly had taken of the two of them in their Mexican regalia. She knew better than to mail it and waited to give it to him in person.

"It's been two weeks. When will we see Charlie again?" Meg asked just before bedtime.

"I'm not sure." Holly looked up from the book she'd been reading and patted the mattress beside her.

Meg climbed onto the bed on top of the covers. "Is it Jordan?"

"Yes." Holly closed the book. "He's a good man. I just wonder how much he'll sacrifice for her."

"Everything. Just like you'd sacrifice everything for me. Right?"

"Absolutely. But you're a joy…and you're stable and strong. It's easy to stick in there for you. Besides, even if I'm sacrificing some things for you, you allow me time with Charlie."

"So, Charlie's sacrificing everything for Jordan?"

"He doesn't know what else to do. Jordan's fragile right now. Charlie's situation is quite different. He hasn't come up with a suitable strategy. He's all alone in this and there are reasons why I can't help him right now."

"You mean his ex?"

"She's part of it."

"She doesn't want them, but Jordan, at least, wants her. Is that it?"

"Jordan doesn't only want her mother but expects her to call them all back home. Sounds like it would blow her away if she found out about me."

"So, Charlie's ex and I are fighting similar battles. I mean neither of us wants our kid."

Holly let out a sharp breath. She didn't respond at first, just looked straight ahead without focusing on anything in particular. "Maybe, but your kid is a fetus and her kid is a teenager."

Meg shrugged.

"Now, Charlie, well that's another story. He has a burden that he's chosen to handle by himself to protect his daughter, maybe both of his daughters." Holly wanted to turn the situation around to Meg. "If your pregnancy is a burden to you, you at least, have people you can talk to and confide in— a support system. Either way, it's a new puzzle. Nobody can put the pieces together for either of you. People can help you and support you and make suggestions, but in the end, it's your puzzle."

"Yeah. I know." Meg put both hands on her belly. "It's a puzzle I don't want. Not now, not without a wedding first, not without an education. Not without Mike."

"I know. You miss Mike, don't you?"

"Of course. What do you expect?"

"I'm sorry. It's been all about your pregnancy and not enough about you."

"Want to know something, Mama?"

"Sure."

"I don't know how to say this so you'll understand."

"Try me."

"I pretend that Mike is still alive and that we're married. I dream about him touching me and putting his head on my belly and talking to our little frog."

"That's pretty normal."

"But, I also dream of us making love. I mean, I never even really got to make love properly. Now I get so horny that it scares me."

"There's two systems working here—heart and hormones. The same thing happened to me. I was so horny I'd wait naked at the front door for your father to come home from work."

Meg's eyes widened as she covered her mouth and giggled. "And did Daddy perform?"

"Oh, yes. Up until the very end when I got so big that we couldn't find a position that worked."

"But, before then—"

"Before then it was glorious but different. Your father spent a lot of time caressing and kissing my belly and talking to you before he got around to pleasing me, and then it was better than ever."

"What do you mean?"

Holly's face flushed. She'd never spoken so frankly. "The pleasure of it all, the release of tension."

"You mean more or better orgasms?"

"Yes. The sex wasn't so much about me trying to please your father or about him trying to please me. We were celebrating each other and the life we'd created. Maybe I shouldn't have told you that. I'm sorry Mike isn't here with you now."

"I'm glad you told me. I'm glad my creation was a celebration. I can't say the same for Frog's—it's more like a nightmare now."

"It doesn't have to be." Holly wondered if she'd said too much. Her pregnancy had been one of love and excitement and joy. She had the love of her life to share it with. The last thing on earth she wanted to do was hurt Meg. "From what you say, your baby was conceived in love. Mike tried to give you all he had. He loved you with his whole body. He made love to you."

"I wish you had known Mike, Mama. I'm sorry now that I didn't share…him, us with you. I don't want a boyfriend now, especially while I'm preggo. The guys at school are like little boys compared to Mike. He didn't want to die. He wanted to live for me. He understood me and he loved me. Thanks for telling me about you and Daddy." Meg bit her bottom lip and looked away.

"Then this baby is a very special gift, a very special gift from someone who loved you."

"That's what you keep saying, but I'm not so sure. Will I ever get over him? I mean did he spoil me for other men? Will I ever meet someone else and fall completely in love and have the kind of pregnancy that you and Daddy had?"

"Yes, Meg, if you let it happen. Time will heal you. Maybe your baby could heal you too. Just look at you and me. It took me a while, but I'm letting Charlie into my life. And all those years I grieved your father's death I had you to fill me up and give me a reason to go on."

"So, someday a second Mr. Right will come along for me as well?"

"Yes, I believe he will. If you choose to be a single mother, you can still have a life. You can shape your life however you want it to be. But right now it's okay to love Mike then someday, when it's right, you'll let him go."

Since Meg's birthday party Holly had read a book a day to keep herself occupied. Charlie had been spending all his free time protecting Jordan, and Meg spent the majority of her free time with Aubrey. Holly had to admit that she carried a twinge of jealously. Although she wondered what could possibly consume so much time, she hadn't been concerned until the day Meg consented to clean up the confetti, deflated balloons, and strands of crepe paper. On a Saturday while Meg and Aubrey studied together, Lisa volunteered to come over and help Holly clean up.

"What are you doing?" Lisa turned the vacuum off and looked at the shreds of paper Holly had thrown across the room.

Holly let out a frustrated growl then sat down on the floor and bawled. Lisa began picking up the scraps of paper and tried to piece them together. "What is this?"

"A pamphlet, *A Loving Alternative.* I found it under the barstool." Holly pointed to the floor in front of the bar, the spot where Meg usually sat to do her homework.

"You mean for adoption?" Lisa sat on the floor across from Holly.

"I guess, yes." Holly looked at Lisa for a moment, speechless. "Why didn't she tell me what's going through her mind? We've always been so close..."

"What did the pamphlet say?"

"It's an agency that helps women face unplanned pregnancy and helps them choose a loving family to adopt their child." Holly placed both hands over her heart. "The front flap showed a young woman dressed in jeans and a striped sweater standing sideways, cupping her very pregnant belly. She looked like a pregnant Taylor Swift with a huge grin. God. So that's what they're doing."

"That's what who's doing?" Lisa asked.

"Meg and Aubrey. They're looking for a home for the baby. Meg is going to give her baby up for adoption."

"You knew that was an option."

"Hell yes, but behind my back? Without consulting me?"

"It's her baby. Maybe she's just exploring her options. Don't jump to conclusions. She's eighteen now, she can make her own decisions."

Holly rested her head on her knees. "Meg and I have been sharing so much lately. I can't believe she's making such a big decision without me."

"Holly—"

"I'm her mother and Aubrey is just a kid—"

"Aubrey is an unbiased, nonjudgmental friend who, from what I know about her, won't force any radical view on Meg. What if Meg doesn't think she can handle a baby right now, but keeps it because you want her to? Think about that and be thankful that Meg is taking full responsibility for herself."

"But, she's not letting me be her mother."

"She's a good girl and you know it. You raised her to make her own decisions, so sit back and leave her be. She's going to make you proud no matter what."

"It hurts, though."

"I know it does." Lisa picked a piece of confetti out of the carpet. "Meg's road won't be easy whether she keeps the baby or not. Don't worry. She's going to need your strength for a very long time, one way or the other."

Holly looked up and smiled. "You're right. Finish the vacuuming and I'll fix us a cocktail." She looked at her watch. "We have a good hour before Charlie's afternoon call."

Charlie's calls had increased to three, sometimes four a day. Jordan refused to go back to school stating she didn't have any friends there and that the girls were hicks who thought riding around in a pickup with boys who stuffed their cheeks with chewing tobacco was cool.

"Whatcha doing, my beauty?" Charlie sounded cheerful for a change. He was out of the Raleigh traffic and heading west on HWY 64 toward Pittsboro.

"Well, Meg finally consented to let me clean up the Mexican decorations, so Lisa is here and we've made a big stab at it. I have a feeling we'll be finding confetti for years to come."

Charlie laughed. "I can relate. Jordan found some confetti

in my laundry basket."

"How did you explain it?" Holly laughed, trying to imagine the look on Charlie's face when the confetti surfaced.

"I told her I went to Mexico while she had dinner out with her mom."

"And she believed you?"

"She shrugged. I don't think she cared. Hey, let me call back later. I didn't mean to take you away from Lisa."

"She's just about out the door. We just finished a blender of frozen Margaritas. Hold on a minute." Holly smiled and waved to Lisa. "Thanks for helping clean up."

Lisa blew Holly a kiss and let herself out. Holly put the phone back to her ear. "Busy day? You're calling later than usual."

"I met with Jordan's psychologist."

"And?"

"He doesn't think that keeping Jordan out of school is in her best interest but agrees with me that she may not get an education without a private tutor. So, that's the next thing on my to-do list. I'd like to find a tutor who could also be a nanny of sorts."

"You mean a companion?"

"Do you think such a thing exists?"

"You're looking for a miracle, Charlie. But, why don't you search the internet? I bet there are sites for all sorts of caretakers—from babies to seniors to pets. Maybe tutors as well."

"I'll give it a shot. Where would I be without you?"

Charlie spent his free time with Jordan, but it wasn't as if they spent time together. Jordan secluded herself in her room with her iPod and computer. They rarely spoke and when they did an argument most likely ensued. Not only did Jordan refuse to go to school, she was totally against the idea of a home tutor or a companion. Eventually, Charlie put his foot down and gave her the choice between school or tutor. She chose the tutor.

Several days later Charlie's miracle materialized. He'd surfed the internet and found a young teacher who specialized in homeschooling medically fragile children. Before Charlie contacted her, he noted that she was available from early morning to late night and occasionally for twenty-four to forty-eight-hour stints. Her background check and references were sterling. She sounded too good to be true.

At first, Angie Nolan's arrival alarmed Charlie. She drove up in a bright yellow Volkswagen Beetle convertible with bumper stickers that read ARE YOU BETTER OFF THAN YOU WERE TWENTY-FIVE TRILLION DOLLARS AGO and another one, I AM CAPTAIN KIRK'S LOVE CHILD. Her purple hair wasn't as surprising as her pierced nose, tongue, and right eyebrow or the tattoo that rose from her back and covered the left side of her neck. Her outfit was the thing that most intrigued Charlie and Jordan. On that warm, sunny morning, Angie wore a black wool mini dress with aqua leggings, one leg pale aqua with dark aqua stripes, and the other dark aqua with light aqua polka dots. Silver peace signs hung from her ears and neck and bangle bracelets covered her forearms from wrist to elbow.

Charlie delayed leaving for work until he felt sure Angie would work out. Jordan took to her right away and after a few minutes, Charlie felt assured he'd made the right choice after all.

On his way to work, he called Holly and they laughed at his preconception.

Later that afternoon, Holly took her phone out to the deck to enjoy the warmth of the sun. The weather had changed from thirty degrees with sleet and snow to eighty-degree sunshine in less than a week. She couldn't stop thinking about Angie and

Jordan and their first day together and hoped that Charlie would call to fill her in. She startled when the phone rang. She didn't give Charlie a chance to say, hello.

"I'm dying to hear how Jordan and Angie got along."

Charlie chuckled. "Hello to you too."

"Sorry. I've been wondering about them all day."

"We definitely chose the right tutor. Jordan not only likes her but is in awe of her."

"In awe, how?"

"It's hard to say, but it's the look in Jordan's eyes. Angie slips in and out of French, English, and urban slang as if it's normal. She's like the accepting big sister Jordan never had. They hit it off immediately."

"That's wonderful."

"Yeah, I think she's just bizarre enough to get Jordan to pull herself out of her depression."

Holly sighed with relief. "But can she teach academics?"

"Seems so. Jordan has a pile of homework.

"So, where are you?"

"I'm looking out the front window. Jordan's saying goodbye to Angie and her boyfriend so I don't have long to talk."

"Her boyfriend's with her?"

"Someone just dropped him off. His car broke down and he left it in a garage in Pittsboro. Guess they live together, but I didn't get into that. Anyway, he's a computer geek with dreads half-way down his back. His name is Jack and when Angie introduced us, we shook hands and he called me Dude."

That made Holly chuckle. "So, they're both a little kooky, huh?"

"Yeah. I have to go, they're getting into the car, but Holly?"

"What?"

"She smiled at me when I got home."

"Angie?"

Charlie clicked his tongue. "No. Jordan."

The smile seemed like a breakthrough. Jordan began sharing her feelings and relating information she'd learned from Angie. In less than two weeks she finished the required courses for her junior year. Angie checked with the school administration and discovered that Jordan could finish her senior year by completing just three more classes, earn a high school diploma by July, and begin college in September.

"What do you think about Jordan skipping her senior year?" Holly asked on one of Charlie's early morning commutes.

"I don't want her to skip it, but she said she'd rather die than go back to that hick school."

"Do you think she's testing you?"

"Absolutely. But, the thing I worry about most is that she doesn't have friends. She's never had a friend. Angie is the closest thing to a friend she's ever had and, well, I feel like I'm paying her to befriend Jordan. Plus Angie suggested this, not Jordan."

"And Jordan picked it up and flew with it?"

"Yeah. Jordan thinks that finishing high school and entering college a year early will please me."

"Will it?"

"Yes and no. My greatest fear is her emotional immaturity. That could badly hinder her relationships once she gets to college. I can't imagine that she's mature enough to take care of herself."

"Sounds like you need to talk with Angie," Holly said. "Things might be worse for Jordan...I mean if you throw her into a situation she's too immature to handle."

"You're right, Holly. While she seems to be making progress in her therapy, she's still on an anti-depressant."

Holly hesitated a moment and thought carefully how to phrase her words. "She could be on that antidepressant for the rest of her life."

"That's something I can't think about right now."

Charlie's calls to Holly became solely limited to his commute to and from the office. Although Holly encouraged his calls and waited expectantly for them, after a few weeks she wondered if they had a romantic relationship or simply one of empathetic listening. Charlie needed to talk and Holly was always there to listen. Holly had allowed the relationship to thrive in her mind and she imagined that he did as well, but when Lisa told her that she didn't mean any more to Charlie than Barbara had, Holly began to worry.

The next Sunday Holly met Lisa at the mall. During lunch at Firebird's Lisa blurted her opinion. "If Charlie cares for you at all, he'd make time to see you. Didn't you tell me in the beginning that this Angie was available for twenty-four-hour stints? So what's his excuse?"

"It's not that simple. Charlie needs to be responsible for his daughter and that means being with her now. He certainly doesn't want to abandon a troubled child until he's certain she's beyond his help. And it hasn't gotten to that."

"Well, what if it never gets to that? What if the two of you never see each other again?"

Holly sat silent, weighing Lisa's words. It did seem strange that Charlie couldn't drop by for a meal or meet her at a restaurant on his way home from work. She wanted to defend Charlie, but she didn't feel like arguing in his defense. She wanted more from Charlie, even more than what Lisa wanted for them. Holly took in a deep breath and said, "I don't know, Lisa. But, he's worth the wait."

"Holly, please. There's a new doctor in Brody's practice. He's a little younger than you. Brody can fix you up. You can't sit here and pine away for Charlie. He's not Prince Charming. He's using you."

"He's not using me."

"Well, how long has it been since you've seen him? And how many times have you seen him? This is ridiculous. This has been going on since Christmas and you've seen him three times and only one of those times for a date."

"A glorious date. It's not even April yet. We'll be getting together soon. Honestly. And anyway, it took ten years for a man to come along that interested me. If he isn't the right guy, I guess some other Prince Charming is going to have to come and break my door down."

On Charlie's way to work the next morning, he called Holly as soon as he backed out of the driveway. "You're not going to like what I have to say," he told her. She held her breath. He'd decided to take Jordan on a trip half-way across the country to look at a few colleges and universities Angie had lined up.

"Wait," Holly said, "I thought you said Jordan was too immature to skip her senior year and start college."

"I did, but there's a thing called a gap year where kids defer on starting college for a year and either travel or do some sort of volunteer work. I finally put my foot down and insisted she wait."

"Well, that's good news, but can't she wait a few months to look for college?" What Holly actually wanted to say was, 'What about us? How long do we have to wait?'

"She could, but it's always good to get a head start. Besides, "We'll just be gone a couple of weeks..."

A couple of weeks and then what? Maybe Lisa was right. The relationship wasn't going anywhere. What was she supposed to do? Wait forever? Holly gritted her teeth until her jaw ached. She tried to think rationally. Jordan continued to make progress. Charlie said she had a spark and he had to give it all the fuel he could. For the first time, Holly felt deep pangs of disappointment. She sat at her vanity gazing at her reflection in the mirror, listening to Charlie ramble on. She sat up straight and mouthed the words, What about me? What about us?

"I'm going to milk it for all it's worth. Jordan wants to look at Iowa. They have a school of veterinarian medicine, but I don't think that's the direction she's interested in…I think she just might be trying to either please me or manipulate me because I tried to get Jessica to apply there and she violently refused."

Holly tried to concentrate on Charlie's chatter. "Do you think Jordan may be looking for greener grass?"

"Absolutely." Charlie paused. "You don't agree that I'm doing the right thing, do you?"

"That's for you to decide, Charlie. Remember, I don't know Jordan."

"I'm sorry, Holly. I just needed to run this by somebody other than the psychologists."

"I know you do. I wish I could help…"

"You are helping. You're letting me rant. And you've helped me decide to give my folks a surprise visit while we're in Iowa."

"Charlie. You've never mentioned your parents."

"I guess I haven't. We've been a little out of touch."

"Because of the divorce?"

"Partly, but mostly because of me. I'm a pretty big disappointment to them." Charlie chuckled. "That's another thing we have in common—your parents are strict Catholics and mine are small town conservative Methodists. Divorce isn't in either vocabulary."

"Do they know about Jill?"

"They've probably figured out most of it. Over the years they just let me make excuses for her. Now, for the first time, I'm ready to tell them everything. I want them to know my fractured reality…and I want them to know about you, about the possibilities for our future."

~*~

Everyone in Charlie's family, as far back as anyone could remember, graduated from The University of Iowa. Charlie's father majored in pharmacology and the day after graduation he took a job at the only drug store in his hometown. Nine years later he owned the store and opened a second across town. Charlie's older brother followed suit and became the junior partner. After six years, the successful pharmacies were sold to CVS making Charlie's father, then fifty-four, and his brother, who'd just turned thirty, millionaires.

Charlie's sister carried on the Iowa tradition and graduated with a degree in Elementary Education the same year the pharmacies sold. Charlie brought up the rear graduating with a degree in Political Science the same year, his mother, who had put her education on hold to raise her family, finished her junior year in the nursing program.

Charlie was a good father because he'd been raised in a happy, loving home. He'd wanted nothing less for his daughters.

~*~

Meg continued her search for colleges also. Both she and Holly wished that they could join Charlie and Jordan on their journey but with Jordan still unaware of her father's relationship with Holly, that dream was impossible. Holly hoped this trip would bring Jordan out of her depression. Maybe she'd mature by looking toward the future and be able to accept the reality of her parent's separation and pending divorce. And just maybe, she'd be able to accept Holly as an important part of her father's life.

Holly wondered how she would keep herself occupied in

Prince Charming's absence, especially now that Meg spent much of her free time with her confidant apparent, Aubrey.

The day Charlie and Jordan left town, Holly came in from work to find Meg at the dining room table engrossed in her laptop. Before she could speak, Meg threw her pen across the kitchen and slammed the laptop shut.

"Am I interrupting something?"

"I don't know if I can do this."

"Do what?"

"Take online courses until I'm recovered from this aliment and the frog is old enough to be left with a sitter. That is if I keep the croaker."

"You can do anything you put your mind to."

"But do I have the mind to do this?"

Holly kicked off her shoes and sat across the bar from Meg. She just stared. She hadn't allowed the thought of Meg with a child sink in. She'd tried to block it out, hoping she'd awaken one morning to find that all of this had been just a dream. It occurred to her then, that if Meg was thinking about a babysitter, she must be thinking about being a mother.

"Mama?"

"Sorry, I was just thinking."

"Me too. Since I haven't decided on a major, I guess I could take as many required courses as possible online for a whole year and start fresh at a college or university the next fall. That way I could earn credits and take care of the frog at the same time. It wasn't in my plan before Frog happened. But, what do you think about the idea?"

Holly got up and opened the refrigerator. "And live at home?"

Meg let out a huff. "Do you want me to move into a home for unwed mothers? There's a few of them around."

"Of course not. I want you and the baby here where you both belong," Holly said. But did she believe that? She felt a surge of guilt. Here she was in a budding romance or at least a romance trying to bud. She'd told Meg that she'd sacrifice everything for her, but could she sacrifice everything without feeling that Meg would be taking advantage of her? Why did she have to meet Charlie now? If they could have met next Christmas maybe everything would be easier and wonderland would be feasible.

"Mama, you keep fading out. Where did you go?"

"I'm sorry. I can't get my mind off Charlie."

Meg packed up her laptop and papers and picked up her pen from the floor before starting for her room. "I feel sorry for you. I thought things would be better by now. Looks like Jordan and I have really wrecked things."

"First of all nothing is wrecked...just waylaid. Like I keep telling you and everybody, if Charlie is meant to be, he'll stick around and everything will work out. But he's struggling now, trying to patch up the damage his ex-wife left behind. He's a good father. If you want to feel sorry for someone, feel sorry for him, not me."

Meg put her things away then waited in the hall while Holly poured coffee into a mug and headed for the living room. When Holly sat on the sofa Meg sat on the floor at her feet. "This is the hardest thing we've ever done, isn't it, Mama?"

"Yes, darling, this is the hardest thing we've ever done."

"I'm so frustrated. This baby cut a great big hole in my life. It's like a hurdle I can't jump. All my friends will be going off to college without a care in the world and I'll be stuck at home with a baby. This baby may be a gift for somebody, but it's sure not a gift for me and definitely not one for you."

8

The constant rain and dreary skies seemed to stunt spring. The Japanese Cheery trees that usually bloomed in March were barely blooming in April. The Redbud and Dogwood showed just a hint of pink buds. The muted tints of the landscape cast a yoke around Holly's already burdened heart. She'd taken a walk after lunch and on her way back her cell phone rang. She panicked, thinking something had to be wrong with Meg, but happiness replaced the panic when she saw Charlie's face on the screen.

"Hello, sweetheart. I just have a minute to talk while Jordan's on a tour of the Iowa campus with a student advisor."

Holly couldn't catch her breath at first. She swallowed so hard that she got the hiccups and then the giggles. "Sorry," she finally squeaked out. "How are things going?"

"Very well I'm pleased to say. All the family gathered at my folk's place last night. Jordan went skating with her cousins and I had a rather revealing conversation with everyone."

"Revealing?"

"I simply told them the truth. That healed so many wounds and misconceptions. They want to meet you and you know how much that pleases me."

"That's wonderful news, Charlie."

"I miss you more the further away I travel."

"It seems like you've been gone forever."

"Seems like we've been apart forever. I need you Holly or maybe I should just come right out and say I want you."

"Charlie…"

"I can't tell you how sorry—"

"You're doing the right thing," Holly said. "There's no need to apologize."

Charlie's long breath whistled. "You know what they say about April?"

"Something about a young man's heart turns to love?"

"Eleven more days. A time for us to be reborn. I mean it, Holly. I'll make this up to you."

"We sound like an old movie."

"We are an old movie. And I'll prove it to you as soon as we get back."

"I'll wait for you, Charlie."

"Maybe you're a fool."

Holly bit her lip and felt her eyes fill with tears.

"Holly? Are you alright? Of course you're not alright. I'm sorry. I shouldn't have called and upset you. I'll make time for you, honestly, as soon as we return. I will."

"I'm just sorry that we have to keep saying, I'm sorry."

"If it makes any difference, I was serious when I told you that I loved you. It's true. I love you so much that I ache for you."

"I love you too, Charlie. It's just that we haven't seen each other since February."

Although Holly loved hearing from Charlie, his confessions of love were beginning to seem ludicrous. She wanted to tell him she loved him in the throes of passion. She began to wonder if that moment would ever materialize.

When Holly drove into her driveway after work, she saw Lisa standing on the front stoop holding a neon pink umbrella above her. She held an envelope to her chest and her face shone brightly against the murky backdrop of the charcoal sky. Holly pulled the car into the garage and stepped out. "Come on in, little miss sunshine. Why are you standing in the rain? Why didn't you let yourself in?"

Lisa followed Holly into the house through the garage door. "I wanted you to see me standing there with this little envelope in my hand."

"Why? What's in it?" Holly asked.

"Fix a couple martinis or maybe a piña colada and I'll tell you." Lisa held the envelope behind her back.

Holly looked at Lisa, her face full of delight. "How did you know I needed a friend today?"

"The gloom. I need a friend today as well." Lisa looked paler than usual and thinner.

"Is everything alright?" Holly hung Lisa's umbrella on the doorknob. "You've lost weight."

"Maybe a couple pounds." Lisa looked down at her delicate build. "I spend my energy trying to keep warm."

"Tell me about it. Three days of summer and we're right back to winter." Holly slipped off her wet shoes and sweater and started unbuttoning her blouse. "Remember when all we wore around the house were soft Levi's and white cotton blouses? Whatever happened to that? Excuse me a minute. I need to get into a pair of sweats. I'm soaked to the skin. It wasn't raining when I started for the car, but it turned into a monsoon a block from the parking deck." Holly headed toward the bedroom. "You can start the martinis. Make mine *Tanqueray*. I don't have any rum to make piña coladas."

Lisa hid the envelope between the cookbooks before taking two martini glasses and a beverage shaker from the china cabinet.

"So what's the mystery?" Holly combed her hair with her fingers on her way to the kitchen.

"What mystery?" Lisa went to the freezer and filled the shaker with ice.

"The envelope? Where is it?"

"Where's the vermouth? I couldn't find it in the liquor cabinet."

"I'll tell you where the vermouth is when you let me see the envelope." Holly laughed.

Lisa retrieved the envelope but held it away from Holly until she produced the vermouth. "Okay. Now close your eyes and think of the sun warming you from head to toe. Inhale deeply and imagine the aroma of orchids, salt air, and sunscreen…"

"Are you going on a second honeymoon?" Holly asked while she retrieved the vermouth and set it on the bar next to the gin. "Now, give me that envelope."

Lisa stuck the envelope down her blouse and smiled impishly while she mixed the drinks and shook them gently before pouring them into the glasses. She passed one to Holly. "Sit down and then take a big gulp."

They clicked the glasses together and sat side-by-side at the bar. "Okay." Holly held her hand out. "The envelope…"

Lisa handed it to Holly.

"What's this?" Holly spread pictures of surfers, huge ocean waves, candlelit outdoor restaurants, waterfalls, and mountain hiking trails.

"It's Maui and we're going."

"When, how? I don't get it." Holly searched Lisa's face.

"Brody agreed to be a last minute substitute for the keynote speaker at a very important conference on lung disease when the sponsoring pharmaceutical company offered him an oceanfront condo in Maui and now, listen carefully, a corporate jet."

"You're kidding? How wonderful for you."

"How wonderful for us. The plane seats six. The condo has two bedrooms. You have to come along. Really. It's just for three nights—this coming weekend. We leave Thursday evening and get back Monday night."

"I don't know…" Holly sipped her martini.

"You never take any time off. Here's three nights on a tropical island with all expenses paid."

"All expenses?"

"Yes, Brody's actually doing a favor for a colleague by substituting to teach a workshop on such short notice. Besides, what will I do all day by myself? It'll be so much fun having you along."

Holly set her cocktail glass on the bar and focused on the tiny icy particles swirling through the liquid like Lisa's suggestion swirled through her mind. "You and I haven't done anything like this in a long time."

"I know. We're way overdue." Lisa flashed Holly a reassuring smile. "Remember how much fun we had shopping in New York City just before Christmas one year and our secret trip to Epcot without the kids when they were in kindergarten?"

"And the time Brody took the kids to Sliding Rock a few years after Marcus died and we flew down to an 'N Sync concert in Atlanta?"

"We're still that crazy, you know."

Holly smiled. "I know. It's just that…."

"You always wanted to go to Hawaii with Marcus. I remembered that." Lisa sat back in her chair. "You can't miss Maui because of an unfulfilled dream, besides you wanted to go to Hawaii's Big Island and that's not where we're going."

Holly looked at the martini and remembered going to the travel agency with Marcus. She remembered calling the agent the next week to cancel when she'd learned the seriousness of Marcus' condition.

"Anyway, all that aside, you need a break from winter, from Charlie, and even Meg."

"You're probably right, but going all the way to Maui, almost half way around the world, isn't at all what I want to do right now."

"Holly, what you want to do right now, you can't do, so what the hell? Why sit home and pine? It's a free trip. When you get back, Charlie will still be gone and Meg will still be cavorting with Aubrey. And you'll have a suntan. Maybe even one without bathing suit lines."

Holly let out a belly laugh. "I will if you will."

Over the next two days Holly tied up loose ends at work in preparation for the long weekend away, but her emotions were tangled. One minute she imagined strolling on a sandy beach with Lisa, both of them in bright sarongs, sunglasses, and big straw hats—living life as if they hadn't a care in the world. But the next minute she felt her decision to go must be some kind of retaliation for Charlie's absence and Meg's secrets with Aubrey.

Holly found it difficult not being first in Meg's life, especially now, while she was in a crisis. What is, is, she reminded herself. She had to trust Meg to do the right thing, even if Holly didn't know what the right thing was. Whatever Meg decided to do, Holly would stick by her and support her all the way.

Life had once been so simple. She and Meg tucked neatly in their quiet, peaceful Victorian surroundings. Every chair and plate and spoon perfectly placed. Holly reading by an open fire with Meg's giggles and shrieks her only interruption. Although thinking of Charlie warmed her heart, Holly knew he would bring a certain amount of activity, be it thrilling or challenging, to disrupt her rather complacent life. It wasn't as if her life was dull or that she'd changed her mind about allowing Prince Charming to carry her away, it was about change. Things were going to be different with or without Charlie. Meg was going to be a mother and Holly was going to be a grandmother even if Meg chose adoption. It all seemed too much to think about. Holly knew she wasn't in control of her future. Maybe a getaway to Maui was exactly what she needed. That made her smile—she deserved this escape. She'd been given a chance to escape the real world and experience a fantastic one. She conjured up dreams of sunny beaches and warm island breezes, but it wasn't until Thursday afternoon that she felt the first pin pricks of excitement. Meg promised to call if even the tiniest problem arose. And if Charlie called, well, he'd be in for a surprise.

When Holly turned onto the street where she lived, she saw Nana's and Bug's car parked on the curb. "Lord..." she said as she pulled into the driveway. When she parked in the garage and turned the ignition off, she had to make herself get out of the car. Inside, she found Nana, Bug, and Meg standing forlorn at the front door.

"Holly," Nana said. Sorry to barge in unannounced, but we...I need to talk. And I want to make amends for the way I treated Meg and you when you last visited. She reached out to her. "Come, dear. May we sit down?"

"Of course you can." Holly looked at Meg who looked at both grandparents, but didn't speak. "Can I get you anything? I can put on a pot of coffee."

"No, no, just let's sit a minute. I need to tell you something."

Nana and Bug sat on the sofa while Holly practically dragged Meg across the room. When Holly sat on the recliner, Meg sat at her feet and rested her head on Holly's knee.

Nana kept her back straight and looked at Bug a moment before she spoke. "I'm sorry, Megan, that I called you a harlot..."

"I'm sorry I said what I said." Meg wiped tears from her cheeks.

"You have nothing to be sorry for. I deserved it, honey. I deserved every word you said. I'm not going to make any excuses. You just reminded me of myself."

"How?" Meg looked first at her grandmother then at

Holly.

"It's time to get this off my chest." Nana wrung her tanned hands. Her body shook like a quaking aspen.

Bug scooted closer to his wife of forty-nine years and put his hand on her knee. "Go on. It's time." He looked to Holly and Meg and smiled. "They'll understand."

"Well, a few months before I married Bug..." Nana looked straight at Meg, "I found out I was pregnant. I didn't know what to do. I didn't want to be humiliated by my family and society, so...I had an abortion. I did it behind Bug's back. He didn't know about the pregnancy, but it was his baby. I didn't tell him because I thought he'd leave me. Eight years later we had Marcus and our relationship was grand, so I told him then and he understood and forgave me."

"Nana..."

"There's more. I feel guilty to this day, not for getting pregnant, but for the abortion. I killed our baby because I didn't want to face humiliation. It was a selfish act that led to more selfish acts. Even though Bug wanted a baby, I avoided getting pregnant for near seven years. I didn't think I deserved a baby. When I accidentally got pregnant with Marcus I felt like God had given me a second chance. I vowed to be the best mother. Then Marcus got sick and died...I...I felt like God was finally punishing me. God allowed me a second baby only to poison him with cancer and rip him away from me in the prime of his life."

Meg began to weep and Holly stared at her mother-in-law gravely.

Nana went on moving from one word to the next without stopping. It seemed that once she got started, she couldn't stop. "The abortion nearly ruined my relationship with my family, my friends, and most of all, Bug. I held onto the guilt and it festered inside me. I'd been so afraid that I would be labeled a harlot, a horrible stigma, and I was so disappointed in you because I always knew you and your mother were much better women than I, so when you told us that you were pregnant, I saw myself fifty years ago. I felt like your pregnancy happened to punish me again. I didn't want you—I don't want you to live a life of regret."

Meg knelt at her grandmother's side and hugged her. "Oh, Nana, thank you for telling me this. I didn't get pregnant on purpose. I didn't get pregnant to hurt anyone."

"I know that now, honey."

Meg pulled away from the embrace and stared at her grandmother. "I still don't know what I want to do, but abortion is obviously out of the question. I wouldn't have one even if I'd found out before it was too late."

"You'll do the right thing." Nana put her hands on Meg's face and kissed her forehead. "I hope you'll forgive me and let me be your grandmother again."

"Nana, I love you. I thought you didn't love me." They embraced again.

"I'll always love you...no matter what. I promise."

Meg pulled away again and sat back on her heels.

"I have something for you." Nana reached into her purse and pulled out a small velvet box. Bug gave this to me on your father's first birthday and now, I want you to have it."

Meg opened the box and took out a golden locket. She opened it and asked, "Is this Daddy?"

"Yes. That's your father."

"Look Mama, it's a picture of Daddy when he was a baby and a tiny lock of his hair. I love it, Nana and I love you and Bug too."

9

The scent of leather and hyacinths surprised Holly when she stepped inside the cabin of the corporate jet. "So this is how the rich live," she said as she ran her hand along the smooth surface of a walnut cabinet that sported a crystal decanter, an assortment of golden and garnet wines, and a vase of spring flowers. When her feet sank into lush, Carolina blue carpet she couldn't wait to sink her toes into it. Two rows of seats separated by an aisle faced each other—eight spacious reclining seats in all. Holly and Lisa chose the two that faced forward on the left while Brody chose to sit facing them, separated by a pull-down table.

"Get ready to be catered to." Brody sat back with his hands clasped behind his head. "We are in for one incredible voyage."

"Bring on the aperitifs and hors d'oeuvres. I am so ready for this." Holly flushed both Meg and Charlie from her mind. "What, is, is, and I am going to enjoy every minute of it."

The plane skimmed just above a thick blanket of gray clouds which had just begun to turn light on the surface and reflect the orange, pink, and lavender of the sunrise. They'd flown for nearly twelve hours with just one stop in LA to refuel. When the sun shined in Holly's eyes she opened them to the glorious rays. "Ahh...it's breathtaking."

"The captain said we're just about to begin our descent,"

Brody said. "There's fresh coffee, shall I bring you both a cup?"

"Please," Lisa said after a yawn.

"Me too." Holly smiled. "Thanks, Brody. It's been a long time since a handsome man waited on me."

Lisa giggled.

Brody returned with three coffees. "There are some pastries and fruit up front. Anyone interested?"

"Not after that huge dinner last night." Holly brought the coffee cup to her lips. "There's enough food in this little plane to feed all the passengers on a Boing triple seven."

"I'll wait and have breakfast on the beach." Lisa's eyes twinkled in the morning light.

The plane entered the clouds and bumped over air currents before emerging into the early morning calm of a tropical blue brilliance.

Holly felt tears begin to build as she gazed at the water below. Every shade of glistening green and blue stretched as far as she could see. The colors penetrated her, calmed her, thrilled her. It seemed like heaven, seemed like she was a part of the blueness or that the blueness was a part of her. She felt lightheaded and giddy. "I love this place."

Lisa and Brody had moved to the opposite side of the plane. "Well, you're looking out the wrong window," Lisa said. "Come over to this side. I can see palm trees."

Holly glanced Lisa's way but couldn't separate herself from the embracing blues of the sea.

The plane tipped its wings to make a U-turn and Holly lost sight of the brilliant blue. The plane skimmed the ground just above the rocky coast on one side and a patchwork of gnarled branches connecting windblown trees into secret canopies that led to civilization—coconut trees, pineapple plantations, hotels, swimming pools, golf courses, and brightly colored umbrellas stacked and ready to protect fragile bodies from the stinging rays of the sun.

Baggage

As Holly stepped from the plane, before she could shake off the emotion evoked by the color of the sea, a bronzed woman dressed in a sarong and halo of shiny green leaves placed a lei of orchids around her neck. Before she could utter a "thank you," a short, dark man dressed in a uniform, ushered her along with Lisa and Charlie into an awaiting white limousine.

The driver handed Brody a card. When they pulled away, he read it, arched a sly brow, and chuckled. "It says to help ourselves to the champagne."

Holly stared out the window, searching for the ocean, but it seemed as if they were driving through a jungle of trees.

"Holly? Are you with us?" Lisa asked. "There's champagne."

"No thanks," Holly said without turning away from the window.

"Well, I think I'll wait until at least noon to indulge in alcohol then I'll start with a tropical concoction with an umbrella in it." Lisa shrugged.

The limo turned onto a pink cement driveway lined with yellow and pink frangipani trees and stopped at the front door of the Ocean Front Paradise Condominiums. Holly stepped out and looked to the top of the ten story plain white building. She caught a whiff of a gardenia-like fragrance and looked around until she finally noticed the delicate frangipani. "It's those trees. I want a bottle of that scent to take home." She inhaled deeply as the fragrance intermingled with the blue brilliance that had settled into her mind.

Brody held the door open and pulled a key from his breast pocket. "Room number eight-twenty. That must be on the eighth floor." The lobby stood empty so they wandered through it until they found an elevator. When the doors opened, Brody stepped aside. "After you, ladies."

The dimly lit elevator creaked its way up then opened to an unadorned hallway carpeted in artificial turf. They crept in silence to room eight-twenty. Brody hesitated before unlocking the door. "This isn't exactly what I'd expected."

"Let's take a look inside." Lisa shrugged and flashed a frown.

When Brody opened the door Holly walked straight through the large living space and out onto the balcony completely oblivious to the grandeur of the inside and the pots of red and yellow hibiscus at her feet. She stood gazing with one hand over her open mouth and the other clasped around the wrought iron railing with a trailing branch of fuchsia bougainvillea. The magnificent blue overwhelmed her once again and she gasped in a breath of the salty air. Her eyes stung as her body slowly slumped. "Marcus."

"Holly? What is it?" Brody asked. He caught her before her knees hit the ground.

She felt light-headed and let Brody and Lisa help her up. "It's so beautiful. It's like a dream."

"Are you sure you're okay?" Lisa exchanged a glance with Brody.

"Yes. I'm fine. The sky, the beach, the flowers…it all caught me off guard."

Holly smiled at Lisa then at Brody. "Thanks for catching me. Maybe I need a little nap before I hit the beach."

Holly took a glass of iced water into her room and sat on the side of the bed. Why, amidst all the beauty, had she called out for Marcus? Was it because she hadn't gotten the chance to share this with him or was it another cruel reminder that he was gone? And what about Charlie? Shouldn't she be calling out his name?

She drank most of the water and let it soothe her mind. For the past twenty years, Marcus had been a sure thing—even in death he'd been a positive memory for her to cherish. Had she hung onto the marriage vow for too long? Was she afraid that Charlie would erase Marcus from her heart? She gazed at the endless blue and couldn't determine where the ocean stopped and the sky began. It's now, she thought. Today is now, yesterday is now, and tomorrow is now. She started to understand something about herself as a peacefulness descended upon her. She smiled when her head hit the pillow.

Holly woke up from a dream filled with color, but she couldn't remember which colors or any of the details except the images changed patterns like a kaleidoscope. She slipped into a bikini and a sarong. When she entered the living area she took a long look around and didn't recognize anything except the glass wall and French doors. The carpet perfectly matched the sandy beach below. When she sat on the sofa all she could see was water and sky like an IMAX movie. She liked the openness, the feeling of being outside. She retrieved her Nikon from her camera bag to capture the view. Only a freestanding bar separated the living and dining area from the kitchen. Even though all the furniture and appliances were white, Holly didn't feel starkness. Hawaiian print pillows in pink, teal, and orange added just enough color to make the room feel warm.

She found a note with her name on it propped on top of a bakery box on the bar. She ambled past the glass-topped dining table, picked it up, and read, "Meet me on the beach. There's a Mai Tai with a red umbrella waiting for you."

Holly giggled while she opened the box. "Yum," she said, and picked through a selection of muffins, donuts, and bagels. She settled on a plain bagel hoping to find some cream cheese in the fridge. Unfortunately, there was just butter and a selection of jams, so she toasted the bagel then smothered it with butter and a little strawberry jam. When she ate her fill, she stepped into her silver bejeweled flip-flops, grabbed her camera, and headed to the beach.

"Here she is," Lisa said to the man standing behind a bar made of thatch. "This is Holly. And Holly, this is Kanoa."

Holly snapped a picture of each of them.

"Aloha. Pleased to meet you, ma'am. Welcome to Maui. I'll have your Mai Tai ready in a sec."

Holly scrutinized the shirtless, young man and smiled at Lisa. "Wait. Just exactly what is a Mai Tai?"

"Dark rum, Cointreau, apricot brandy, lime, and just a little lump of sugar." Kanoa's deep dimples emerged as his smile broadened.

"I'd hoped for something with coconut."

"Ah, let me please the young lady." Kanoa picked up a coconut from beneath the counter, stood back, and whacked the top off with a machete. He lifted the nut to his nose and inhaled. "Fresh and sweet. Why don't I concoct you a Lava Flow?"

Holly giggled. "And, what is that?"

Kanoa answered slowly without losing his broad smile. "Just a light rum with a little coconut rum blended with strawberries, banana, pineapple juice, and coconut cream."

"Is that fresh coconut milk sweet?" Holly put her hands on the edge of the counter.

"Very sweet." Kanoa popped a straw into the coconut and handed it to Holly to taste.

"Yummy." Holly looked at Lisa and back to Kanoa. "Okay, so, can you just add a jigger of rum and one of those white orchids and a white umbrella to this?"

"For you, yes, ma'am." Kanoa laughed. "We'll name it the Hawaiian Wedding."

Holly rolled her eyes, stepped back, and whispered to Lisa, "What have you told him about me?"

Lisa chuckled while turning her palms upward.

"You sit and I will serve you." Kanoa placed the coconut in a holder and proceeded to prepare the drink.

"The next time you whack off the top of a coconut could you warn me? I want to get a picture." Holly tilted her head.

"Yes ma'am," Kanoa said, laughing loudly.

"Feeling better?" Lisa asked while Holly removed her

sarong and settled into a padded chaise lounge.

"Lots. Thanks."

"You were thinking of Marcus, weren't you? I mean when you collapsed?"

"The beautiful view caught me off guard. It made me realize how lonely or empty I feel. This is new, this feeling of longing."

"Is it because of Charlie?"

Holly gazed out at a white sailboat. "Charlie and Meg I think. Maybe Marcus as well. I don't have Marcus, Meg is slipping away, growing up, and well Charlie...Charlie isn't really here yet." She touched her heart.

When Kanoa delivered the Hawaiian wedding, Holly took it with both hands and set it on the wooden table beside the chaise lounge. "I have to get a picture." She stood and took several pictures of the drink from different angles. "Gorgeous. Thank you, Kanoa." She sat back and exchanged the camera for the wedding white drink.

"It's on the house if you don't like it," Kanoa said, shaking his head as if in appreciation that anyone would want to photograph one of his creations.

Holly removed the orchid and fastened it behind her right ear before lifting the coconut to her lips and taking a sip. She smiled up at Kanoa. "Delicious."

"The flower behind your right ear means your heart is free, available. If you keep it there you will have an island romance." Kanoa laughed as he returned to the bar.

Lisa swallowed the last of her Mai Tai and retrieved a bottle of water from her canvas bag. "Charlie finally opened you up to love again, but the relationship is stalled. Maybe that's why you feel empty."

"And Meg growing away at the same time makes the emptiness deeper."

"But, Meg isn't growing away from you. She's growing up and making a very adult decision."

"I can't disagree." Holly took another sip of her drink before lowering the back of the chaise lounge to stretch out under the shade of the coconut palm that towered out of the sand beside her. "I think I'm just figuring out where these men need to be in my life."

"What do you mean?"

"Don't laugh, but it all started when the plane flew through the clouds. It was something…spiritual, sort of. It's difficult. It had something to do with the endless blues and greens of the water as if I'd never seen an ocean before. Whatever happened, had to be some kind of sign…" Holly wrinkled her nose and looked at Lisa. "Like I have permission to let go of Marcus and let Charlie in at the same time. It's not easy to explain."

"Maybe it's permission to let other men in, not just Charlie. You know, Holly, you've had one date with Charlie and that was what…five weeks ago? You never played the field before Marcus came along and that's it. If this relationship ever gets off the ground Charlie will only be the second man you've ever had sex with. There's nothing wrong with playing the field while Charlie gets his act in gear. Right?"

"I guess."

"You haven't had sex in ten years, for God's sake. Look at it this way—you could have a few practice runs while you're waiting on Charlie. Have fun. Don't pine away for a guy you're not sure will ever be free. I'm serious. Just keep your options open. Okay?"

Holly laughed. "Just shut up. How many Mai Tai's have you had already?"

"This is my second."

"Okay, I'll keep my options open, but I'm certainly not going to put an ad in the paper. Are you happy now?"

"Yes. You could have a fling right here in paradise." Lisa held her arm out and swept it across the beach.

"I came along to keep you company. If I have a fling, you'll be all alone, unless you have a fling as well..."

"Maybe I will."

Holly sat up straight. "Are you serious?"

"Probably not. But, who knows?" Lisa flashed a seductive wink. "Besides, I sowed my wild oats before I met Brody. You didn't."

"That's true. Maybe that's why things didn't work out for Brody and me."

Lisa shrugged. "Guess we'll never know."

"Wanna take a walk down the beach before lunch?"

"Sure. Just let me slather myself in sunscreen."

Holly gulped her drink and it made her feel giddy immediately. "Squeeze some into my hand and I'll get your back."

Holly started to tan as soon as she stepped outside, but poor Lisa with her pale complexion and fragile skin had already turned pink. It didn't seem fair to Holly that someone who worshiped the sun as much as Lisa didn't have a darker complexion.

They both left their flip-flops and sarongs behind and marched off down the beach clad only in bikinis. Holly felt good in a bikini and she felt cocky walking down the beach. She looked good—not as tight as she was a few years ago, but no cellulite and her breasts were large enough to be proud of but small enough that she didn't feel like she was exposing too much skin. She felt Lisa's eyes on her and stopped walking. "Are you thinking what I'm thinking?"

"I think so." Lisa stretched to stand as tall as her petite frame would allow. "I think we look hot and we're proud of it."

"Me too. Are we silly?"

"Nah."

They chatted and laughed as they strolled the narrow sandy beach toward an endless line of hotels.

Holly retrieved a ball from the surf and tossed it to a toddler who stood with fingers wiggling and arms stretched toward the water then stopped to exchange a few words and a laugh with a young woman who looked to be supervising a group of children. "I hope all those kids aren't hers."

"Another *19 Kids and Counting?*" Lisa arched an eyebrow.

"I'm going for a swim. Are you with me?" Holly asked.

"Go ahead. I'm happy just to walk in the surf."

Holly waded into the waves before diving into the salty crystal water. When she came up for air she faced a young blond man.

"Hello. How do you do," he said in a British accent.

Holly wiped the water from her eyes and giggled. "Ah, fine…hello, excuse me, I didn't mean to—"

The man smiled and reached out his hand. "Jonathan Spencer here and I'm afraid I'm behaving awkwardly forward."

Holly shook his hand and felt unexpected arousal. "Holly Gaynor." She nearly stammered on her own name.

"Pleased to meet you, Holly. I presume your birthday is on Christmas. I couldn't help notice you walking down the beach. You are celestial."

Holly let go of his hand, swallowed hard. She stared up into eyes the color of the ocean and wondered if he had complimented her or if calling her celestial had been his pick-up line.

"You've lost your flower." Jonathan scooped up the orchid that fell from Holly's hair and held it out to her.

Without thinking she slipped the orchid between her breasts with the stem protruding under the string of her bikini top.

"Holly," Lisa called. When Holly gathered her senses, she turned to the shore. Lisa called out again. "Take your time. I'll meet you in the room."

"No, wait, please," Jonathan shouted back then turned to Holly. "I didn't mean to take you from your friend. Shall we catch up to her?"

"Sure." Holly noticed Jonathan's bathing suit—not a Speedo, but something close. She also noticed his flat belly, marginally developed abs, and that bulge at the top of his thigh she called a kick muscle. She figured he played soccer or rugby. When they caught up to Lisa, Jonathan extended his hand.

"Jonathan Spencer and you are Holly's friend…"

"Lisa Adams. It's a pleasure to meet you, Jonathan Spencer. Any relation to the late Princess Diana?"

Jonathan arched his brow. "Are you asking if I'm a Lord or Viscount? Certainly not, unfortunate for me, I do say. Actually, my family roots are in Nottingham, so I'm more likely related to Robin Hood."

"But, you're not just an ordinary man, are you?" Lisa asked.

"Ordinary and rather dull, I'm told. May I buy you ladies a couple of drinks or maybe a meal and you can decide for yourselves?"

"Thanks, but no. We have plans for lunch." Holly felt something stir inside that she knew wasn't the rum. She had second thoughts about refusing his offer so quickly.

They made their way back to the chaise lounges. Jonathan looked at Holly. "It would please me if you would walk with me, just to the shore."

Holly searched Jonathan's face and when she'd convinced herself that he was safe she agreed. She adjusted her bikini and took in a deep breath.

"Excuse us, Lisa." Jonathan took Holly's hand as they strolled toward the unending waves. He turned to Lisa. "I'll have her back in a jiffy. Are you sure I can't get you a drink?"

"No. I'm fine." Lisa stood mesmerized as she watched Holly and Jonathan walk to the shore and let the waves slap against their legs.

After a few minutes, Jonathan walked Holly to his beach chair. "I would like to spend some time with you."

Between the rum, the sun, and the longing in Jonathan's blue eyes, Holly felt dizzy. "I don't know," she said instead of coming right out and telling him the truth. She had to restrain her desire to reach out and touch his sunburnt chest.

"He pulled a backpack from the chair, took a card from his wallet, and said, "Well then. I won't pressure you. Take my card and if you change your mind give me a jingle at The Four Seasons." He took both her hands in his. "You will change your mind, won't you?"

"Perhaps I will." Holly turned and glided back to her chair feeling as if she would explode.

"What was that all about?" Lisa sat up straight and flashed Holly a curious smile.

"He asked me to the opening of an art show…this evening…then dinner."

"And you said?"

"I said, no."

"No? Are you insane?"

Holly breathed a defeated sigh. She put on her sunglasses and watched Jonathan gather his belongings. "Maybe. He's what, twenty-one? I'd rather introduce him to Meg."

"I think he's older. Besides, this isn't forever. He lives in England, for heaven's sake. This is an opportunity of a lifetime."

"He may be older than he looks, but he's definitely not a day past twenty-five. I should be flattered that a gorgeous younger man is drooling over me." Holly couldn't contain her giggles. "I just might change my mind."

"You have to change your mind." Lisa clasped her hands. "I told you that you need to have a fling."

"And now, I agree," Holly said with a mischievous smile. "So, maybe after lunch, we should strut over to that nude

142

beach to get an all-over tan before I call to accept his invitation."

"I'm all for it. It'll give Brody something to get excited about." Lisa did a seductive shoulder shimmy. "We should drink on the beach more often."

Holly glanced at Jonathan's business card. JONATHAN SPENCER, FINE ART, LONDON KNIGHTSBRIDGE. She handed it to Lisa and winked.

"Well." Lisa turned the card over. "Is this painting from the show he wanted to take you to?"

Holly took the card and studied the front. An angelic figure swirled through pale blues and greens. The image caused her to jerk forward and grab her waist. "I presume so."

"You can change your mind," Lisa said. "Or you could just show up."

"Maybe…" Holly sat on the chaise lounge and watched as Jonathan disappeared down the beach. She let out a sing-song sigh. "I'd like another drink before lunch if it's alright with you."

"Of course. I'm one ahead of you anyway."

Holly picked up the empty coconut shell and held it high. "Kanoa."

"Coming right up."

"Wait, Kanoa. May I take an action shot?"

Kanoa held a coconut in one hand and his machete in the other and posed while Holly clicked the shutter several times before changing the shutter to motor drive. "Okay, whack the top off," Holly shouted as the shutter clicked in rapid succession until Kanoa presented the drink to her on a woven bamboo tray.

Holly handed the camera to Lisa, took the drink, and posed next to the palm tree. She sipped the drink then flashed a sharp look at Kanoa. "A little heavy on the rum this time?"

"Two jiggers makes the coconut sweeter." Kanoa bowed before he turned back to the thatched bar.

Holly thought about the look on Jonathan's face when she placed the orchid between her breasts. Had she ever done anything so daring? She actually had him right in the palm of her hand. "Lisa, he desired me, didn't he? I mean, didn't he? He did. I know he did," she said with a dreamy smile. "I wonder what it would be like to... Oh, Lisa. I've been stirred. I feel wicked, aroused. Or is it the rum?"

Later that afternoon, Holly and Lisa crept onto the nude beach. After they secured their blanket on the sand they removed their sarongs, sunhats, sandals, and finally their bikini tops. They sat on the blanket to survey the beach and the other sunbathers.

"We're sitting here topless," Lisa said, "and no one is gawking at us like they do at the public beach when we have our tops on."

"I noticed the same thing." Holly stood up and stepped out of her bikini bottoms. "We're less conspicuous with nothing on. Come on, let's go for a quick swim."

Lisa did the same and joined Holly in the surf. Before they were waist deep in the cool waves something brushed past Lisa's leg. "Look. It's a manta ray."

Holly spotted the manta in the clear water and then another and another. Soon half the crowd gathered to ogle at the glorious creatures as they gracefully glided by and even splashed skyward out of the water like whales. When the pod disappeared into deeper waters the group shared the adventure and reveled in delight.

Walking back to their blanket, Holly chuckled. "What fun. What absolute good fun that was. Everyone is nude and we all celebrated a pod of gigantic manta's like we were kids dressed in uniforms at Sea World."

"So much for being daring and sexy on a nude beach," Lisa said with a frown. "No one cared. No one even noticed us."

"Guess if we want the kind of reaction we came here looking for we need to go back to the public beach clad in the skimpiest bikini we can find."

"I think I kind of like this reaction better." Holly stretched freely and swung in a circle letting the sun caress her entire body. "I'm definitely getting an all-over tan."

"Me too." Lisa giggled. "Won't Brody be surprised?"

"Oh yeah, I'd like to be a bug on your wall tonight."

The next morning, Lisa met Holly in the living room of the condo holding her silk robe away from her chest.

"Well, I'm anxious to hear about your escapades last night." Holly fanned her face with her hands.

Lisa grimaced and opened her robe. Her breasts were crimson compared to the pale pink of the rest of her body.

"Ouch. Guess we overdid it in the sun yesterday." Holly frowned. "So, about last night…was it a bust?"

"Not at all. Brody doctored me with *Noxzema*." Lisa flashed a subtle wink. "He spent a long time with these sunburnt girls. Plus, he got pretty aroused when I told him how we'd strutted down a nude beach. It was fiery, Holly, like we were twenty again."

"Wow." Holly giggled. "I don't need to hear any more."

That afternoon, Holly looked for Jonathan on the beach to no avail. She felt guilty turning him down, but it hadn't been the first time. Most of the boys or men she'd turned down since she'd been allowed to date had threatened her in some way. Brody, Marcus, and Charlie had been different. She'd felt at ease with them right away. She felt at ease with Jonathan as well, even attracted to him although he didn't fit her "Mr. Right" requirements. He was too blond and too young, yet he owned a charisma that had seeped into her veins like a fever. That night, she dialed his hotel. He didn't answer and she declined to leave a message.

Sunday afternoon, Holly and Lisa sat at the Blue Marlin Harborfront Grill where they downed a hearty lunch of crab-stuffed mushrooms, peel and eat shrimp, and washed it all down with oyster shooters made with pepper vodka.

"I can't believe it." Holly brought her napkin to her mouth when she spotted Jonathan.

"Holly," he said as he stepped from the main dining room to the patio. He turned to an entourage of eclectics and said, "I'll just be a minute."

Lisa stood. "Hello, Jonathan. Excuse me. I'm going to visit the ladies' room."

"You don't have to leave." Jonathan placed his hand on her shoulder.

"I know I don't but I'm going to. It's good to see you again."

After a few minutes, Holly joined Lisa in the restroom. "Jonathan invited me to The Four Seasons for a nightcap tonight. He seems serious about showing me his paintings."

"And you said, yes, didn't you? I knew you wanted to see him again. But, just a nightcap, not dinner first?" Lisa badgered.

"I just don't have any desire to have dinner or, I don't know. Romance just isn't a part of my interest in this guy. I do want to see his paintings. I told him I had dinner plans, but that I could slip away at ten."

Lisa blinked repeatedly as a smile grew across her face. "You're going to sew some wild oats, aren't you? This is so exciting. And on our last night. What could be better?"

"I might change my mind once this vodka wears off, but right now, yes, I'm as serious as can be. What shall I wear? Probably something I can slip out of easily."

Lisa beamed. "What made you change your mind?"

"I don't want to go home with regrets. He's a handsome man. That first time on the beach...I had his tongue hanging out in three seconds." Holly stood straight, raised her chest until her breasts about popped out of her halter-top. "You're right, Lisa. I can't count on Charlie. I dearly want to count on him, but Jonathan is just too good to be true. I have to take a chance on him and have a little fun, besides, you said I needed the experience."

"You are absolutely glowing." Lisa squealed in delight but her smile quickly turned to a look of concern. "Are you certain he's safe? I mean, I don't want you to disappear like those American girls in Aruba."

"Honestly, you harp on me for saying no, and now you're worried that he isn't safe? It may just be a drink and some paintings. I'll be fine. I'll take my cell and call you if I get into a jam. Or maybe I could just leave it on so you can hear everything. Better yet, let's have a *ménage a trios*."

Lisa stared at her with cow eyes. "I don't think you should drink any more vodka."

10

Holly picked at dinner. Her stomach felt like a jellyfish sloshing inside a wave. She had reservations about her rendezvous with Jonathan, but not enough to back out. At first, she felt guilty because of Charlie, but since their relationship hadn't gotten off the ground in over three months there wasn't much to be guilty about. Excitement easily replaced the hesitation. Turning forty had seemed a turning point, yet the only celebration had been the beginning of middle age unless she counted those few minutes with Charlie in the parking lot. She felt amused by her actions. If she wanted to be in wonderland, she needed to step right in.

Just to be on the safe side, Holly agreed to meet Jonathan in the lobby of the hotel. He stood waiting for her at the front door dressed in a white linen suit, a tan silk shirt, and light brown loafers without socks. Before the doorman opened the taxi door, Jonathan handed the driver some bills. She knew she'd made the right decision when he held both hands out to her and kissed her on the cheek. After exchanging greetings, he held her elbow and guided her into the air-conditioned lobby. She shivered when the revolving door swung behind them.

"Don't worry," Jonathan said. "The bar is on a veranda, overlooking the ocean."

"Good." Holly noticed that Jonathan's eyes changed to gray much the same way as Charlie's changed with the light.

She took in a deep breath.

"I was afraid you wouldn't show up." Jonathan let his hand slide down to the small of Holly's back. She felt suddenly self-conscious that he might see her left breast pulsing recklessly with the rhythm of her heart.

"You look beautiful," Jonathan said as they made their way through the lobby and out the back door into the warm night air. "Turquoise must be your favorite color."

Holly searched his face.

"Your swimming costume was turquoise also."

"I thought you were an artist." Holly gave him a curious look.

"I aspire to be one, why?"

"My bikini is teal and this dress is aqua." Holly smiled as she ran her hand over the spaghetti strap of her gauzy cocktail dress.

"It's all shades of turquoise to me." Jonathan leaned toward her and touched the necklace that caressed her neck. "Quite unique, this necklace,' he said. "When you see my paintings you'll understand my appreciation."

On a whim, Holly had decided to wear the blue and teal beaded necklace she'd made that had never sold. It matched her dress perfectly and now that she thought about it, it did resemble the swirls of blues and teals in the painting on his business card. Standing in the warm air, her body broke out in chills. While they waited to be seated, Holly couldn't think of one thing to say. Her breath caught when she looked up at Jonathan.

"You must be a Pisces." Jonathan looked closer. "Or maybe a Scorpio?"

Holly laughed to herself wondering if young people still used Zodiac signs for icebreakers. "I'm afraid you were correct on the beach when you said I was born on Christmas. I'm a Capricorn."

"Really? Born on Christmas? Your name gave me a hint,

actually. Ah, you're a Capricorn. So, you can dance out on the edge of a cliff and not fall off."

Holly wondered if she appeared that transparent. "You could say that I'm pretty stable," she said, knowing that she was on the edge of a cliff right then.

The host seated them at a small table overlooking two lighted grand fountains, a grove of coconut palms, and the moonlit ocean beyond. Large round pillars supported the wood-shingled roof of the open-air bar and multiple bamboo ceiling fans gently stirred the dry air just enough to cause the candles on the tables to flicker. The sweet aroma of tropical flowers wafted around them, but when Holly glanced around the deck she saw only green leafy shrubs and trees.

"May I bring you a drink?" The host asked as he handed Jonathan a menu and wine list.

"Certainly." Jonathan glanced at the wine list then at Holly. "What's your fancy?"

"*Tanqueray* martini, straight up, with olives on the side please."

"Yes ma'am. And for you, sir?"

Jonathan closed the wine list and handed it to the waiter. "*Glenlivet* with a splash of soda, *Schweppes*, if you have it."

"Yes, sir. Thank you." The host picked up the menus and walked to the bar.

"Such discriminating tastes."

"I'm attracted to women who are sure of themselves, like you." Jonathan winked.

Holly looked away, toward the ocean. "This view is gorgeous, isn't it?" She breathed in the salty air and breathed out as much anxiety as she could.

"Yes, it is indeed," Jonathan said, leaning back in his chair. He studied her face as if to memorize it or analyze it.

"Is this trip strictly for business?" she asked.

"It is. Unless you indulge me."

Holly tried not to smile. She looked out at the ocean

again. "Indulge you how?" she asked, coyly. "I'm having a cocktail with you and then you're going to show me your paintings."

The waiter delivered the drinks. When he walked away Jonathan lifted his glass. "To a beautiful woman."

Holly clicked her glass against his. She felt beautiful and pleased that this charming man had noticed. Feeling a sexual urgency, she changed the subject. "Are you the only artist in the show you invited me to attend?"

"I'm afraid that I am."

"Why are you afraid?"

"What I paint on the canvas is my soul. When others view it..." Jonathan paused a moment. "When others critique it, I feel exposed, or something closer to being flogged or ripped open. Who's to say what's good or right or bad about my feelings?" Jonathan looked intently at Holly. "I paint for myself—what I see and feel. I guess one might say that my paintings are my naked heart and who has the right to scrutinize my heart?"

"Were you scrutinized?"

"Always." He put his elbows on the table and held his glass with both hands. "I don't mind if my technique is critiqued. I try to stay open-minded. I'm open to learning new processes."

"Then how would you sum up this show?"

"All of the paintings sold. I'll leave it at that." Jonathan half grinned. He took a swig of his scotch then placed the glass back on the table.

"Doesn't that make a show successful?" Holly sat back and swung her hair so that it fell over one shoulder.

Jonathan's eyes dilated until there was just a rim of blue. "You are stunning."

Holly smiled, averted her eyes. "You're changing the subject."

"Sorry. Where was I? Ah, yes. Financial success is one

151

thing, but most people will buy a painting because it matches their décor. When I sell to those kinds of people I feel as if I'm selling my child to a slave market." Jonathan paused, frowned as if he'd just thought of something he didn't want to share. "There have been women in my past who were mistakes and disappointments—probably because I set the standard too high. I met a lovely woman who seemed to be the epitome of my dreams. I tried to paint a portrait of her. Before I finished, she dumped me. I thought I was going mad. I took my brush and tried to destroy the painting by covering it in blue paint. When I finished, I looked at the canvas. There was the image of all the things the women in my life lacked, and it enlightened me. I took another canvas and another and painted twenty hours a day for a week—each painting better than the last, each painting expressing something..."

"Philosophical?"

"I want you to see my work. Maybe you can help me understand it. Will you come to the gallery with me?"

"That's why I'm here." Holly licked her upper lip seductively, sipped the martini, and set the glass aside. She smiled and leaned forward to show off more cleavage.

"Excuse me. Let me settle the tab."

Holly looked out past the fountains and lighted palms to the black ocean. A million stars dotted the sky and surrounded a sliver of a moon. She closed her eyes and blocked out everything except Jonathan and the desire she'd wished for to change her life when she passed through the portal of turning forty. A shiver ripped through her.

"Shall we go?" Jonathan extended his hand. She reached up and took hold, pulling herself up, her face only inches from his, her eyes locked with his until she had to look away. They walked in silence through the lobby then down a long hall. When they reached the gallery, he pulled a key from his pocket, unlocked the door, and held it open for her. The lights were dim as he made his way to a closet to turn the gallery lights on over the paintings.

Holly walked from one painting to the next stopping in front of each one. Jonathan followed without speaking. When she'd gotten all the way around, he stood behind her and asked, "What do you think?"

"They're...enchanting, ethereal. I feel as if I'm a part of them." She gasped. "I'm genuinely moved by the images.

Jonathan pressed his face into Holly's hair and curled his arms around her. She felt his warm breath on the back of her neck and she leaned into it.

"How do they move you?"

"Like I've been...inside them. Like I know them...in a Biblical sense. Is that weird?" Holly wrinkled her nose. "It's difficult to explain. I've never been moved by art before. I feel as if I've had...an erotic or ecstatic experience." She felt embarrassed laying her naked emotions before him, no longer playing a teasing game.

"These paintings move me much the way you moved me when I saw you stroll down the beach. You are the essence of the images on these canvases. It's as if you are one of these paintings come to life."

Holly pulled her arms out of Jonathan's embrace and crossed them over his, touching his biceps. She felt the jellyfish slosh in her belly again. "Do you think they look like...me?"

"Do they look like you?" Jonathan pressed closer and swayed them from side to side. "I don't see as much as I feel. That's what art is all about—feelings."

"So they don't look like me?"

"Not physically, no, but emotionally, they feel like you. That's the truth, not a line. That's what I thought when you popped up in front of me in the surf. I haven't shaken that feeling."

"I take that as a great compliment." Holly closed her eyes and let Jonathan continue to rock her. She felt more secure than she'd imagined she could be under these circumstances. He'd taken her to the edge of the cliff, and she stood on her toes, ready to jump. She felt secure that she was ready to make the dive.

Jonathan released her from his embrace then turned her around to face him. "These paintings are fragile, delicate, ethereal, as you say…much like the necklace you've created. They are you and you are them. And I am captivated by you. I think you embody the soul of what I could only imagine."

"I'm not your imagination. I'm real. Where would your imagination like to lead me?"

Without speaking, Jonathan took her hand and she followed like a child enchanted by the Pied Piper. She'd never felt so light. So free. So desired.

Once inside his suite, Jonathan turned on every light. He removed his jacket and loafers and walked slowly toward her. She trembled when his eyes beckoned. When she was just a breath away, he devoured her lips with his. His hands moved deliberately as he explored her face, her ears, her hair, and stroked her back and shoulders so gently that she felt beloved. She stood limp, oblivious to zippers and buttons as Jonathan undressed them both with a calm passion that seemed to mirror what she'd seen in his paintings. She eased onto the bed and he slipped in beside her. His kisses wet her hair, her neck, her breasts. He entered her quickly, but gently, and she watched his face as his thrusts became rapid. She felt him inside her mind and the whirling, angelic images, the blues and greens of the paintings and the ocean saturated her and carried her to an emotional place of sublime splendor.

Their orgasm sent her mind flashing back to her First Communion. She saw herself in her white dress and veil, walking away from the alter feeling confused over the ritual, trying to believe that she had indeed become one with Christ and His Spirit. As she eased herself away from Jonathan, she realized that the emotion she should have felt then was what she felt now. She hadn't only made love with Jonathan—the universe had made love with her. Then it hit her, the feeling she'd carried in her head but didn't quite believe—Marcus was with her in the now as much as Jonathan and even Charlie. It was time for her to accept the part about until death do us part. She suddenly understood that the opposite of death is not life—the opposite of death is birth. Life goes on. Life never ends. Life is eternal. Holly smiled as she scooted to sit on the edge of the bed. She looked back at Jonathan and smiled as she watched the color of his eyes shift through shades of turquoise. "We're all swirls of blue in this ever present now."

Jonathan rose up on one elbow. "This wasn't about sex."

"No. It was about life," Holly said as she stood before him unashamedly proud of her body. "Your paintings evoke loss and expectation. I see myself in them—my past and my future. They're like…eternity." She picked up her panties and began to dress.

"My God Holly, you understand." Jonathan got up and pulled on his trousers. "Before you leave me, I have a confession."

"About what?"

"All the paintings didn't sell. I held one back—the best one. I couldn't bear to part with it." Jonathan took a box from the closet and pulled out the painting. "I want you to have it."

Holly held her breath. Delicate figures appeared to be dissolving into swirls of blue and emerging as one. "I can't accept it." Holly stared at the painting. "It is your best. No, it's too much. I saw your prices."

"It would please me…" Jonathan stepped forward. "Besides, this one is priceless—like this experience with you."

"Then I shall cherish it. Thank you."

Holly returned to the condo to find Lisa and Brody sitting on the balcony. When they stood to greet her, she held up her hand. She removed the painting from the box and propped it against a chair. She blew them kisses before going into her room. There was nothing to tell and no words to express her feelings. The doors to wonderland stood wide open. The universe had swung them off their hinges.

The next morning Holly got out of bed and went to the glass wall so she could see the beach. It was early but the shore had already filled with people and umbrellas.

"Holly?" Lisa called from just outside the door.

Holly stretched and smiled knowing that Lisa would give her the third degree. She opened the door and Lisa held out a tray with coffee and donuts. "I want to hear everything."

Holly took the coffee, held the cup to her lips, and teased Lisa with her eyes.

"You weren't gone for long." Lisa put the tray on the end of the bed. "Something happened didn't it? I can tell. The painting is gorgeous. Did he give it to you?"

"The evening was...surreal. It's difficult to explain. Jonathan's paintings were the window I could look through to see the wonderland I asked for on my birthday."

"Excuse me?" Lisa leaned forward.

"Everything meshed." Holly sat on the bed next to the tray and picked up a donut. "What I'm trying to say is, everything fell into place—Marcus, Charlie, me...life. It's all deep and spiritual. I just need to hold onto this, this awakening." Holly winked and took a bite of a cream-filled donut leaving a layer of powdered sugar on her lips. She licked it off. She could see that Lisa wanted more, but there was nothing left to say.

Lisa smiled. "I guess that's all I need to know. I'll use my imagination and try to guess the rest, but you look every bit as changed as I think you asked to be when you turned forty."

Baggage

11

Severe jet lag made it difficult for Holly to drag herself from the bed Tuesday morning. She hadn't heard from Charlie in a week and she couldn't help wondering why he hadn't called even though her memory of the blue brilliance of Maui inspired her not to worry. After all, she'd danced with the universe and Charlie had already been crowned prince. She needed to relax and let her life play out. What is, is, and it was luminous.

That afternoon when Holly came home from work, the warm afternoon sun flooded the deck in golden light. She was about to relax outside with a glass of chardonnay when Meg came crashing through the front door.

"I'm so happy you're home." Meg threw her books on the kitchen bar then threw her arms around Holly. "How was it?"

"Grand. Maui is the best island in the Pacific, or so a bartender told me. The weather was gorgeous, surprisingly dry for a tropical island. I missed you so much, honey."

"I missed you too. I have so much to tell you." Meg followed Holly outside.

"Well, I want to hear it all." Holly sat on the swing.

"You know, Mama? I thought I wanted to be in some sports related profession." Meg paced while she talked and scrunched her nose. "But, now, I'm thinking of being something like Sara Without an H."

"You mean a nurse?"

"Not exactly. But, maybe a school teacher or a guidance counselor or a social worker. I want to be somebody who can help people."

"That's very admirable, sweetheart." Holly smiled. "I'm proud of you."

"Thanks. I sort of started something like that on Friday, but it's caused another problem for you to help me solve."

"Okay. What's up this time?"

"The stupid prom."

Holly laughed and wine dribbled down her chin. "What about it? I thought you'd decided not to go."

"Aubrey and Tia want me to go with them, but I'll be almost thirty-two weeks pregnant by then. I'm afraid that I'll look pregnant—look what happened while you were gone." Meg pulled her shirt out of her jeans and showed Holly the pooch of her belly. "I have a baby bump."

"Yes you do but not a very big one." Holly resisted the urge to laugh again. "Come and sit beside me and tell me the problem."

"I have a date." Meg finally stopped pacing and sat down.

Holly took a long look at Meg before she spoke. "I don't know what to say. I mean how will it look?" As soon as she spat out the words she wished she could have taken them back. Was she ashamed of Meg? Did she fear that her date would try and take advantage of her like Tia said boys do? Meg still didn't look pregnant, but her baby bump would most likely increase rather quickly now.

Meg scooted away from Holly and crossed her arms. "I know what you're thinking. You think I'll embarrass myself and you. Well, I've thought about that. Even though I don't look pregnant, it's not like everyone doesn't know that I am and since I go to school and basketball games pregnant, why can't I go to the prom pregnant?"

The two sat in uncomfortable silence. Holly had to think

158

for a moment. She didn't know if she was being unreasonable, overprotective, embarrassed for Meg, or just plain old-fashioned.

"Are you ashamed of me, Mama?"

Holly hung her head. "I didn't think so."

"Then what?"

"I guess it's the part about going on a date pregnant that caught me off guard. It's something that hadn't entered my mind. I didn't even know you were…friends with any boys."

"Well, it looks like I'm friends with one now."

"Is he a boy I know?"

"No. He's what people call special."

"Special, like in challenged?"

"I guess. His name is Sam and he's sweet, just a little slow. He's the brunt of lots of jokes. He asked a couple of the popular girls to the prom, but they turned him down. A lot of the kids laughed and made fun of him. I could tell his feelings were hurt, so I stepped up in front of the creeps and asked Sam if he wanted to take me, and he said yes."

Holly set her wine down and wiped a tear from the corner of her eye. "That's so dear of you."

"No, it's not, not really." Meg put her hands together, laced her fingers until her knuckles turned white. "You, Brody, and Sara Without an H all say that Frog is a gift. I'm trying hard to make it one. Okay?"

"Okay."

"And I hate it when kids who have everything are so mean to the kids who don't. I might not have figured that out or even cared if I wasn't pregnant and see the way some kids look at me." A tear trickled down Meg's cheek. She looked at Holly with lips quivering. "Frog is making it possible for Sam to go to his senior prom."

"Let me squeeze you. I know how rough things are for you right now, but you make me so proud and so happy."

"That's what I want to do with my life—help make

people happy."

Holly sniffed. "You said you wanted my help with something?"

"Will you go shopping with me? Will you help me find a gown that I won't look stupid in?"

"Of course I will."

"Thanks, Mama. You're the best mother ever. I'm glad you liked Maui. I want to hear everything."

Holly sipped her chardonnay, wondering where to start and how much to tell. She decided to start with the blue brilliance of the ocean and sky, show Meg the painting, and somehow leave the part about Jonathan out. Someday she would tell her the whole story, but not today.

12

Almost as soon as Charlie returned home, he called Holly. "Hello beautiful. We're back in Pittsboro."

"You're home? You sound out of breath. Are you alright?"

"Yeah. I just ran half a mile…so I could get away from Jordan. She wanted to soak in a hot bath so I told her I needed to run."

"I'm glad you're home. How'd it go?"

"Way better than expected. I have so much to tell you."

"So, everything worked out for Jordan?"

"That and then some. The healing has begun and not just for Jordan. Jessica was the surprise. She did some growing up as well. I feel as if I have two different daughters now."

While Charlie gave Holly a blow-by-blow commentary, she reveled in the realization that this trip had been necessary. She listened and interjected responses and comments. She giggled. The longer he talked the more certain she was that things were going to get better for them.

On their way to the University of Wisconsin, Charlie and Jordan had stopped for lunch in a rural area south of Madison. Across from the restaurant Jordan spotted a pasture with several horses and foals and took off running. By the time Charlie caught up with her, she was petting one of the foals.

She glanced over her shoulder and flashed a smile. Her usual demure, depressed expression had changed to one of optimistic joy and Charlie thought she looked suddenly quite grownup with her long thick curly dark hair blowing in the breeze. "This is what I want to do with my life." She'd told her father. "I want hundreds of horses in rich green pastures. Not racehorses. Show horses, maybe, or the kind of horses in the equestrian competitions in the Olympics or just maybe a dude ranch."

Holly hadn't heard Charlie so euphoric. She let him ramble. She shared his joy.

After visiting The University of Wisconsin, Charlie and Jordan pulled up to Jessica's sorority house in Champaign, Illinois. They could see her pacing on the porch. When she saw them drive up she stopped pacing and folded her arms across her chest. "It's past nine," she shouted. "And it's freezing out here." Both he and Jordan knew how difficult the next few hours were going to be. They weren't mistaken.

Since Jill had kicked them all out, Jessica had turned into an even darker version of her mother. Her anger seethed. She'd lost her patience with Jordan and Charlie and she used sex to get what she wanted—including a spot on the varsity cheerleading squad. When Jordan showed up in a pair of multi-colored leg warmers that Angie had given her, Jessica accused her of looking like a four-year-old. An argument immediately ensued and Jessica ended up with a swollen, blood-shot eye from the corner of the book that Jordan hurled her way.

Somehow, amidst the insults and accusations, Charlie had helped them understand their anger and resentment. By the end of the visit, Jordan and Jessica were friends again and had come to grips with their situations. Charlie admitted to Holly that he'd been shocked to hear Jessica say that she'd learned to use sex for power just by watching her mother. She'd been proud that she'd fucked her way into her sorority and was

162

about to fuck her way into cheerleading. After Jordan tossed the book, Jessica broke down in Charlie's arms. He sensed an epiphany of some kind although Jessica hadn't spoken a word.

He'd gone on to reassure his daughters that the three of them were still a family and it was alright to be angry. Their mother simply didn't know how to love them the way they needed to be loved. While Jessica agreed, Jordan defiantly held to the expectation that her mother would one day realize her mistake and let them return home.

The day before Charlie and Jordan arrived back in Pittsboro, Jessica called. "I didn't make cheerleading, Daddy, but it's okay. If I make it next year, it will be on talent, not by fucking my way in. I'm not going to be like Mom anymore."

When Charlie finished his chronicle, he took in a deep breath and blew it out slowly. "I've missed you, Holly."

"I've missed you as well, and I have so much to tell you."

"Is Meg okay? Is there something I should know? My God. I've been hogging the conversation."

"You're fine. I wanted to hear every word. Meg's great. She's handling everything so well. I'm so proud of her."

"Tell her I said, hello."

"I will. She'll be happy to hear that you're home."

"Holly, please say that you're free Saturday and Sunday," Charlie blurted. "I'm down on one knee, begging."

"I have a date with Lisa to go shopping on Saturday, but I can reschedule." Holly suddenly began to shake.

"How about a weekend in the country?"

"We tried that once. Are you sure you want to try again? Is Jordan ready?" Holly babbled then stopped and held her breath.

"Well, it's a different country this time. Jordan is doing well enough to stay by herself. I'm sure she'll be fine for one night."

"A different country? Are we flying off somewhere?"

"No, I was pretty certain, well, I don't mean to take your affections for granted, but I was hoping we could stay at the bed and breakfast at Fearrington Village. I have a room on hold for Saturday night."

"Fearrington? How lovely." Holly felt her heart bouncing off her ribs.

"So, is that a yes?"

"Yes, yes. It's a yes. But what about Jordan?"

"I'm on an adrenalin high right now. I think it's going to be okay to slip away this weekend. Let's see how it goes with Jordan for the next couple of days. If everything is as good as I think it is, she'll be alright. If not, I'll get Angie to stay with her. And Holly...it's way past time for us."

"Charlie..."

"Done. Unless you hear from me, I'll pick you up at eleven-thirty Saturday morning. Shall I make reservations for lunch?"

"Lunch?"

"You don't want to miss a gourmet country meal, do you? You're going to need all the energy you can muster."

"Are you bragging?"

"I'm promising."

Holly slapped her chest to quell her exhilaration and catch her breath. "I'll be waiting on the doorstep." She held her hand over her heart long after she hung up the phone and remembered the surreal experience she'd had with Jonathan. Her expectations were high that her weekend with Charlie would be much more tangible.

Late Saturday morning Holly stood on her front porch dressed in a pair of white satin jeans, a flimsy ecru blouse with pink satin edging, and a pair of pale pink sandals. Although it was mid-April, the warm weather of the past couple of days had plummeted, so Holly wrapped a cream-colored wool shawl around her shoulders. She wore her hair straight and unrestrained—the same way she felt.

She thought about Maui and Jonathan and how much of it she should share with Charlie. Jonathan wasn't nor hadn't been a romantic attachment, and it wasn't a fling either. The distinction might seem trite to Charlie. She hoped he wouldn't be jealous. She smiled and let out a soft chuckle. Three months ago, sex had been the furthest thing from her mind, and now the thought of it obsessed her.

When Charlie pulled up, Holly tried not to run for the car.

He got out of the Porsche and met her halfway down the walk. "Good morning, gorgeous." He took her suitcase.

Holly thought he looked the part of a fine English chap in his white trousers and navy sports coat. "You certainly are a welcomed sight."

Charlie opened the trunk and placed her bag inside. Before closing it, he took her in his arms and they clung like magnets for a long while before he kissed her. Holly kissed him back with the same wild hunger, feeling the fluttering in her chest slow to deep thumps as she relaxed in his arms. Their kisses grew deeper until she knew they'd better stop before they had a repeat performance of the last time they got into such a passionate state.

Charlie closed the trunk and then led Holly to the passenger door. He held her elbow while she climbed in.

Once in the driver's seat, Charlie turned the key and backed into the street. Holly noticed how the new green of the deciduous hardwood trees and shrubs brightly contrasted with the darker evergreens. Pink and white dogwood trees and the bright blossoms of the redbud fulfilled the promise of new life. Holly turned to Charlie and imagined that new life bursting through the open door to wonderland.

"What a beautiful morning." Holly reached over and placed her hand on Charlie's knee.

"And what a beautiful woman to share it with." Charlie smiled. "I sound kind of corny, don't I?"

Holly giggled.

Fearrington Village stood just about halfway between Holly's house and Charlie's in a pastoral setting, complete with a white wooden fence and Fearrington's famous Belted Galloway Cows and Tennessee Fainting Goats—black and white animals that looked like *Oreo* cookies. The main house nestled in a small forest of trees and manicured gardens. Orange, peach, and scarlet tulips just a day or two past their peak, but still bright as neon against their slender green stalks, waved in the gentle breeze as they drove the winding road to the plantation style house.

The décor inside left Holly feeling as if she were standing in a luxurious, yet cozy, home which could have belonged to an ancestor. The European antiques, artwork, and shiny dark heartwood floors covered with rich Oriental carpets reminded her of a magnificent version of her own home. She breathed in the rich aroma of a hundred and fifty years of southern hospitality.

After checking in they followed a walk of sun-soaked paving bricks where tiny lavender flowers overran their borders.

The Granary Restaurant had been recently restored. The heartwood floors gleamed brightly against the soft yellow walls which had a hint of avocado or chartreuse or maybe just a reflection of the great trees shading the windows. Yellow and red plaid country-style curtains, vermillion red windowsills, and one lime-green chrysanthemum in a tiny jar on each table gave the room a homey feeling.

As they passed the rustic wooden tables and mismatched cane chairs, Holly couldn't help but notice the succulent shrimp, festive salads, and Eggs Benedict that filled the plates of the guests. "Sir Charles, this is magnificent, but I'm not so sure I can eat."

"As I told you, we're going to need sustenance to get us through this weekend." He winked. "We have so many activities that we've neglected."

Holly felt hot blood crawl up her neck and explode onto her cheeks and nose. She felt faint and chuckled.

"What is it?" Charlie asked as the host led them to a table with a view of an English-style courtyard.

Charlie held the chair for Holly and she sat facing a huge window. She waited to speak until Charlie sat across from her and the host walked away. "I was just wondering about those fainting goats. Do you think they actually faint?"

"We'll have to investigate that in our free time this afternoon." Charlie winked. "Why? Do you feel faint?"

"Yes, and giddy."

"And we haven't even gotten to the champagne."

"I'd be in a spin if I drank champagne on an empty stomach."

"Then you'd better eat up. Our room will be ready at one."

Holly looked at her watch and counted the minutes until then.

They both ordered the almost-too-gourmet omelet of the day—Parisian ham, mushrooms, goat cheese, spinach, caramelized onions, and roasted potatoes. Charlie devoured his while Holly nibbled around the edge and drank two cups of coffee. They lingered at the table, bragging about their girls and the way the three of them were handling their problems.

"You must be one heck of a father to have brought your girls through their anger."

"They did most of it on their own. They just needed a spark to let go of their frustrations. Now, I believe they see each other in the same boat. They've turned into confidants…friends even." Charlie smiled and sat up straight—the humble, proud father.

"I can't wait to meet them." Holly blotted her lips on a linen napkin.

Charlie reached into his breast pocket and pulled out a

photograph. "I won't bore you with pictures, but I wanted to share this one with you." He handed the picture to Holly. "It was taken the morning we left Jessica's."

In the picture, the two girls stood arm-in-arm with their heads touching and wide smiles on their faces—one fit and shapely with straight blond hair and bright green eyes and one, less developed, a few pounds overweight, and with frightfully frizzy chestnut hair.

Holly held the picture with both hands and pondered it. "Jessica's eye looks a little sore, but they're beautiful and they look like they love each other."

"Right now they do, but it's been a long time coming."

"Are they ready for me?" Holly asked.

"Jessica is, but Jordan's just beginning to heal. She's been quiet much of her life, not depressed, just not overly happy."

"Honestly, Charlie, things are going to get better. I can feel it," Holly said, still gazing at the picture.

Charlie reached across the table and covered Holly's hand with his. "As you wish."

Holly thought she would burst into tears, but she managed to hold back. She clung to Charlie's warm and confident hand hoping that Jordan and Jessica were ready for her to step into their lives and share Charlie's affections. She wanted Charlie...but she didn't want to interrupt his restored bond with both of his girls.

"Shall we go?" Charlie looked at Holly's nearly full plate then looked up and smiled at her. "Good thing I ordered a picnic basket for later."

They walked outside and down another brick sidewalk lined with pale pastel pansies, white daffodils with coral trumpets, and a row of tall trees in full spring blossom of violet-pink, too vivid to be real. Their room sat behind the main house and faced an expanse of green. Workers were busy arranging tables under white tents on the far lawn.

Holly hugged Charlie's arm. "It's so beautiful here. It's

like we're a world away from home."

Charlie unlocked the door and Holly stepped inside. "It's wonderful. It's more than I could've ever imagined."

The first thing Holly noticed was the canopied bed. How she'd wanted one when she was a girl. "Someone has lit the fireplace. It's so, romantic, isn't it? I mean to have a fireplace in the bedroom."

"So, the room pleases milady?"

"Yes, Prince Charming. Your lady is pleased."

While Holly investigated the rose pink and cream décor Charlie picked up a bottle of *Perrier-Jouet* from a silver ice bucket.

"Champagne." Holly spun around. "The flowers on the bottle match the room."

Charlie gently eased the cork from the bottle and filled two flutes. When he handed one to Holly he bowed slightly and smiled.

Holly covered her face with both hands then ran her fingers through her hair before taking the glass.

"To us." Charlie lifted his glass.

They stood silent and gazed into each other's eyes before slowly lifting the flutes to their lips.

Charlie went to the door, took the do not disturb sign off the inside handle, and placed it on the outside of the door. Holly sat in one of the easy chairs in front of the fire.

"There's plenty of food," Charlie said when he sat in the chair next to her.

Holly smiled. She realized that Charlie had made every effort to impress or please her or both. She couldn't help thinking about being with Jonathan in an elegant, yet stark room and no conversation—only comprehension of something so profound that it was incomprehensible. The pleasure of the memory aroused her and she felt her breathing turn slow and deep.

"Holly?"

"Sorry, I'm just so overwhelmed." She sipped the champagne, gazed into Charlie's crystal blue eyes, and tried to erase Jonathan from her thoughts. "What kind of food?" she mumbled.

"Cheese, pâtés and terrines, fruit, fresh-baked bread, chocolate truffles, shall I go on?"

"What about chocolate-covered strawberries? I saw them on Fearrington's web page."

"I thought we'd save those for last." He winked.

Holly giggled. 'To celebrate?' she wanted to ask but refrained. Surely, everything would be wonderful tomorrow afternoon when they packed up to go their separate ways, but she didn't want to jinx the romance by asking.

An Australian sheepskin rug covered the wood floor in front of the fireplace. Holly removed her shoes and let her feet sink into the smooth wool. Charlie stood and removed his jacket and shoes and socks then refilled their glasses. He chuckled. "What does Meg think of this?"

"She's so excited. I can't believe that she's so happy for us while she's battling with her emotions."

Charlie looked down. "If she's anything like you, and I think she is, she'll find her happiness on her own."

Holly closed her eyes but tears surged through and found their way down her face. "Thank you for those words. That's just what I needed to hear."

"I love you, Holly," Charlie said as he set his glass down and wiped away the moisture from under her eyes with his thumbs. He cupped her face in his hands. "I love you and I want to show you, no matter how awkward this rendezvous is." He leaned forward to brush his lips against hers.

Holly placed her hands over his and they kissed with their lips and then with their mouths. When Holly pulled away she saw a tear running down Charlie's face and they kissed again.

Charlie's hands were still on her cheeks and he kissed her so gently that she felt treasured and adored. He slowly ran his fingers against the sides of her head and let long strands of her shiny hair slip through his fingers.

Holly inhaled and moved her hands to Charlie's chest. She felt pleased that Charlie was taking this slow. His hands moved to her neck and then her shoulders then her waist. Slowly, he pulled her blouse up over her head and let it drop to the floor. He touched her breasts through her cotton camisole and she felt his hands quiver. She watched him as he gazed upon her body and she smiled in delight. He brushed her shoulder, neck, and face with his lips then let his open mouth linger gently on hers as if he was breathing her essence into his soul.

Holly took a step back, removed her camisole, and placed her hands on her belt buckle just below her navel.

Before she could unbuckle it Charlie said, "Wait. Let me look at you." He traced the outline of her torso with his index fingers while his eyes focused on her breasts and then the silver ring that pierced her belly. He touched her belly ring first and then ran a finger across her flat and firm abdomen. His fingers inched up her sides to her chest and he gazed, again, at her full breasts. "May I?" he asked.

She nodded.

His warm hands cupped her breasts and she let her head fall back and held her breath. She felt as if he would devour her and that's just what she wanted. Charlie raised his head and looked into her eyes. "You please me," he said.

Holly took a step back on wobbly legs to remove her jeans and silk underwear while Charlie unbuttoned his shirt and pushed it off his shoulders.

"You're so beautiful, Holly—perfect in body and soul."

She sat down on the sheepskin and watched him undress. He knelt in front of her, then sat back on his heels.

"You're beautiful too." She spoke in a whisper as Charlie caressed her shoulders and eased her to lie back. He kissed her gently then hovered over her in a push-up position. He bent his arms until their faces were a breath away then rose up to gaze into her eyes. He repeated this until Holly was so aroused that she pulled him to her and kissed him deeply, drawing him into her, feeling physically and emotionally connected. The logs in the fireplace crackled as sparks flew up the chimney.

When Holly thought she couldn't take a second more, Charlie took her to a higher plane then a higher one until the pleasure became gloriously unbearable, but she didn't want it to stop. She longed to stay on the edge of ecstasy. She balled her fingers into fists as she arched her back. Charlie held off until Holly grabbed the sheepskin rug and began to moan. They let go together in an explosion of pent-up emotions and mutual desire.

They remained connected and drank up each other's pleasure until the logs in the fireplace beside them turned to embers.

"I should stoke the fire," Charlie said.

"Not yet." Holly looked at him. "Please don't let go of me."

"I'll never let go of you, Holly. Never."

They'd entwined themselves like fragile vines of wisteria, twisted together by sun and wind they had no control of. Holly couldn't remember being so content and so complete. She thought about the candles on her birthday cake, the hope she'd placed in them, and now, the deliverance of her wish. She thought of the brilliant blue and realized that she and Charlie had made love with the blessings of the universe.

Charlie watched in silence as if he knew exactly what she was thinking. After a long moment, he spoke. "I love you, I love you, I love you. I wish I could come up with something clever, but, my darling, I stand before the jury with not one word eloquent enough to express the way you fill my soul. Will you forgive me for my lack of enviable prose?"

Holly glimmered. "Thank you."

"Thank you?"

"Thank you for you, for this place, for this day, for loving me so tenderly." She kissed his cheek. "I don't need enviable prose. I need the kind of honesty that you just gave me."

"When I first saw the beauty of your body, I felt like Pygmalion and Galatea the artist who fell in love with the sculpture he'd created, not that I had any influence in creating you. It's just that you are so serene. I can't take my eyes off you. You look every bit a goddess, Venus de Milo herself, or when I saw your breasts, Aphrodite."

"Charlie, I need to tell you something, speaking of artistic creations."

"What is it?"

"I took a little trip while you were away."

"Good for you." Charlie smiled as they disentangled themselves. "Where did you go?" he asked as he put a log and some kindling on the spent fire before snuggling next to her again.

"Maui."

"So that's where you got your beautiful...and sexy tan."

Holly looked at Charlie with intent, feeling somewhat nervous suddenly. She told him about Lisa and Brody and about the corporate jet, about the condo and the view of the ocean and sky like an IMAX movie, and she tried to explain the experience of gazing out on the endless colors of blues and greens of the ocean from the window of the plane. She told him about the trip to Hawaii she and Marcus had planned in the months before he took sick.

"I met a young man in Maui, an artist..." Holly put a hand to her head. "Jonathan Spencer. You might be interested in his work."

"What kind of work?"

"Oil paintings—the most glorious collection of paintings I've ever seen." Holly watched her hands shake as she spoke but proceeded to tell Charlie almost everything about Jonathan's paintings and their encounter. She didn't hold back on talking about the pleasure they'd shared, but she tried to focus on the art and the way it enraptured them and led them into exploring one of the pleasures of life.

"Charlie, to be honest, I was upset that our relationship wasn't more than telephone conversations. I met Jonathan on the beach and it took me two days to accept his invitation into his bed. It was a fling. Maybe I was trying to hurt you but as it turned out, it wasn't Jonathan that made love to me. I never connected to him. I connected to a force something akin to the universe itself. Like a prelude to a dream and you, Charlie, have made that dream become a reality. The experience prepared me for you, enabled me to accept and understand that my commitment to Marcus ended when he died. What we just shared was no less fantastic than my wildest imagination." Holly stroked Charlie's face with her fingers. "Can you understand?"

Charlie reached up and took a napkin from the coffee table and blotted his eyes. "Yes. I understand. Thank you for telling me." Charlie kissed Holly's hand and held it against his lips. "It makes me love you all the more. And Holly, I'm sorry to have gotten so caught up in Jordan that I let you down."

"Apology accepted. In a way, Jonathan was the framework of a dream. In that dream I made love to Marcus for one last time, I made love to my vision of you, and in return, the universe made love to me, gave me my freedom from Marcus and the permission to love you. I honestly believe that. Jonathan was nothing more than a muse."

"You were sent to me, spiritually speaking. I honestly believe that. And if it took a sexy young artist to help you see that so be it." Charlie smiled.

Holly moved to her hands and knees and kissed him from head to toe.

"You'd better watch yourself."

Holly stopped nibbling on his toes and looked up. "Why?"

"Your breasts hanging down and swinging like that just could arouse me enough to—"

"What? Ravish me? Again?"

"Any better ideas?" He pulled her to him and rolled them to their sides.

"Two days after we met, I wished for you when I blew out my birthday candles. Since then, you have built such a fire in me that I can think an orgasm." Holly smiled. "I can't imagine how I went for ten years without sex, but I couldn't imagine being in love like I am now. I have ten years of orgasms pent up in me. There must be thousands of them."

"Well then, we'll have to keep a tally, won't we? Do you think we can reach a hundred by tomorrow night?"

"Tomorrow night? I can reach that by midnight." Holly giggled. "Can you keep up or do you need some Cialis?"

"I'll bet I can make you say uncle before I do."

"Oh, I like that challenge."

"Hot damn." Charlie sat up. "I need a little break first. Wanna take that cheese plate and the rest of the champagne and get into the whirlpool tub? I'm starving."

"So am I. I wasn't that hungry before we started this lovefest."

Charlie laughed. "I told you that you needed all the energy you could get into your body. I win the first round."

By Sunday afternoon, they'd missed the English afternoon tea in the Farm House lobby, dinner in the Fearrington House Restaurant, the sunset, the gala wedding just outside their window, the moon rise, the meteor shower, and the country breakfast on Sunday morning. The cheese and fruit plates were empty as well as the chocolate truffle plate. They'd opened the second bottle of champagne and Charlie drained the last of it while Holly munched on chocolate-covered strawberries and hot black coffee.

"We should get dressed." Holly frowned.

Charlie sat playing with the foil from around the top of the champagne bottle. He rolled it up and twisted it around his pinky. "Just one more thing." He walked to Holly's side of the bed and knelt. "Holly Marie Gaynor, I take thee as my precious wife. I promise to love, cherish, and adore you from now and into eternity. Will you marry me back?"

Holly couldn't stop the torrent of tears. She let out a peep of a sound and nodded.

Charlie slipped the gold foil ring onto Holly's third finger, left hand.

"I pronounce us husband and wife."

"May we live in our enchanted union forever," Holly said and covered his face with kisses.

Holly admired the foil wedding ring as they paused at her front door. She insisted that Charlie come in so they could break the news to Meg together. She opened the door and called Meg. "I'm home. Charlie's here too."

"I'll be right there," Meg called from her bedroom.

Charlie set Holly's suitcase next to the front door and looked at her. "You're sure we'll get a positive response."

"One hundred percent sure." Holly pulled Charlie's face toward hers.

"So how was your trip to the country?" Meg smiled as she came into view of them kissing. "Fantabulous wasn't it?"

They turned to her and smiled.

"I guess that was a stupid question. I can see the answer written all over your faces."

Charlie held out his hands to Meg and she took them. He looked into her eyes. "I just wanted to stop in for a minute. I asked your mother to marry me and she did."

"What? You guys got married…without me?"

Holly held out her hand. "We're married in our hearts."

"We'll set a date for a legal wedding before the end of summer."

Meg hugged Holly. "I'm so happy, Mama." She turned to Charlie and threw her arms around his neck. "You are our Prince Charming."

Charlie kissed Meg's cheek. "So, I have three daughters now."

Meg stood next to Holly and put her head on her shoulder and her arm around her waist. "This is just like a fairytale, isn't it?"

Holly kissed the side of Meg's head. "Thank you, sweetheart, for sharing my happiness."

"Charlie, I've been trying to get her interested in men for years. Why would she think I'm not happy about this?" Meg winked at him and he winked back.

All day Monday Holly tried to contain her giddiness, tried to be the professional office manager she was. By nine-fifteen, the whole office knew about her engagement. She managed to finish her work, but she just couldn't stop her heart from zinging, or wipe the smile from her face, or stop the twinkle in her eyes. She repeatedly brought herself back to the reality of her office routine. She imagined walking hand in hand with Charlie on a sunny beach somewhere along the Aegean Sea or standing before Claude Monet's gardens in Giverny. She remembered the rose-pink room at Fearrington and her first thrilling gasp when Charlie put a finger to her belly ring.

She couldn't stop thinking about the wedding. She imagined Meg, Jessica, Jordan, and Lisa dressed in aqua, teal, turquoise, and sapphire. She wanted something different from her first wedding, which, at the time, had been perfect, but she didn't want to repeat the big, formal church ceremony and Latin Mass. When she married Marcus, her attendants wore red. Holly remembered the way her mother had tried to talk her into pink citing that red just wasn't appropriate for a spring wedding. But Holly won out and her mother acquiesced. Weeks later when the *Raleigh News & Observer* announced the Gaynor wedding, "The Red Wedding," as the Triangle's wedding of the year, her mother finally approved of Holly's choice.

Holly's dreaming turned to Charlie. She knew that their wedding would be uniquely their own, maybe on a beach, maybe just the two of them in Seychelles or Sri Lanka—a pink wedding amidst the blues and greens of the ocean and sky. Holly laughed. At least she'd please her mother this time around if she chose pink. She shook her head and brought her mind back to the present. Charlie—maybe he'd drop by unexpectedly. Maybe they could slip off somewhere cozy and share a few intimate moments. She felt as if her face would crack from her perpetual smile. All afternoon, she glanced at her watch. It surprised her that Charlie hadn't called. On her way home, she began to worry.

13

Holly's apprehension manifested itself when she returned home from work to find Meg, Aubrey, and Tia sitting on the sofa, hands folded and heads down.

"What is it?" Holly turned on the lamp and sat beside Meg.

Meg licked her lips before turning to Holly. "You don't know?"

Holly felt a cramp in her heart. "Do I want to know?"

"Charlie didn't tell you?"

"I haven't talked to Charlie since he left last night. Tell me what I need to know."

"Mama, maybe you'd better pour yourself a martini."

"Stop this, Meg, you're scaring me. Just tell me."

"I thought you would come home mad at me. That's why Tia and Aubrey are here—to protect me. I thought you'd heard it from Charlie." Meg looked up and sucked in a loud breath. "Let me see where to start. God, Mama."

"I'll tell." Tia leaned forward. "When Charlie got home yesterday Jordan was gone. She left a note that said she hated him for lying to her and she called him all kinds of names and said she didn't want to be his daughter anymore."

"No. Poor Charlie. What precipitated this?

"Somehow she found out about you," Meg said, "and got angry because she thought you wrecked her parent's marriage. That you were the reason her mom kicked them all out. She accused Charlie of fucking a ho at a sleazy motel…then asked him if he was the one who got me pregnant."

"Wait…" Holly's hands were shaking. "I'm certain that Charlie didn't tell Jordan about me. How did she know he was with me? And how did she know about you?"

"That's why I'm afraid you're going to be mad at me." Meg pulled at her ponytail.

Holly waited.

"Somehow, Jordan made friends with Vanessa. Before Vanessa stopped being friends with me, she knew the story about Charlie Prince being called Prince Charming. Anyway, Vanessa met Jordan Prince on Sunday at some friend's house and asked her if her father's name was Charlie—if he was the famous Prince Charming."

"No, sweetheart, don't blame yourself. Telling the story about Prince Charming was completely innocent. Come here…" Holly took Meg in her arms and hugged her close. She felt Meg's whole body tremble as she wept. "So, I presume everyone at school knows the accusations against Charlie?"

Meg grimaced. "Yeah."

"Everybody knows," Tia said. "Meg got snubbed and called horrible names…and so did you. All the kids are making up nasty stories about you and Meg and Charlie all doing it in the same bed."

"Oh, God. No." Holly let out a loud sigh. "It's not your fault, Meg. Charlie's daughter has been depressed since her mother abandoned them almost a year ago. She blamed Charlie until last week. I can't imagine what happened since then."

Meg sobbed and coughed and tried to catch her breath. Aubrey sat stunned.

"Vanessa stopped being friends with Aubrey and me because we tried to protect Meg from the bullies." Tia looked at Holly. "Vanessa tried so hard to hurt Meg. She really did it this time."

"Listen, Jordan's being treated for depression, but Charlie seemed to think that she was better and more understanding of the divorce. Now, Vanessa, that's another story. I didn't know she could be so mean."

"It all started when Meg told her that she got pregnant by a married man," Aubrey said.

Meg spoke between gasps. "There's more. Charlie needs you, Mama. When he got home last night and read the note, he called the police. The sheriff found Jordan, Vanessa, and another girl driving out of McDonalds and three squad cars surrounded them and escorted them to Vanessa's friend's house where Charlie was waiting. She fought and kicked and swore at both Charlie and the sheriff. She bit the sheriff during the struggle and they had to restrain her. An ambulance came and took her to the psyche ward at UNC."

Holly buried her head in Meg's hair and wept with her. "I have to call Charlie."

"Will he be mad at me?" Meg asked.

"No way. He'll feel all the guilt. That's the kind of man he is."

"I'm sorry that all this happened, Mama. Charlie was so happy yesterday."

Holly picked up the phone and dialed Charlie's number.

"Oh, Holly. I'm so sorry." Charlie sighed and Holly could imagine him pacing with head down and hand rubbing the back of his neck. He sounded exhausted. "I was about to call you."

"I heard about yesterday when you got home. Is there anything I can do?" Holly's eyes locked with Meg's.

"How did you find out? I was trying to keep you out of this until things settled."

"You sound terrible. Did you sleep last night?"

"No. Tell me what you know."

"Somehow Jordan met a girl who used to be friends with

Meg. She broke off their friendship when Meg told her that Mike was married. I guess she wanted to hurt Meg."

"Oh, my God. Is her name Cheryl?"

"No, Vanessa."

"There was a Vanessa there last night. I couldn't figure out how they knew so much. Now, things are falling into place. So, you've already heard Jordan's accusation?"

Holly hesitated. "That you had two playmates...me, and Meg?"

"God. That came from Vanessa?"

"That's what it sounds like."

"How's Meg taking all this?"

"Not well. She's pretty upset. Vanessa evidently told the whole school. Meg thinks it's all her fault because she told her friends the Prince Charming story."

"Is she there? Put her on the phone."

"He wants to talk to you." Holly handed Meg the phone.

Meg took the phone and held it against her thigh. She looked to Holly. "What should I say?"

"Just listen."

She put the phone to her ear. "Hello."

"Meg, I, I'm so sorry about this. Listen to me, honey. None of this is your fault, okay?"

"But, I—"

"But, nothing. I should have told Jordan the whole truth in the beginning...then none of this would've happened. If you're not too upset with me I'd like to drop by later. Will that be okay?"

Meg took in several small breaths to prevent sobbing. "Yes," she said and cleared her throat. "Remember Mom's motto, what is, is."

"I love you, Megan Gaynor. You're one hell of a girl. I have to go. Tell your mom that I'm bringing a surprise over in about an hour. Tell her not to cook. I want to take us all out...for pizza or something simple."

Meg turned the phone off. "He had to go. He said to tell you that he was bringing us a surprise later and that he wants to take us to dinner."

"Did he say anything about Jordan?"

"No. He said what you told me he'd say. That it's all his fault."

Aubrey stood up. "We should go home now, okay Tia?"

"Thanks, guys" Meg swallowed hard. "I couldn't ask for better friends."

Tia hugged Meg and Holly then held her head in her hands and bawled. Aubrey comforted her as they walked to the door. Before she closed the door Aubrey turned to Meg. "You're the best," she said.

Charlie rang Holly's doorbell an hour later. Holly was there in an instant with Meg on her heels. Holly held the door wide. "Charlie," she said and looked at a beautiful young woman standing next to him.

"Holly, Meg, this is my daughter Jessica." He looked to Jess. "And, Jessica, this is Holly and Meg Gaynor.

Jessica reached out her hand to Holly. "Mrs. Gaynor. I'm pleased to meet you."

"It's wonderful to meet you. My, this is a pleasant surprise. Please call me Holly."

Jessica turned to Meg. "Hi, Meg, pretty rough day, huh?"

"Pretty rough, yeah. It's good to meet you though. I think I've known about you for a lot longer than you've known about me."

"Daddy just told me yesterday, but I'd already heard about you and your mom from my sister. She called me after she ran away to Cheryl's house."

"Who is this Cheryl?" Holly asked.

Charlie rubbed his forehead. "Jordan met her a few weeks ago then forgot her. It wasn't until I told her I was going away for the night that she thought about looking her up. Cheryl lives near us and has a few horses. While Jordan visited her on Saturday, her cousin, Vanessa, dropped by. You can figure out the rest."

"I knew Vanessa was upset with me," Meg said, "but I didn't think she'd make up vicious lies."

"How is Jordan?" Holly asked, fearing the answer.

"We'll tell you in a minute," Jessica said. "But will you please hug my father. He needs you, Mrs…I mean, Holly."

Holly threw her arms around Charlie and held him while he burrowed his face in her hair.

Meg turned toward the kitchen. "We're eating here, Charlie. I put a frozen lasagna in the oven. I don't want to go out in public tonight. Hope that's okay."

Charlie didn't respond. Meg turned to see his shoulders shake.

Meg and Jessica exchanged a sad glance. "Come into the kitchen with me, Jessica. We'll give them a few minutes."

Holly continued to hold Charlie. "I'm so worried. Is Jordan—?" Before she could finish her sentence, Charlie's warm mouth covered hers. The moment wasn't romantic. It was more like guilt and mourning.

When they finally broke away from the kiss, Charlie looked at his feet but held onto Holly's waist. "I didn't want to tell you last night. You were radiant when I left. I didn't want to ruin that. I wanted you to have at least twenty-four more hours of bliss."

"But, you knew I'd be here to comfort you, didn't you?"

"Just thinking about you comforting me was enough. And, yes, you're right, I did need you. All night I craved your sympathy and support. But I pictured you in a snow globe, all safe and happy and protected from the harsh outside world of that glass ball."

They kissed again, with more passion and pressed their bodies together.

"I never want to leave your side, Holly. Never." Charlie

kissed her forehead before he stepped back.

"Tell me about Jordan? Is she why Jessica is here?"

"Come sit with me." Charlie led Holly to the sofa. They sat close together and held hands. "Just when I thought things were looking up, this happened. Jordan was doing so well—so well that she stopped taking her antidepressant the day after she and Jessica mended their relationship. She didn't tell anyone until yesterday afternoon when she casually told Jess over the phone, just before she packed her bags and ran away to Cheryl's."

"So that's what precipitated it?"

"That, and the fact she caught me in a lie. I told her I had a business trip. It wasn't a complete lie. Hell, it wasn't a lie at all. You and our future is my business. I didn't think she was ready to hear that, and now, well, she heard about us from the wrong person and she thinks I lied about where I went. I planned to tell her this week. I thought that, by now, she'd be okay with it."

"How is she today?"

"Sedated, but no longer restrained. You can't imagine seeing your child out of control and a policeman wrestling her to the ground and putting her in cuffs. When he tried to stand her up she kicked him and then bit him hard enough to draw blood."

Holly tightened her grip. "I'm so sorry...for both of you."

"She called Jessica late yesterday afternoon to tell her what Vanessa said. Thank God for that, because that's how we found her. Good thing we live in a rural community. The sheriff knew that a woman with a teenage daughter and a few horses lived down the road from us. Everything would've been fine if Vanessa hadn't been there, but it was just a matter of time before they met."

"I've known Vanessa for years. I never knew her to be vindictive." Holly paused. "A couple of years ago Vanessa's father impregnated a minor, divorced her mother, and married the girl so he could avoid a rape charge. Vanessa got pretty angry. She blamed the girl for breaking up her parent's marriage."

"Transference?"

"Sounds like it."

Jessica and Meg came back into the living room. Jessica sat in the recliner next to the sofa. "Daddy, Jordie, and that Vanessa girl must have made up the story about you having an affair with Holly and Meg. But why did Jordan believe it?"

"And how did she know that you were with Mama?" Meg asked.

"I imagine that she just came to that conclusion." Charlie looked at Holly. "I've never taken a business trip before."

Meg eased herself to the floor and buried her face in her knees.

"I'm sorry, Meg," Jessica said. "I didn't mean to make things worse for you."

"You didn't." Meg looked up and smiled. "Blame it on my hormones. They're out of whack. I need to go to bed."

"Without dinner?" Holly asked.

"I ate some yogurt and crackers earlier. I'm just so exhausted." Meg stood up. "I'm really happy to meet you, Jessica. I hope we can get together before you leave."

"Sure," Jessica said. "I'll be here for a few more days. Hope you feel better."

Charlie stood to hug Meg. "Will you forgive me? I'm so sorry you got the brunt of this."

"It's okay. If I wasn't pregnant, Vanessa wouldn't have said what she did. We're kind of all in this together." Meg turned away then looked back over her shoulder. "Goodnight everybody." She sauntered down the hall like a goalie who'd just missed the winning puck in the last second of the championship game.

Jessica brushed tears from her cheeks. "Daddy?"

"See what a lie will do?" Charlie said. "I never wanted to

hurt any of you and now, well—"

"You didn't lie, Daddy. You withheld some personal information. You did what you thought was best."

"And Jordie decided to believe the worst. I guess she wasn't as well as I thought."

"Especially since she went off her drugs," Jessica said. "Why did she do that?"

"Probably because she made up with you and was feeling happy." Holly looked to Charlie. "You think?"

"That's what the psychiatrist thinks."

"This reminds me, I need to ask you something." Jessica pulled her hair away from her face and wound it around one hand. When Charlie looked at her, she let go of her hair and let it fall to one side. "A few years ago Mom told me that you aren't Jordie's father." Jessica stared at her father. "Is that true?"

Holly felt uneasy. She touched Charlie's knee then pulled her hand away.

Charlie took in a deep breath and let it out slowly. "I stayed there by your mother's side all through her pregnancy. I held Jordan and fell in love with her before your mother even touched her. My name is on Jordan's birth certificate. I did the night shift from the day Jordan was born. I fed her formula because your mother refused to breastfeed. I answered her when she cried out in the middle of the night. I read stories and tucked her in every night, just like I did you. I just wasn't around when she was conceived. As far as I'm concerned, I'm Jordan's father—and happy about it no matter what's happened."

Jessica held her stare. "I'm so sorry, Daddy. When we walked away from Mom, you could've left Jordan with her, but you didn't. So, Mom literally threw Jordan away like garbage."

"No, she let me have both of my daughters."

Charlie wrapped his arms around Jessica.

187

"Mom brainwashed us. We never realized that we had the best father in the world." Jessica broke away from the hug. "Jordie doesn't know, does she?"

"Not to my knowledge." Charlie frowned.

"That would be the last straw, wouldn't it?" Jessica asked. "If Jordie knew that neither biological parent wanted her, she would die."

Charlie covered his face with both hands.

Jessica asked softly, "Am I your biological daughter?"

"Of course you are." Charlie looked at Jessica with a frown. "I can't imagine that you're not. I never suspected that you weren't." He paused. "We can check our DNA to be certain, but—"

"Don't worry. I don't want to know. You're the only father I want."

"Thanks, Jess. The question surprised me and I'm not one hundred percent sure. I love you as much as I love Jordan."

"I know you love us. Jordie just can't love us back." Jessica looked at the ceiling. "What I don't understand is why she won't talk to me? She called me, crying, to tell me what she'd found out about you. She talked to me then like I was her friend."

"But, you stuck up for me, didn't you? You didn't buy into the lie."

Jessica closed her eyes and pulled at her hair. "I didn't think about that."

"She probably wanted you to be her ally against your father," Holly interjected.

"It probably would've been better if Mom had moved out. Then Jordie might believe that Mom is the one who left us." Jessica curled her hands into fists and thought a moment. "When we packed up and left, it looked like we were leaving Mom."

"You're right."

"I have an idea." Jessica sprang to the edge of the sofa.

"You know since Jordie won't talk to you or me maybe we could get that hippie-chic to visit her. Do you think Jordan would listen to her?"

"Good idea," Charlie said and his face began to relax. "I need to call her and let her know what's happened. She just may be able to breakthrough."

Neither Charlie, Jessica, nor Angie could pry a word out of Jordan. She refused to speak to anyone, including the nurses and doctors. Charlie sat beside her bed and explained his life to her, asked her forgiveness, expressed his love, but mostly just sat in silence hoping for any indication that Jordan recognized his presence. Angie tried her best to be Jordan's best friend—asked her if she needed anything, and waited for hours on end to see if Jordan would answer. When Jessica visited she talked non-stop. She told Jordan how she felt about their mother, both now and while they were growing up. She told her how lucky they were to have their wonderful father. She told her how she supposed Charlie must have felt during those lonely years when their mother ignored him and them. She told her about Holly and that if she let her, Holly would be more of a mother to her than their real mother had ever been. She told her about Meg's pregnancy, and Mike. She told her that Mike and Meg's father were killed by the same disease. And she told Jordan to stop being so self-centered. She reminded her about college and her love of horses. She talked until she got a sore throat. But Jordan just sat and stared.

The few days Jessica spent in town proved to be uplifting for Meg, who wasn't used to the little rich-bitch image Jessica had at her disposal. She took Meg to Saks Fifth Avenue at the mall and a few specialty shops and boutiques and introduced her to designer sunglasses, shoes, and expensive perfumes. She told her to hold her head high and keep an expression on her face as if she knew a juicy secret about every person she met. Meg saw through her, but at the same time enjoyed their camaraderie.

On Saturday morning Meg and Holly were surprised when Jessica showed up in her father's sports car. "Daddy said you wanted to take her for a spin," she said, dangling the keys before Meg.

"If I remember correctly, your dad said that he'd take me for a spin."

Jessica laughed. "Had Vanessa seen you tooling around in it with Daddy, her story would've been believable."

"Don't remind me." Meg made a choking face.

"Are you certain it's alright with your father?" Holly asked.

Jessica shrugged. "Don't worry, he'll be fine with it. Besides I'm celebrating today."

"Celebrating what?" Meg asked.

"It's sort of sad. The cheerleaders were practicing the day before yesterday. Someone stumbled and the whole team went down. The fly girl fell face first and fractured two vertebrae. She's okay but had to have a fusion. I'm sad because she's a sweet girl and the best one out there. Anyway, they needed a replacement and they chose me. They just called an hour ago." Jessica did a little happy dance.

"Wow. Congratulations." Meg said. "The day we met your dad he told us how good you were."

Jessica's eyes twinkled and she chuckled. "My mom has been holding me up over her head and flipping me down ever since I was born. It always horrified Daddy watching her throw a baby around like that. That was one good thing about Mom—she taught me balance and not to be afraid of heights."

"Count your blessings." Meg flashed a smile.

"Yeah, guess I need to start doing that. Hey, do you want to drive or shall I? Daddy will be here in a minute—I think he's driving the speed limit. Come on. It'll be fun. We can go to that gourmet market you told me about and get stuff to fix dinner tonight for Prince Charming and Lady Holly."

Meg looked at the still dangling keys for a moment longer and then grabbed them before turning to Holly. "See you later, Mama. Tell Charlie that I'll try not to put a scratch on his Porsche."

Later that night, after Charlie and Holly shared a quick cup of coffee they sat down to a grand six-course dinner in Holly's formal dining room. Jessica and Meg dressed in black with white aprons and served a meal fit for a king, or at least a prince and his lady, complete with French cheeses, pâtés, edible flowers, and candlelight.

After the meal, Jessica and Charlie visited Jordan one last time before Jessica had to return to school. She had to tell Jordan one more thing. "You have your phone. Call me anytime day or night. I just want you to be happy. I want you to see how Daddy and Holly and Meg and me are already the best family. I want you in that family with me, Jordie, because I love you." When Jordan turned away, tears streamed Jessica's face and she ran from the room and down the hall. Charlie walked away without saying a word.

Early the next morning Charlie and Holly took the rather introspective Jessica to the airport.

"I usually can't wait to get back to school, but today...I don't want to go back. I don't mean ever, it's just that nobody has gotten through to Jordie. She's got some big mental hang-ups, doesn't she?"

"She's hurting. It's going to take time for her to heal." Charlie stared straight at the traffic ahead.

"And then she has to get angry? I mean, after she stops hurting? Only she already got angry, but that was over Mom, not you and Holly. And then she went catatonic." Jessica leaned forward, between the front seats of Charlie's truck.

"I'm glad Jordie threw that book when you two visited me in my dorm room. It made me wake up and realize the negative effect Mom had on us. All my anger and pain vanished when Jordie brought it into the light. That's what I kept telling her all week. So why doesn't she see it?"

"Maybe her scars go deeper than we know."

"It hurt me to see her in restraints. I hope I never see that again." Jessica sat back and readjusted her seatbelt.

"Hopefully when you come home for the summer, Jordan will be better." Holly glanced back at Jessica and saw her tears. "Oh, Jess…"

Charlie looked at Jessica in the rearview mirror and heaved a heavy sigh.

14

Later that morning Holly found it difficult to switch gears from Jessica's teary goodbye to Meg's excitement over prom gowns. Aubrey and Tia had purchased their gowns in the previous weeks but wanted to shop with Meg and Holly to insure Meg would get the perfect gown. Meg dragged them from shop to shop. Nothing suited her and she about gave up when Tia stepped from the petit department in Nordstrom. "I think I found it. Look."

Meg's face flashed a look of surprise. "It's cute, but I'm too tall for a petit."

"This is the perfect dress, besides it's longer than the other short dresses on the rack. Try it on." Tia insisted.

Meg held the dress up against her and looked at herself in the mirror. "Maybe." She took the dress into the dressing room while Holly, Tia, and Aubrey exchanged hopeful glances. The bright raspberry dress had an empire waist and straps that crisscrossed in the back. The skirt hung in tiny, pressed pleats two inches below her knees.

When Meg emerged from behind the curtain she was all smiles. "I love it. It's so…elegant."

"And gorgeous," Aubrey said. She pulled out her cell phone and snapped pictures of Meg posing in front of a full-length mirror. "You don't look one bit pregnant yet. Are you sure there's a baby in there?"

"I think it's wrapped around my backbone." Meg placed

her hands on her belly. "I do have a little baby bump and there's room in this dress for it to grow."

"That's why I knew this dress was *the* dress." Tia put her hands on Meg's belly. "Hey, little froggie. *You* are going to the prom."

On the way home the girls chatted about shoes and handbags and hairdos the way Holly expected teenagers would. She breathed a sigh of relief. Meg looked radiant. What resilience she possessed. She'd dealt with the kids at school by holding her head high and not responding to their crude remarks. She followed Jessica's instructions and plastered a smile on her face that confused the cruel kids so much that they left her alone. She was excited about the prom and life in general and seemed to have come to grips with her present situation. Her idea of becoming a guidance counselor or social worker sounded more suitable every day. Holly felt fairly certain that Meg had made a decision about Frog—she just hadn't shared it with her.

On the night of the prom, Sam, along with the girls and their dates, drove up in a shiny black stretch limo that Aubrey's parents rented for the occasion. Sam shuffled slowly to the door, looking back over his shoulder a few times before ringing the bell. He wore a simple black tux with a dark pink rose in his lapel.

Holly watched with trepidation as Meg went to the door and opened it.

Sam sheepishly handed Meg a white florist's box tied up with pink ribbons. "Hi, Meg. You look awesome."

Holly watched as the boy with his wide smile and bright eyes stepped into the foyer. Even though he possessed a pleasant appearance, it wasn't difficult to see why other teenagers would cast him out of their social circles. He fiddled with his lapels and rocked back and forth on his heels.

"Thanks, Sam." Meg opened the box and lifted out a halo

of tiny pink roses and baby's breath. "It's gorgeous," she said and turned to Holly. "Can you help me with this, Mama?"

Meg smiled. "I'm sorry, Sam, this is my mom. Mom, this is Sam."

"Hello, Sam." Holly smiled as she removed the hatpins from the box. "It's a pleasure to meet you."

"Hi, Meg's mom. He pulled a small digital camera from his breast pocket and held it out to Holly. "My mom asked for you to take some pictures of me with Meg and the other kids. Okay?"

"Alright." Holly took the camera and hung it from her wrist. "Let me fix the flowers in Meg's hair. Why don't you get the others to line up in front of the hydrangea?" Holly placed the halo of flowers on Meg's head and fastened it with the pins. She thought of her idealized wonderland and Meg as her little princes. She wanted to give her an empire where there was no pain and no shame.

Sam gathered the other kids and then came back to Meg and Holly. "Aubrey said you liked roses. I'm wearing a rose for you." Sam pushed out his chest and touched the flower.

"Why, thank you, Sam." Meg smiled at him. "How nice of you."

Holly bit the inside of her lip to keep her tears at bay. "Okay, you two. Let me snap a few pictures of just the two of you first then I'll photograph all six of you together." Holly had her camera as well and took as many pictures as the kids allowed alternating the two cameras.

After the photoshoot finished, Sam extended his elbow to Meg and walked her to the limo with a proud smile.

When they reached the open door, Meg turned back and blew Holly a kiss.

Holly hoped that Meg would one day look back on this moment and realize that this single act of kindness had defined her future. Because of this pregnancy, Meg considered a path of empathetic caring service. At the most difficult time in her young life, she had reached out and accepted Sam in such a way that no one else probably ever had. Holly waved until the limo was out of sight and then she broke down.

From what little Charlie had said about his place in Pittsboro, Holly imagined a rustic, split-level, cedar-sided edifice in a hardwood forest. He'd told her that the house had been constructed by a building contractor using scraps and leftovers of wood, vinyl flooring, carpet, and cabinets with the result as bizarre as if it had been built by a madman. The charm, for Charlie, had been the roofline and multilayered decks on the front of the house. And, of course, the land was just big enough to accommodate a horse and a small stable. Charlie had mentioned relocating the driveway and planning the landscaping, but other than that he hadn't discussed the progress with Holly.

Charlie invited Holly to visit the weekend after Jordan's admission to the hospital, the day after Meg's prom. Holly hesitated for several reasons. First, she didn't feel comfortable sneaking behind Jordan's back and second, it didn't seem right that she and Charlie would indulge in the pleasures of the flesh while Jordan suffered. Holly agreed to visit on one condition—that Meg accompany her.

Meg drove the dirt roads while Holly navigated from a map Charlie had drawn. "Turn left just after that mailbox with the flag on it," Holly said.

"It's a good thing we're doing this while it's still light. It's kind of eerie back in here." Meg made a face and made herself laugh. "I hope we're at the right house. We're so far out in the woods that somebody might meet us with a gun for trespassing. Did Charlie say the driveway was this long?"

"He said it snaked around."

"And it's uphill. I wonder how he got out when it snowed." Meg veered to the right then to the left as the drive twisted and turned and ended a ways from the house in front of a retaining wall.

When they got out of the car, Charlie called from the deck. "Welcome to my castle."

"My goodness, Meg. Would you just look at this place?" Holly spoke softly so Charlie couldn't hear.

"Looks like we have to climb up there." Meg slapped her hands on her hips. "How many steps are there?"

"Count them as we go."

There were twelve steps before the first landing, eight before the second, and four more before they reached the lower deck.

"Only four more," Charlie said, smiling.

Meg looked up. "There's an elevator out back, right?"

"No elevator, but if you'd continued to follow the driveway and took the right fork in the road you would've ended up at the back door."

"Thanks for telling us now," Meg said, faking a pant.

Charlie grinned. "Steps are the best exercise a person can get."

When they reached the deck Charlie kissed Meg on the cheek and Holly on the lips. "I wanted you to get the full effect of all the hard work I've put into this place."

"I'm in shock. It's better than paradise," Holly said, trying to take it all in. "It just doesn't sound like the house you described."

The sun hung low and couldn't be seen from the road, but from the deck, the treetops danced in golden light. Charlie had turned a gravel driveway into a series of raised beds with flagstone pathways around and between each one. Patches of bright yellow daffodils jutted through the forest like parades of fairies with trumpets. Holly felt as if she were overlooking the courtyard of an Italian villa.

"It's beautiful." Holly leaned against the railing and surveyed the garden. "I bet it's glorious when everything's in bloom. What else have you planted?"

"The daffodils were a surprise. From what I've found online, they were most likely planted many years ago and then multiplied. I think they're called creeping daffodils. When I bought the place there were the remains of a rotted out cottage just behind the house, so this land had to be inhabited a long time ago."

"You just gave me an idea for a short story I need to write for English class," Meg said, clasping her hands under her chin. "The teacher set three boxes on her desk and asked us to pick a notecard from each box and come up with a story. I picked, young woman, oak tree, and preternatural. That's an oak tree isn't it?" Meg pointed to the stately tree shading the deck.

"Yes, it is. It's a white oak."

"In class on Friday, I googled oak tree and found out that in Celtic mythology the oak is considered the tree of doors, sort of a gateway between worlds. I don't know which kind of oak, though." Meg squinted and thought a minute. "Anyway, that's not important. What if a widowed young woman planted the daffodils over her husband's grave, knowing that in a hundred years they would spread out like a carpet and welcome you and Mom to live here and have the happily-ever-after life she didn't. She looked at the oak and saw the future."

Holly and Charlie looked at each other and smiled until Holly had to look away. With the absence of conversation, Holly heard the songs of the croaking frogs and the distant call of a Mockingbird. For a moment Meg's story seemed real and Holly wanted to know the sad woman and hear the end of her story.

"I'd like to read it when you finish," Charlie said, breaking the silence.

"Okay, but only if I get an A on it."

"So, what did you plant?" Holly asked again.

"Lilies, mostly, and other summer bulbs." Charlie took a deep breath before finishing. "Next week I'll plant seeds, perennials, and see what comes up."

"A garden is always a surprise." Holly smiled and tried to imagine the burst of color that would begin in a few weeks.

Meg gasped. "Quick. Turn around. Look at the sunset."

The thick, gray clouds changed before their eyes to deep purple with streaks of coral as the bright golden sun turned a dark gold and sunk silently behind the trees.

"It's wonderful, Charlie." Meg smiled. "It's like God is looking down on this place and saying, 'It is good.'"

Charlie took Meg in his arms and hugged her. "Thank you, sweetheart. I think you're an angel in disguise."

"I don't think there's such a thing as a pregnant angel." Meg pulled away.

"I think you're wrong, kiddo." Charlie smiled and blinked away a tear. "So, tell me about the prom. How'd it go? Your mom sent me a few pictures last night on email. You looked wonderful."

Meg chuckled. "It was good. Sam had a blast, I think, even though I couldn't dance—doctor's orders, you know, except slow dance, and Sam wasn't exactly into that. He got down with Tia—she taught him some funkdafied hip-hop and how to dance like a gangsta. His mom will probably never forgive us. On the way home, Aubrey and this guy, Jason, started making out in the limo right in front of the rest of us. We were laughing then Tia started chanting, 'Don't make a froggy, don't make a froggy,' but they just kept on kissing." Meg looked skyward. "I'm glad I went."

Charlie chuckled. "Shall we go inside?" He held the door open.

Holly walked around while Meg and Charlie talked. As soon as there was a lull in the conversation she said, "It looks like you've put a little work into this."

"I had it gutted and installed drywall and hardwood floors. It needs a decorator now."

From the front door, Holly could see the sparsely

furnished L shaped living room that flowed into the dining room. A black granite topped bar separated the kitchen from the dining area. A large bay window in the dining area and several floor-to-ceiling windows in the living room with views of the trees that hadn't leafed out yet made the rooms appear stark. Holly felt a chill and shivered.

"I'm sorry. Let me turn on some heat." Charlie switched on the gas log fireplace and the orange and blue flames added the only color to the room. "As you can see, I worked on the outside first. We just have the necessities inside. I couldn't get the girls interested in interior decorating."

"It's a beautiful, open area. I like it." Holly spoke as she walked from the front door through the living room and into the kitchen. "The appliances are super. I like stainless steel. It's chic."

"I was afraid that it would be too austere for your taste." Charlie frowned. "I bought it before I met you."

"Well, I love it. I'd have it in my place if all the appliances hadn't come with the house. I couldn't afford to replace what was there. No, I love this look. Really, I do."

Charlie grinned at Holly. "Since we're surrounded by trees, it's a little dark and gloomy inside. That's why I painted all the walls white."

"That sounds like an apology," Holly said. "Or an excuse."

"I know just the person who can color this place up." Meg smiled.

"You don't have to continue to be the matchmaker." Holly stood behind Meg and rested her hands on Meg's shoulders. "Charlie and I are engaged already, or did that slip right out of your mind?"

Meg looked at Charlie and rolled her eyes again.

"I was counting on a little help, from both of you, when Jordan..." Charlie's forehead puckered. "Come upstairs. It's sparse also.

Baggage

Holly and Meg peeked into the girl's rooms then followed Charlie down the hall to the master suite which was four white walls, a king bed with a walnut frame, and two wicker trunks. Charlie opened a window and looked out. "When we moved in the humming of the cicadas comforted me. I slept with the windows open. It's just frogs now, but most of the day we're serenaded by songbirds."

When Charlie didn't turn away from the window, Holly went to his side and spoke softly. "You're worried about Jordan, aren't you?"

"Worried as hell." He turned and held Holly's hand. "How about some turkey Tetrazzini and Caesar salad?"

"Yes. I'm starving. You know I'm eating for two." Meg shrugged.

Charlie served dinner on an old, wobbly wooden table with four chairs that didn't match.

"This is what I expected the whole house to look like." Holly rocked the table when she sat down.

"I managed to hire a company to finish the inside while Jordan and I were away. Believe me, it was a nice surprise to come home to finished walls and floors and cabinets that matched."

"It's lovely, Charlie, and it has so much potential."

Charlie laughed. "Yeah, that's what I paid for—potential."

"I can't imagine you wanted to buy our house," Meg said. "It's so different."

"I thought I wanted to live in Chapel Hill." Charlie picked up his napkin. "Your house is in a nice neighborhood and we could've moved in without having to remodel."

"But we snatched it out from under you." Meg grinned.

"And I'm glad you did or I wouldn't have met you."

Meg cocked her head. "Didn't Jordan want a horse then?"

"She didn't want anything then except to go home." Charlie balled the napkin in his palm. "It wasn't until we looked at this place that she decided she wanted a horse. That's what sold it. She was finally interested in something and I encouraged her. I told her mother that I would build a stable if she bought the horse. And you know the rest."

"I'm sorry for Jordan that the horse died." Meg looked at Charlie with a frown.

While Holly savored every bite, Meg gobbled the rest of her dinner then asked to be excused. "Thanks for dinner. You're a really good cook for a lawyer. I'm anxious to start writing the short story for class. Is it okay if I go home now?" Meg grinned. "You don't mind taking Mom home, do you, Charlie?"

"Not at all. What time is her curfew?"

Meg bit on the nail of her index finger and looked at the ceiling. "Tomorrow's a workday. You'd better have her in by six a.m. so she can get ready."

"Good night, Meg," Holly said as she watched Meg glide out the front door.

"She knows, doesn't she?" Charlie asked, smiling for the first time that evening.

"Knows what?"

"That I need a woman to clean up the kitchen for me."

Holly threw her napkin at Charlie's face and laughed. "That's all?"

Charlie sat back and stared at Holly for what seemed an eternity. "Meg knows that I need you. It's selfish. I don't dwell on what I can give you. I dwell on all the wonderful things you can give me. I like to think about how you and I are becoming us."

"That's the way it's supposed to be." Holly reached out for Charlie's hand. Neither spoke—their eyes conveyed their feelings. Finally, Holly asked, "Can I help you clean up?"

"I didn't invite you here to wait on me. I invited you here so I could breathe you in."

"I know and so does Meg. She left because she knows we

need time alone. She also realizes that this relationship isn't just about sex."

"It isn't?" Charlie winked.

"She knows what it means to be close to someone you love. She figured that out on her own, or maybe with Mike. She also knows the difference between sexual attraction and being just plain horny."

Charlie chuckled. "She's a wonderful girl."

"I keep wishing that she wasn't pregnant. I don't want her to be pregnant. I want her to have a normal life."

"And what's normal? Marrying the man of your dreams and watching him die while he's still a young man? Or knowing that your spouse is making it with everyone but you? At least Meg is dealing with her pregnancy, not hiding away in an asylum with the lights out and the blinds closed."

"I'm so sorry. I guess it's true that there's always someone less fortunate. I didn't mean to—"

"It's okay." Charlie stood, still clasping Holly's hand. "Follow me. We didn't do something right."

Holly followed Charlie up the stairs. He stopped at the bedroom door, swept her into his arms, and carried her to the bed. "I wanted to carry you over the threshold, my beautiful bride, but was afraid to in front of Meg." Charlie sat on the edge of the bed with Holly on his lap. "It will be good to make love in our own bed."

Holly put her arms around Charlie's neck and pressed her forehead against his. "Last weekend was wonderful and I crave your body, but this just doesn't seem right. I mean with Jordan suffering so."

"Maybe. I can't help her right now. I need to take care of us. I wanted you to see this place and know that it's yours if you want it. I bought this bed when we moved here and no one has slept in it with me. I guess you could say that I saved it for you."

Holly slipped off Charlie's lap and stood in front of him.

"Can we just snuggle?"

"Certainly."

He stood to kiss her and she began unbuttoning his shirt.

"Holly—"

"Shh." She removed her shoes and sweater. "Come on, take off your shirt, and lie on your stomach. I'll massage your back."

When Charlie did what she'd asked she began massaging his head and neck and down to his tailbone. When she finished he was weeping and she snuggled against him and kissed the back of his neck until he relaxed enough to sleep. How she loved this man who wasn't afraid to weep in front of her. Holly rested her head against his and drifted off to sleep as well.

When Holly awoke, she could tell that Charlie was still asleep, so she didn't move until he awoke and turned to face her.

"Better now?" she asked.

"Much. But, now you see what I was talking about. You served me. I didn't serve you."

"But, you're wrong. You did serve me."

"I did? How?"

"You're the first man who didn't even try to take advantage of me when all I wanted was to snuggle up."

"And that includes Marcus?"

Holly closed her eyes.

"You're saying that I got tonight right?"

"Absolutely."

"Well." Charlie puffed out his chest. "It's not because I didn't want to ravish you."

"You made a couple of points tonight. Don't spoil it."

"Okay. Understood. How about coffee and Cherry Garcia? I got it especially for Meg."

"Perfect. I'll tell her what she missed."

Baggage

Holly stood and helped Charlie back into his shirt. He kissed her with passion. When she pulled away, she noticed peacefulness in his face that she hadn't seen since a week ago at Fearrington.

When Charlie called on Monday afternoon Holly invited him to an impromptu dinner with Lisa and Brody at City Kitchen Restaurant in Chapel Hill. Lisa had gotten wind that Charlie could get away easier while Jordan was hospitalized and told Holly that it was about time for Brody and Charlie to meet.

"Show and tell, huh?" Charlie joked over the phone.

"Blame it on Lisa. She wants to show you off to Brody…and, well, so do I."

"I guess it's about time. Is Brody expecting Prince Charming or just regular ole Charlie?"

"Regular ole Charlie I presume." Holly was glad Charlie couldn't see her anxious face or her possible look of sadness if he declined the invitation. "It's okay if you can't make it. I know you're under a strain right now."

"Let me call you back. I'm on my way to the hospital. The evening depends on Jordan. But, I really would like a night out, especially if I can rub knees with you under the table."

"Charlie…thanks."

"I'll get back to you as soon as I can."

Holly made a quick call to Lisa then sat tight with her phone in her hand. She tried to clear her mind of all the clutter and visualize the positive.

Meg came in from school and stood in the foyer. "What are you doing?"

"I'm being silly. I guess." Holly looked at the silent phone in her hand and then at Meg.

"Silly? Why?" Meg set her books on a chair and removed her jacket.

"Lisa wants Charlie and me to meet Brody and her at City Kitchen. I ran the invitation by Charlie and he's going to call me back. For some reason, I'm nervous about it and I can't think of a thing to do except sit here and hold this stupid phone."

"I don't think you have to worry about Brody and Charlie getting along."

"No, I'm worried that Jordan will somehow prevent Charlie from socializing tonight." Holly placed the phone on the coffee table. "He's with her now."

"Are you afraid that Jordan will tear you and Charlie apart? Because I am."

Holly flashed a lackluster smile. "I don't think anything or anyone could tear us apart, but Jordan certainly could make life a little rough if she doesn't get well."

Meg looked at Holly and blinked a few times before turning around and picking up her books and coat. "Tia's coming over to study world history with me. We have a big test tomorrow—worth fifty percent of our grade for the whole semester. Is it okay to make nachos?"

"Of course it is. Are you studying about Mexico?"

Meg huffed and went to her room to change clothes.

At a little past seven, Charlie called. "Am I too late?"

"Not for me. How is everything?" Holly asked hesitantly.

"Some big news, at least I think it's big."

"What?"

"Jordan's talking…"

"Well, that's good isn't it?"

"It's a step in the right direction. Her silence got to me. She's angry and I take that to be a good thing, but she's angry at the wrong person. Anyway, I'll explain more later. There's nothing more I can do here. The longer I stay the worse I feel."

"Charlie…"

"She's torturing me and I'm torturing myself sitting

beside her. I imagine her just snapping out of it one day and I'd like to be here when she turns to me, and says, 'Daddy,' because I know she will one day."

"I love you, Charlie. You're doing the right thing and you're doing it out of love, not duty."

"Thanks. Hey, can I pick you up? I'm driving out of the parking deck right now. I can be there in five minutes."

"That would be perfect." Holly relaxed and excitement replaced her apprehension. For the first time in over ten years, she would get to meet Lisa and Brody for dinner with a man by her side. She knew Charlie would put Jordan at the back of his mind and show Brody just how charming he could be.

City Kitchen is a meet-and-greet type of place with its noisy bar, especially when there is a UNC or Duke game on the TVs. When Holly and Charlie entered the restaurant, they joined Lisa and Brody at the bar. Brody stood, shook Charlie's hand, and kissed Holly on the cheek. Lisa folded her hands under her chin like a star-struck teenager in front of Shawn Mendes. After the introductions, small talk, and a round of cocktails the host seated them in the main dining room where the atmosphere turned to a romantic cosmopolitan ambiance. Ceiling lights hung like large amber tulips adding to the ambiance. The only other light came from votive candles on recessed shelves along the walls and on the tables.

"This is a beautiful place," Charlie said after taking a good look around. "It gives me some ideas for my place. What do you think, Holly?"

"I love the warm glow and candlelight."

Charlie took Holly's hand and smiled. "What Holly's trying to say is that my place is a bit stark at present."

"You've got the right woman to warm things up." Brody winked at Holly.

The four feasted on the international cuisine and fine wine and enjoyed the conversation that didn't revolve around the girls and their calamities. To Holly's delight, the conversation turned intellectual as they discussed literature, theatre, travel, the economy, and theorized solutions to the world's problems.

At the end of the evening, Brody shook Charlie's hand warmly. "Holly's told us some of what you're going through. If there's anything we can do, please let us know. Lisa and I are here for both of you."

"Thanks. More evenings like this would be..." Charlie looked from Brody to Holly.

"Lovely," Lisa finished Charlie's sentence and continued. "We have to do this again and soon. Brody and I love to entertain. Maybe you two could come to our place one night next week."

"It would be a pleasure." Charlie hugged Lisa. "Holly is fortunate to have loving, caring friends."

When Holly kissed Brody goodbye, he whispered in her ear. "Congratulations. You've got a winner there."

On their way back to Holly's, Charlie stopped the car along the entranceway into the subdivision and leaned his head on the steering wheel.

"What is it?" Holly asked.

Charlie turned to her. "Tonight was a vision of our future and I don't want it to end. I want to take you home with me...forever. What are we going to do?"

"We're going to make the most of what we've got. We're going to have to make some difficult decisions and we're going to make them together—and that includes Meg's as well as Jordan's future."

"Well then, let's make a decision right now."

"Okay. What?" Holly smiled suspecting that Charlie might suggest something mischievous.

"Let's decide to spend as many evenings as possible at my place and while we're deciding, let's decide to call it our place."

"Alright. I'll meet you at our place tomorrow at six."

Baggage

"No, you won't. I'll pick you up at five forty-five."

15

At first, Holly tried to believe that the evening sex she shared with Charlie was purely sexual healing for him, but she quickly realized that she was there because she wanted to be there and not just because Charlie wanted her to be there. They both needed an emotional break from reality, so on succeeding evenings, Holly spiced things up by serving sexy cocktails in seductive clothing. She wasn't going to let either herself or Charlie feel guilt because they were enjoying each other while Jordan suffered.

Meg had done her best to support Holly by getting dinner invitations to Aubrey's and Tia's on Monday and Tuesday, but the next couple of days she'd decided to hang out by herself. Everything in Holly's life was moving forward except Jordan.

On their fourth afternoon together, Holly and Charlie made love with their usual vigor. The sun set while they were in the throes of passion and the room turned dark. Holly stretched across the bed to turn on a light then propped herself up on an elbow.

"You are so beautiful," Charlie said. "Thanks for turning the light on to remind me."

"You're welcome, sir."

"You know? I don't know if I like you better in the buff or in that little sweater without a bra. I'd love to take you out in public in that skimpy outfit you wore tonight."

"Are you crazy?"

"I'm proud of you. I want to show you off—all of you."

"You silly boy." Holly curled up in Charlie's arms with her head on his chest. "I'm getting used to this. What are we going to do when Jordan comes home from the hospital?"

"I'm a little worried about that." Charlie repositioned the pillow under his head. "I also worry that she'll never recover."

"Shouldn't there be a diagnosis by now?"

"That's just it. The doctors are still holding to the idea that this is some long-term stress-related depression and it's just a matter of time until the medications will bring her out of it or until she snaps out of it by herself. They've ruled out clinical depression and bipolar problems."

"Do you think she will...snap out of it?" Holly asked delicately.

"That's my wish and the doctors are encouraging this thinking. That's why I talk to her even when she screams back at me. Deep down I hope that something I say will somehow set off a spark that will bring her out of this. She's so angry she won't listen. Jess calls, but Jordan won't answer. She's turned Angie away, which bothers me. Jill refuses to visit—said she lost her patience after the first five minutes."

Holly snuggled closer. "I love you, Charlie. Have I told you that today?"

"Ten times at least. I'm so happy that we decided to spend these evenings together. We owe Meg, you know. She's such a champ about it."

"This is Meg's dream, and believe me, she takes credit for it every day, Prince Charming." Holly stroked Charlie's chest while they basked in quiet intimacy until Holly's phone pierced their tranquility.

Holly leaped from the bed to retrieve the phone from her purse. Before she could say hello, she could hear Meg screaming.

"There's blood all over the bed and I think the baby's pushing to get out! My belly hurts...sharp pains in my chest.… Meg stopped to gasp and cry. "I don't know what to do. Mama, help me. Please help me."

"Charlie, quick call 911. Meg's bleeding and in pain—maybe her water broke. She could be in labor."

Charlie shot from the bed. "It's too soon, isn't it?"

Holly nodded and jammed her foot into her jeans. "Meg, listen to me, put a pillow between your legs."

"I…I…can't, move," Meg screamed out again. "This pain…is paralyzing me."

"Meg, listen to me. Charlie's calling 911 and we're on our way. Are you still bleeding or was there just one big gush of blood?"

"I don't know…I'm cramping, really bad. Please help me. Somebody, please, help me."

Charlie tucked his shirt into his Levis then took the phone from Holly. "Meg, we're on our way. Hold on. Just hold on. The paramedics may get there before us. I told them to knock the door down if it's locked."

Holly finished dressing and Charlie handed her the phone. They ran to the car and tore off down the road. Meg continued to scream in excruciating pain. Holly tried to comfort her. "Charlie, give me your cell phone and talk to Meg on mine."

Holly exchanged phones and called Brody. Fortunately, he answered on the first ring. He was out the door before Holly hung up.

"He thinks he can get there before the ambulance," Holly said. "He has a key to the house. Thank God."

Charlie sped the fifteen miles down 15-501 running the red light at the entrance to Holly's subdivision. They were the last to arrive and could hear Meg screaming before they got out of the car.

Meg had been moved to a gurney and Brody assessed her as they moved quickly. One of the paramedics held a doppler to Meg's abdomen and Holly could hear the rapid beating of the baby's heart. A green oxygen mask covered Meg's face and fluids streamed through an IV. Meg looked like a wounded wild animal caught in a trap.

Holly ran to the side of the gurney and squeezed Meg's hands.

Meg continued to scream and cry and Brody tried to calm her. "Meg." Grit your teeth and listen. Your water broke and the previa is bleeding, but not badly. You're going to have this baby soon." He looked to the paramedics. "Let's go." Brody stepped back to let the paramedics take over. "I'm going to call Dr. Gilbert, see if she can meet us at the hospital.

As they wheeled Meg through the living room, Holly began to weep and Charlie comforted her.

"They'll both be fine." Brody turned to Holly while the EMTs lifted the gurney into the ambulance. "Her labor is progressing rapidly, but I think we have time to get her to the OR. I've already called in the team and the room will be ready when we get there. Let's just hope Dr. Gilbert calls back soon."

"The OR?"

"I'm pretty sure that Meg will need a C-section, because of the previa. We can't let her reach the third stage of labor. She can't push. She could hemorrhage and lose the baby. I'm going to ride with her in the ambulance. We'll meet you at the emergency department door, alright?" Brody hopped into the ambulance and they pulled out with lights flashing and siren screaming.

Luckily, the hospital was just minutes away. Holly watched the paramedics whisk Meg out of the ambulance and push her through a set of automatic doors before she could climb out of the car. She told the admitting clerk Meg's name and threw her insurance card on the desk before following a woman in blue scrubs to the Labor and Delivery OR waiting area.

When they arrived, the woman rested her hand on the back of a chair, "Just wait here and someone will be out to speak with you shortly. Can I call someone for you?"

"No, my friend is parking the car. He'll be here in a minute."

"Alright. Can I get you some water or coffee?"

Holly sniffled, rubbed her chin with her thumb. "I'm fine." But she couldn't stop the flood of tears.

The woman handed Holly a box of tissues just as Charlie arrived.

"Any news?" he asked.

"Not yet."

The woman in scrubs smiled at Charlie. "I'll leave you now. Are you sure I can't get either of you some coffee?"

"No, thanks," Holly said through blurred eyes. "You've been very kind."

"Everything will be fine. Just hold on." The woman smiled and turned to go.

"I'm scared to death, Charlie. I don't want to lose her. There was too much blood. Did you see it?"

Charlie wrapped his arms around Holly. "Trust Brody and the other doctors. I'm sure they've been in similar situations. They know what to do."

"I can't lose her, Charlie. I can't."

"Don't think that. Try to think positively."

"She could lose the baby—"

Brody entered the waiting room wiping his hands on a green towel. "Meg and the baby are fine."

Holly burst into tears and jumped up to hug Brody. "Fine?"

"While the nurses were prepping Meg's abdomen, she pushed the baby out precipitously. She's had a significant blood loss, but the bleeding is under control and we're replacing the blood now. When she passed the placenta, it came out in shreds. Dr. Gilbert didn't answer my page until after the baby was out. She's on her way, but I'm afraid she missed the party. There's a gifted third-year OB resident who's taken over. She's going to do a D&C to make sure that pieces of the placenta haven't adhered to Meg's uterus."

"A resident?" Holly asked in a panic.

"I told you, Dr. Wells is brilliant. Meg is in excellent hands."

"Is she awake?"

"Awake and groggy. They gave her a sedative as soon as the baby was delivered. You can come to the OR door and speak to her. The nurses are cleaning her up and putting her on a sterile field. Come with me."

"And the baby?" Holly feared the answer.

"I'll let Meg tell you about the baby."

Meg's hair had been tucked into a paper OR bonnet and the oxygen mask still covered her face, which had paled to snow-white.

"Meg?" Holly called softly.

Meg turned her head toward the door, pulled the oxygen mask down around her neck, and gave a goofy grin. She spoke slowly and tried to keep her eyes open. "The frog...isn't a frog...after all. It's a girl."

"A girl? How wonderful." Holly tried to control her breathing.

"I love you, Meg." Holly gasped. "I'll be right here, darling, waiting for you."

"Hang in there, kiddo." Charlie waved but Meg had already drifted off to sleep.

The anesthetist returned the oxygen mask to her face. "Sorry, I had to put her under. Dr. Wells is finished scrubbing."

"Hello...Mrs. Gaynor?" A tall dark woman dressed in green from head-to-toe walked from the scrub sink with hands up and elbows dripping. "I'm Andrea Wells. Your daughter is going to be just fine."

Inside the OR a nurse handed the doctor a sterile towel and when she finished drying her arms the nurse helped her into a sterile gown and gloves.

"Thank you for helping my daughter." Holly choked out the words.

"You're welcome. That's my job. We've just witnessed a wonderful success. Meg did great and the baby looks excellent. She may be a little bruised. She came out feet first like she was sliding down a water slide with her arms over her head."

"We're going to have to ask you to step out now. I'll meet you in the waiting room as soon as we're finished."

"Where's the baby?" Holly asked, addressing anyone, everyone.

Brody closed the door. "Let's go and see your granddaughter. "She got a big thumbs up from the neonatal team. They'll keep her in the NICU until she's big enough to go home."

"How big is she?" Holly asked.

"Three pounds-fourteen ounces, I think they said."

Holly put her hand over her mouth. "That's so tiny."

Brody chuckled. "She's thirty-three weeks and healthy—probably the biggest baby in the NICU. All she needs to do is grow. How about I walk you and Charlie back to the elevator and point you in the direction of the NICU? My job here is finished. I need to get back to Lisa and my in-laws. Don't hesitate to call—at any hour. Meg's procedure will take twenty or thirty minutes and then she'll go to the recovery room for about an hour."

"Brody, I'm so glad you were here for this." Holly reached out to hug him.

"It prepared me for my own grandchild's birth." Brody flashed a proud smile and shook hands with Charlie. "Wait until you see her. She's a miracle."

Holly and Charlie followed the directions to the NICU. Holly's steps were forced. Her feet felt shackled. She didn't want to leave Meg, even if she was in the hands of an excellent resident. And she wasn't quite sure she was ready to meet Meg's daughter. While in the elevator, Holly pressed her face into Charlie's chest and sobbed.

"It's okay, Holly. Go ahead and cry it out." He held her until the door opened on the fourth floor then led her into a small waiting room. He held her, stroking her hair until her body relaxed and her heart stopped galloping.

"Thanks, Charlie. I needed that." She pulled a tissue from her bag, dabbed her eyes, and cheeks and neck, and blew her nose.

"Are you ready to meet your granddaughter now?"

"Yes and no."

"What do you mean?"

"I'd like to know Meg's plan first. Do you think she's decided to give the baby up? I mean she wouldn't let me buy anything for the baby. She said she wanted to be financially responsible for it, but she didn't buy anything either—not a crib or a toy, nothing."

"Maybe she just thought it was too early."

"I don't know. She's never shown an interest. At least not to me." Holly fought back more tears. "I didn't see it before, but it's as if Meg had everything under control and didn't need me to…"

"Hush, now." Charlie held tight to Holly's shoulders. "Don't go worrying about things you don't understand. There's something more important to do right now."

"There is?"

"Yes. We need to meet the little girl who used to be a frog."

Holly introduced Charlie and herself as the grandparents of the Gaynor baby to the NICU receptionist. Once inside, the receptionist instructed them in the visitation policy, told them they could find their baby in Pod E then showed them how to scrub to their elbows before each visit. Holly felt a little lightheaded walking past four other pods before finally reaching E. Charlie grasped her hand at the door and a nurse beckoned them to a bed space across the room.

Holly felt as if she were in another world—outer space, maybe. Monitors beeped and flashed, alarms buzzed and rang and there was so much equipment around some of the beds that Holly couldn't see the babies. The lights were low except for one over her tiny granddaughter.

"Hello," a nurse standing beside the baby said. "My name is Carolyn. You must be the grandparents."

Holly couldn't speak. She just stared at the baby. Charlie looked to the nurse. "This is Meg's mother, Holly Gaynor. I'm Charlie. Nice to meet you."

"You too." Carolyn's smile spread a blanket of relief. "So, your daughter goes by Meg?"

"Yes." Holly leaned heavily against Charlie.

"First of all, the baby's doing great. Does she have a name?"

"No. Meg hasn't chosen one, yet." Holly looked to the nurse feeling the fruit of embarrassment poke from her depths. "Meg didn't want to know if it was a boy or girl until it was born and she wasn't due for another seven weeks."

"That's fine. I just wanted to call her by name, if she had one already."

"And the baby's father died of leukemia in January." Holly volunteered the information trying to save her daughter's reputation.

"Yes, I read that on Meg's chart. I'm sorry for your loss."

Holly clenched her jaw. Meg's loss. Not my loss. Meg's. Will this premature baby help mend Meg's broken heart? Or will she carve out another chunk? Holly bit her lip and willed herself not to cry.

Carolyn showed them the IV in the baby's hand, the monitor wires, the pulse oximeter, and the temperature probe stuck to the baby's belly with a shiny gold heart. She explained how all the equipment worked and how the warming bed kept the baby's temperature normal. She told them not to be afraid and she encouraged them to stroke the baby gently.

Holly touched the baby's hand with the tip of her finger. The baby squirmed and the nurse showed her how to calm her by cupping one hand around the baby's head and the other around her feet. When Holly followed the instructions, the baby relaxed. Holly looked for Meg in the baby's face, but couldn't see any resemblance. The baby was pink with soft, white fuzz on her head and shoulders. She swallowed hard when she thought about Mike. She didn't know anything about his looks. Could he have been blond? Why hadn't she asked? Why hadn't Meg told her? She hadn't even seen the picture of him that he'd given Meg and there weren't any pictures of them together. Maybe that was for the best.

"She's so tiny," Charlie said. "When will she get to come home?"

Carolyn smiled. Holly could tell that she'd probably answered this question a million times. "She has work to do. First, she has to be able to keep herself warm without the warming bed. Next, she has to have a steady weight gain. And last, she needs to be able to take all her feedings by mouth. We'll start feeding her tomorrow by a small tube that goes through her mouth into her stomach. In the meantime, she'll have the IV fluids for nourishment."

Charlie stared at the baby. "How long will it take her to do all those things?"

"When was her due date?" Carolyn asked.

"Fourth of July." Charlie stood straight, like a proud grandfather.

"Well then, I'd say she'll be ready to go home by the Fourth of July."

Carolyn turned to Holly. "Has Meg decided to breastfeed?"

Holly didn't know the answer to that, either. Why hadn't

they discussed it? What possible answer could she give to make Carolyn believe that she and Meg were good people, people who loved each other dearly, people who shared and communicated? Had she been that preoccupied with Charlie that she'd neglected Meg? Holly stood drowning in her ocean of shame.

16

Charlie kissed Holly good night outside Meg's room on the post-partum unit before heading to visit Jordan. His words of encouragement kept Holly treading water, at least. Meg, who'd been in and out of a drug-induced sleep, opened her eyes near midnight and looked around the room until she spotted Holly sitting in a recliner next to her bed.

"Did you see her?" Meg asked in a raspy voice. She cleared her throat. "Is she alright?"

"She's not only alright, she's beautiful—delicate little hands, rosy cheeks, chubby thighs."

"Does she have hair? When I saw her she was covered in blood."

"Yes. Peach fuzz. She's blond."

"Blond?" Meg smiled at the ceiling. "I didn't think I would feel this way."

"What way?"

"Bittersweet, emotional."

"Because Mike's not here?"

"I guess. It's confusing, Mama. And amazing the way something like this can change your life."

"Your daughter will bind you to Mike."

Meg took a tissue from a box on the bedside stand, wiped her face and neck. "I want to see her."

"The NICU nurse said you can come anytime. She asked if you were planning to breastfeed. I, told her…yes because I didn't know. I didn't want her to know that I didn't know."

Meg stared hard into Holly's eyes. She sighed, bit her bottom lip. "I didn't tell you a lot of things." Meg held her stare. "It's just that…I mean, I… There's so much I want to tell you now. I kept things from you, on purpose, not to be mean, but because of Charlie. I didn't want anything, anything at all to prevent Charlie from…staying." Meg pushed herself up in bed and found the nurse call button.

The two sat speechless. Meg looked at the IV in her arm then around the room as if to orient herself. "Mama, I'm not ready to be a…" A knock on the door interrupted her. "Come in."

A middle-aged nurse peeked around the door. "Hello. I'm Ruby. May I help you?"

"I'd like to see the baby," Meg stated, her voice matter-of-fact, her face blank. "Is it okay for me to get up?"

"Certainly. Congratulations. I hear your little one is doing well." The nurse walked to Meg's bedside. "Let me unhook you from your IV, the bag is almost empty, anyway. You'd best go in a wheelchair. I can imagine you still have sea legs from the pain meds." She smiled and looked at Holly. "If you don't mind pushing the chair you two can go by yourselves."

"I don't mind." Holly stood next to Meg and fluffed out her bangs.

"Good. I'll just get a wheelchair. Do you know the way?"

"Yes," Holly said. "I was just there."

Meg didn't speak while Holly wheeled her down the hall and into the elevator. Holly feared that if she spoke, she'd say the wrong thing. She longed to hear the end of Meg's sentence and all the things Meg had kept from her. She worried about how Meg would react when she saw the baby surrounded by IVs and wires.

When they reached the NICU the receptionist asked them to wait at the front desk and told them the baby's doctor wanted to meet them.

"Is everything okay?" Meg paled as she glanced from the receptionist to Holly.

"The doctor will be right out to talk to you." The receptionist's smile didn't reassure Holly.

Holly stooped in front of Meg. "The nurse told me that the baby is fine. Maybe the doctor just wants to explain things or meet you first."

"Megan Gaynor?" A young woman dressed in green scrubs walked toward her.

"That's me. Is everything alright?" Tears welled in Meg's eyes.

"Your daughter is okay. She's just acting like she was born seven weeks early. That's what I want to talk to you about. Come with me. The doctor, who didn't look much older, or different than Meg, led them down the hall, past Pods E and F, into a small room with two easy chairs and an end table with a lamp. She left the door open. Congratulations. You have a beautiful daughter." The doctor looked to Holly. "And you're the grandmother?"

"Yes." Holly felt a twinge of excitement and acceptance that she hadn't until then, let herself feel.

"I just wanted to make sure." The doctor smiled and Holly felt a wave of relief. But, Meg's lower lip trembled.

The doctor went on and on describing the roller coaster type emotional experience Meg would certainly endure, and ended by outlining all the horrible and painful complications which could occur. "The bottom line is this—your baby has developed what we call RDS, respiratory distress syndrome. She started grunting and breathing with her ancillary muscles and her oxygen saturations fell into the seventies. The only treatment is to give her lungs some pressure and oxygen and we're doing that with bubble CPAP. Her nurse, Carolyn, will explain how it works when you visit. Just to be on the safe side, we've drawn some blood to check for infection and started her on antibiotics. Because we don't know which way she'll turn, we've placed central lines into the stump of her umbilical cord."

As the doctor rambled on, Meg seemed to shrink until she looked like Alice in Wonderland after she downed the contents from the bottle labeled, DRINK ME. Holly felt numb. She didn't know how to respond.

When the doctor finished her oration, Holly pushed Meg to the door of Pod E. When Carolyn saw Meg stand up from the wheelchair, she came forward. "Hello, you must be Meg."

"Yes."

"Congratulations on your beautiful daughter. Can you walk okay?"

"I think so. Thanks," Meg said as she searched the room for Frog.

Carolyn looked at Holly. "We've made a few changes since you were here. Little Missy Gaynor decided she wanted her money's worth out of the NICU."

"The doctor tried to explain it all." Holly forced a smile. "I think we're both a little overwhelmed right now."

"Well, come on over and I'll show you the changes." Carolyn pulled two tall chairs to the bedside and helped Meg sit on one and offered the other to Holly. She then lowered the bed so Meg could touch the baby. Holly sat next to Meg while Carolyn walked to the opposite side.

Meg gasped and raised her hands to cover her mouth when she looked at her baby. Holly couldn't believe how much smaller the baby appeared with the added equipment surrounding her.

A corrugated piece of tubing, fastened with strips of dark blue Velcro, crossed the baby's face from ear-to-ear and up the side of her face. Oxygen under pressure blew into her nostrils. Tiny black eye patches protected her eyes from a bilirubin lamp that bathed her frail body in a bright white light. A second IV had been placed in her foot and two central lines protruded from the stump of her umbilical cord. There was a tube taped to her mouth and connected to the barrel of a syringe that dangled by a piece of silk tape from the side of the overhead warmer.

Carolyn turned the bili-light off and gently removed the eye patches so Meg could see her baby's face. "I can take these off for a few minutes. I wish you could hold her, but she's just now stable and we don't want to disturb her."

"Can I touch her?"

"Of course you can." Carolyn encouraged Meg the same way she'd encouraged Holly earlier.

Meg's hand trembled as she reached out. She stroked the baby's thigh. The baby didn't move as she had earlier and Holly felt as if the roller coaster car had reached the top of the incline and was about to go speeding down the other side, totally out of everyone's control. Carolyn took time explaining and encouraging, but it didn't ease Holly's nerves.

Before Meg and Holly left, Carolyn asked if she had given the baby a name.

"No, but you can call her Frog." The corners of Meg's lips curled slightly. "That's what I've been calling her for the past twelve weeks since I found out I was pregnant."

"Twelve weeks?' Carolyn chuckled. "No wonder you haven't picked out a name yet. It was probably just sinking in that you were pregnant. Don't worry, Meg. You'll choose a name soon enough. In the meantime, we'll call her Frog as well."

Holly and Meg didn't speak on the way back to Meg's room. Meg crawled into bed and Holly pulled up the covers.

"Is she going to die?" Meg screwed up her face.

Holly sat on the side of the bed and scooted to face Meg. "I don't know."

"I didn't want a baby, and now I'm afraid she'll die."

"Carolyn told us how well she's doing. We need to believe her. We need to trust that this breathing problem is normal for babies born early. Neither Carolyn nor the doctor seemed worried.

"Mike died when the doctors said he was getting better."

"But, he had a terminal illness. Your little girl is a normal preemie who has to jump some ropes, that's all."

"I'm so confused. My brain is spinning. I thought I had everything worked out, but now, I don't know." Meg let out a wail and cried long and hard.

Holly sat on the bed stroking Meg's back. She wondered what all was going through Meg's mind. "If it helps any, I fell in love with her tonight, blond hair and all."

Meg pulled away. "Mike had brown hair. His eyes were light grayish-green, mostly gray. His mother said that he had white hair until he was in first grade."

"His mother said?"

Meg drew in a deep breath and blew it out through pursed lips. "His mother told him."

"I see."

"Carolyn said that breast milk was better than formula. I hadn't thought about breastfeeding. Maybe I should try to pump."

"It's a good idea."

Meg pushed the call bell again.

Ruby brought a breast pump and showed Meg how to use it and store the milk. Meg pumped for fifteen minutes but just got a few drops of colostrum. Ruby returned and told Meg the colostrum was liquid gold and it might take a few days before her milk came in. Meg fell asleep while Holly took the bottle to the NICU. Holly settled herself in the reclining chair and tried to make sense of Meg's vague comments. She worried about Frog but trusted Carolyn to call if there were any changes. She sat and stared out the window at the yellow lights that dotted the parking deck until the sunlight overpowered them and they faded out.

At seven, the door to Meg's room opened without a sound and Charlie stuck his head in.

"Charlie," Holly whispered. She glanced at Meg, asleep with her mouth open. She tiptoed to the door. "What a sight for sore eyes you are." She leaned into him.

"Long night?" Charlie spoke just above a whisper.

"I didn't sleep a wink. The baby, we're still calling her Frog, took a turn for the worse, but both the doctor and Carolyn, the nurse, said it's a normal course for a preemie." Holly pulled away and looked at Charlie from head to toe. "Doesn't look like you got much sleep either. You haven't been home, have you?"

"Seeing Frog reminded me of the first time I saw Jordan. She was bigger and louder. Jill didn't want to hold her until they were both cleaned up, so the doctor handed her to me. I can't tell you how overwhelmed with love I felt. I knew she wasn't my biological child, but it didn't matter. I was her father and I was the chosen one to protect her. Last night I stopped by Jordan's room. She was sleeping then but woke up later. I wanted to touch her, hold her, protect her the way I did that first night. She turned away. So I talked to her all night. I told her about the day she was born. I told her everything I could remember from that day until today. She tossed and turned and put her fingers in her ears a few times, so I know she heard me. But she didn't speak or even open her eyes to look at me."

"At least she didn't lash out, Charlie. Maybe that's a good sign."

"I worry just as much when she ignores me. All I can do is hold on to hope. I can't live her life for her."

Holly pressed her face against Charlie's chest.

"How did Meg react to the baby, to Frog?"

"Distantly concerned." Holly felt tears well in her eyes. Her vision blurred. "I've cried more since my birthday than in my whole life."

"Some of those tears were for my girls and…me, right?"

"Right."

"Looks like Prince Charming didn't deliver on the wonderland part."

"Nonsense. You've delivered everything I wanted and more." Holly gazed into Charlie's eyes. "We've found our wonderland together." She held his stare. "The girls are going to have to find their own wonderland—in their own time and in their own way. Is that a horrible thought?"

"No." Charlie tried to smile. "It's just that parents want happy, successful children. We want to mold them every step of the way."

"It's hard to let go while they're still so young, though."

Charlie looked to the ground for a moment then back to Holly. "I have to go home and change. This afternoon I have to argue a case in Greensboro. If you need me and get my voice mail, call my secretary. She'll put in an emergency page. I'll stop by on my way home."

"Charlie." Holly gathered the fabric of Charlie's jacket in her hands and pulled his face to hers. She kissed him quickly then watched him walk down the hall in his crumpled suit. At the elevator, he turned and nodded but didn't smile. She leaned back against the wall and let her head bang hard.

"Mama?" Meg sat up in bed.

Holly tried to shake off her worries. "Good morning, darling."

Meg moved to the side of the bed and let her legs dangle. "What did Charlie mean about not being Jordan's biological father?"

"You heard."

"Most of it."

"He is her real father, but he's not her biological father." Holly closed the door and sat in a wooden chair next to the bed.

"Was she adopted?"

"Jordan doesn't know and you're not supposed to."

"Know what?"

228

Holly proceeded to tell Meg Jordan's history.

Meg twisted her hands together. "Wow. He's a great dad. Maybe if Jordan knew the truth, she'd treat him better."

"Maybe. Or it might just push her over the edge."

"Because her real father didn't want her? Oh, God." Meg looked away.

Holly swallowed a lump in her throat. "Do you want to visit the baby now?"

"Carolyn didn't call, so that means she's no worse. I need to pump. We can go after and take the colostrum."

"Okay."

"I want to call the Frog's nurse first." Meg lifted the bedside phone and dialed the NICU and then asked for Frog's nurse as she'd been instructed to do.

"Yes, I'm Megan Gaynor, Baby Gaynor's mother. How is she…okay…no, not yet. I'll be over soon…yes, I'm getting ready to pump right now…I will…thanks." Meg lowered the receiver and looked at Holly with repulsion. "She wasn't very nice."

"What did she say?"

"She said that Frog was stable." Meg stared at the receiver before she hung it up.

"Stable is good news."

The muscles in Meg's face tightened. "She sounded like I was bothering her. She didn't even tell me her name."

"Maybe she was busy. She might be more pleasant in person."

"Did you call Aubrey or Tia last night?"

Holly grimaced. "I'm sorry. I couldn't think of anyone except you and the baby."

"I'd better call them now and Sara Without an H too. We all need to decide what to do."

"About Frog?"

"Yeah. I guess my cell phone isn't here."

"Honey, that's the last thing I thought about last night."

Meg chuckled. "I guess it was a bad scene. So, can I borrow yours?"

Holly rummaged through her purse and then handed her phone to Meg. She sat back to listen, her heart galloping again.

Meg spoke with Aubrey, Tia, and Sara, told them the Frog had arrived and a little about the absence of labor, the trauma of the delivery, and the horror of the NICU, but she didn't reveal any information that Holly didn't already know.

"Aubrey and Sara Without an H will be here at about three. Tia's in a fit because she has to babysit her little brother after school. I'll probably see her tomorrow." Meg screwed up one side of her mouth. "She's pretty excited...like I got a new doll or something. She just doesn't get it. God, Mom, she's the one who should've had a baby."

Meg handed the phone back to Holly. Before she could speak, the day shift nurse came with toiletries and towels and told Meg she could shower when she finished pumping. While she was pumping, Dr. Gilbert stopped by on her rounds with Dr. Wells and a host of residents and interns. Dr. Wells examined Meg, and Dr. Gilbert gave her some discharge instructions. "I have to go home, today?"

"Yes, ma'am. Your insurance only covers one night." Dr. Gilbert toyed with her stethoscope.

"But, I had surgery."

"You did, but a D&C is a day-op procedure. Insurance pays for one night." Dr. Gilbert said again.

Dr. Gilbert's bedside manner hadn't changed since Meg's initial office visit. Holly felt suddenly thankful that she hadn't answered her page the evening before.

"You don't have to leave until tonight." Dr. Wells spoke with her hand on Meg's knee. I checked up on your daughter this morning. The neonatologist said that she's doing well. She's strong and active, which is a good sign, and her lungs have improved. Plus she's just so darn cute."

"Thanks." Meg looked at the group of doctors. Frustration crinkled her eyes. "It's just that she's so little and last night we could see her ribs when she breathed."

Dr. Wells winked at Meg. "She looks better this morning. You'll see."

Before breakfast, Holly and Meg walked to the NICU. Frog did look better, but the nurse wouldn't remove the eye patches so Meg could see her eyes. This nurse wasn't as friendly as Carolyn had been and didn't take time to comfort Meg or encourage her. She relayed the facts and that was that. When Meg reached out to touch the baby, the nurse forbade it, stating that the baby wouldn't be able to rest if Meg kept disturbing her.

"Let's go home, Mama. We can come back after seven. Carolyn said she'd be back tonight."

"Can I give you my cell phone number…and my mom's?" Meg asked the nurse on their way out.

"Sure." She took a paper towel and scribbled the numbers on it and taped it to the side of Frog's bed.

On their way back to Meg's room, Holly asked, "Are you sure you want to go home right away?"

"I don't want to leave, but that nurse…"

"Then rest in your room. You have to pump every three hours anyway. You can take the milk and look in on Frog." Holly looked at Meg sternly. "Honey, don't let that nurse intimidate you. Frog is your baby and Carolyn said you can visit anytime."

"I know. Why does she have to be so mean? I thought nurses were kinder than her."

"So did I, but I guess it takes all kinds. Maybe she's an unhappy person. Who knows?"

"Then maybe they should put her in the psych ward with Jordan." Meg shrugged. "She scares me, Mama, like Nurse Ratched."

Holly laughed. "She's not that bad. Just smile the next time you take milk. Maybe she'll soften up a bit."

"I guess I'll stay until they kick me out."

Back in her room, a breakfast tray sat on the over-bed table. Meg lifted the lid from the plate. "Pancakes, bacon, and scrambled eggs. Wow. I'm hungry all of a sudden."

When Holly kissed Meg goodbye, she told her that she'd pick up a rental breast pump from the company Carolyn had suggested and be back by four.

"Thanks, Mama, for staying with me. I love you."

Holly blew Meg a kiss and forced a smile then turned and walked down the hall and into an elevator before she broke into tears. She'd wanted to hear Meg's plans, but since Meg hadn't broached the subject again Holly hadn't either.

As soon as Holly returned home, she went to Meg's room to clean up the blood-stained sheets and carpet. To her surprise, the room was pristine. The bed looked like one in a luxury hotel with brand new Laura Ashley yellow and blue floral comforter with matching blue and white striped shams and toss pillows. A stuffed lamb with a music box inside sat on a pillow along with a note for Meg and one for Holly. Before Holly opened the envelope she knew who it was from and she sat on the bed and cried. Lisa had thrown out the bloody linens and scrubbed the blood out of the carpet. Holly sat on the edge of the bed and picked up the little lamb. She wound the music box and listened to a song she hadn't heard in decades, *Mairzy Doats*. She hummed and then sang along with the melody. "Mairzy doats and dozy doats and liddle lamzy divey…"

Later that afternoon when Holly returned to the hospital, she found Meg scribbling on a paper towel. She looked up when Holly spoke. "Hello, darling."

"Hi. Did you get the breast pump?"

"Sure did. It's all plugged in and ready to go."

"In my room?"

Yes, ma'am."

"I bet my room is a mess." Meg frowned. "All that blood scared me. I could hear Brody saying that I could bleed to death. That's what I thought when I called you."

"Well, you didn't die, so thank your lucky stars." Holly held out two shopping bags—one with a new pair of sweats, socks, and slippers and the other with a carton of Cherry Garcia.

Meg looked into the bag at the sweats and smiled, but she beamed when she found the ice cream. "Thanks, Mama, I'm starving. Lunch wasn't nearly as appetizing as breakfast." Meg opened the drawer of the bedside table and pulled out a white plastic spoon in a cellophane wrapper. "Aubrey called." Meg chuckled. "So did Tia—about six times. Aubrey should be here any minute and Sara Without an H is coming after work. My nurse said I can stay until midnight."

"How's Frog?"

"The same. That's what Nurse Ratched says every time I ask. I can't wait until Carolyn gets back."

While Meg gobbled the ice cream, Holly sat on the end of her bed. "Meg? Is there something I should know? I mean before everyone gets here?" Holly held her breath, afraid to hear what Meg had to say.

Meg put down her spoon. "Yes, but I don't know where to begin."

Holly sat in a straight-backed chair next to the bed. "How about at the beginning." She couldn't believe she'd said something so clichéd. Nevertheless, it was too late now.

"The beginning. Okay. It seemed impossible that I could be pregnant. Then Brody said I might want to let Mike's doctors know. That's how everything started. Aubrey and I talked about what I should do. She's a sleuth, but she only did

233

what I asked her to do." Meg took in a deep breath. "Okay. Here goes."

Holly tried to relax but braced herself.

"I don't know why, but Sara Without an H seemed like someone I could trust and someone who wouldn't judge me. Aubrey and I decided to talk to her about telling Mike's doctors that I was pregnant. We wanted to know if she thought that was a good idea."

"Did she?"

"Only if it would be good for scientific research. I mean I got pregnant by a man who was supposed to be sterile. She wanted to make sure that my reasons for telling them were really for science and not that proving paternity would vindicate me. I wanted to tell her that both mattered, but what bothered me was that I felt guilty, like nobody believed that Mike could've possibly impregnated me."

"Even me?"

"Yeah." Meg began stirring the ice cream with the spoon. "Even Aubrey asked if Mike was the father or if I was trying to protect somebody—like a teacher or Brody. My counselor at school asked me how long I'd been sexually active and how many partners I'd had. That...humiliated me. Even telling them that Brody had confirmed that my hymen was intact didn't seem to completely satisfy them, like maybe Brody being your friend..."

"I'm sorry, darling. I wanted to help you, but I didn't want to be pushy." Holly touched the ache in her chest. Maybe she should have been pushy or at least demanded to intervene. After all, she was the parent and she felt like a pretty weak, irresponsible one for allowing Meg to handle her situation with the help of teenage girls. Had she failed Meg? Definitely.

Meg took a bite of the ice cream and it dripped down her chin. "I guess I need to drink this—it's melting." She wiped her chin and smiled. "Sara Without an H was right. I needed vindication. I felt weak and I didn't want you to be disappointed in my weakness. You'd called me the perfect daughter so many times, even when I didn't think I deserved it. But, this had to be the worst situation I'd ever been in. I know I didn't have to, but I wanted to prove that I didn't lie about Mike and that I was mature enough to take responsibility for my life and problems.

"The first roadblock appeared as soon as I'd decided to contact Mike's doctors. I didn't know who they were and Brody had already told me that there are harsh punishments for people who snoop around medical records. Aubrey suggested that we just ask Mike's parents who his doctors were." Meg chuckled. "Then we realized that if we contacted them, they would want to know why."

"So, what did you do?"

"Well, I remembered that you'd said they may want to know that they have a grandchild on the way. But then again, what if they didn't want to know? What if knowing that would hurt them? What if they were close to his wife? What problems would it cause her, if she knew about me?

"Aubrey was thinking better than me at that point, so we decided to drop that approach and talk about how a baby would change my life. One thing, I knew I'd lost my scholarship no matter if I kept the baby or not. I wasn't ready to be a mother. I didn't know if I even wanted to be a mother someday in the far off future. So, I decided to give Frog up for adoption."

Holly grabbed at her face and tried not to break down.

"Do you want me to keep her, Mama?" Meg asked as she pushed the ice cream container aside and rubbed her eyes.

"You know I want what you want. I'll support you no matter what you decide. I was afraid that you might…give her up. I'm sure there's someone out there who would dearly love to adopt her." Holly felt suddenly empty. Frog wasn't going to be her granddaughter. The flesh of Meg's flesh would belong to someone else. She thought of Charlie and Jordan and hoped that Frog would have someone like Charlie in her life to love her and cherish her. Maybe this was for the best.

"Mike was the first…and only boy to kiss me. You know that I'd never been out on a real date and never had real sex and then I come home pregnant. I knew that I would be a burden to you and Charlie, and in the back of my head, I thought that Mike's parents might want the baby."

"Charlie and I can cope with you and Frog. There's nothing you can do to break up our relationship."

"I know that now, but I didn't then. Anyway, I didn't know Mike's parents' names or where they lived. I didn't know Mike's number or even if he had a home phone. There weren't many other Jacobi's in the phone book so I called them all. None of them had a son or relative named Michael. I remembered that Mike went to Florida State, so Aubrey and I googled everything we could think of—the alumni association, info in yearbooks, the Orange County listings of deaths. We found his name, but the date of death was the only info we could get. We hit the Orange County Register of Deeds, but that turned out to be a bust. Then I got an idea. There had to have been an obituary notice in the newspaper and if we could find it, we would know his parents' names and where they lived."

"No wonder you stayed glued to your computer."

"We searched all the newspapers in the Triangle and came up with nothing. It took two more weeks before we struck gold. Aubrey and I looked at the obituaries in just about every city in Florida. We figured that if Mike went to Florida State, he must have been a Florida resident. At first, it was exhausting and I wondered if we'd soon try other states. But, I remembered that Mike said his wife went to Florida for Christmas. Since they met in high school, I just sort of figured that Florida had to be home for both of them. His parents just had to be in Florida too. Aubrey finally found it in the Boca Raton News." Meg looked at Holly and smirked. "His wife was listed as Kelly Christine Boswell. She didn't even take Mike's last name—"

"That's kind of a modern thing to do, especially if she's a professional."

"Anyway, his parents are Anna and David and they live in Boca. He has a brother, Gabriel, and two sisters—one is married, Ruth Howard. She lives in Miami and another sister still lives at home. I think his wife still lives in Durham. That's where Mike told me he lived."

Sadness clung like a metal vise around Holly's neck and she didn't have the key to unlock it. She wanted to hear the end but feared her reaction.

Meg continued. "It was because Mike's wife hadn't taken his last name that we couldn't find a listing for her in Durham. I didn't have the nerve to contact her even if we had found a phone number." Meg let out a humph. "I was probably the last person she would want to hear from, but you know what, Mama?"

"I can imagine you wanted to throw your pregnancy in her face and get even with her for dumping Mike when he got sick."

Meg nodded. "Exactly. In a way, I sort of needed to blame someone. If she had stayed faithful, Mike and I wouldn't have happened."

"That sounds like a pretty natural reaction."

"Yeah, but she might've killed me. You know, like in a catfight. I didn't want to provoke her." Meg pushed the overbed tray to the side of the bed. "I still want her to know about Mike and me...and the baby. I may find her someday and tell her what Mike and I did while she was off in Miami with another man."

"You're angry, but you can't blame her for Frog or the loss of your scholarship. You and Mike made a decision and you need to take responsibility. I know you know that."

"How do I get rid of this anger? I just want to pull Kelly's hair out."

Holly leaned back, flashed Meg a cocky wink. "If it helps, so do I."

"Yeah, but you want to pull Mike's hair out too, don't you?"

"We both need to blow off some steam before we end up in an anger management clinic, don't we?" Holly smiled and smacked her lips. "I'm anxious to hear the rest."

"I also found out that his family is Catholic, which generally means they love kids. They wanted charitable contributions to a leukemia foundation rather than flowers— which probably means that they're nice people. The best news was Mike's sister, Ruth, lives in Miami. We decided that if we contacted anyone, it should be her. Unfortunately, there are a lot of pages of Howards in the Miami phonebook, so we started at the top of the list and, lucky for us, found Ruth's number quickly under Dennis and Ruth Howard.

"I wasn't sure what I wanted to say. That's where Sara Without an H came in. As a professional, she told the whole story and after an interrogation, Ruth finally told her the name of the medical group, but she wanted to talk with me. I had to promise not to contact anyone else in the family, especially Mike's wife, and I had to promise to keep her informed. She sounded like some kind of control freak, but I was happy to know Mike's doctors names."

"I just can't believe that you and Aubrey spent so much time playing detective."

"Well, what happened next was amazing and I almost told you, but I wasn't quite ready. I tried to get an appointment with his doctors, but that didn't work. Patients have to be referred so I took a big step and talked to Brody since he was the one who'd suggested telling Mike's doctors in the first place. Brody called the main doctor in charge of Mike's case and he was amazed but skeptical that Mike could've impregnated anybody. He wanted proof. He had Mike's DNA but couldn't release it for paternity without permission from Mike's family."

"And did they cooperate?"

"Yeah. Ruth got written permission from her father by telling him the doctors needed it for research, which was the truth. Unfortunately, because of my placenta previa, the doctors at UNC couldn't get Frog's DNA until she was born. Dr. Wells drew blood from the umbilical cord last night. It's going to take a week or so before the results are back."

"Brody's such a good man. He tried to be a father substitute when your father died."

"I know." Meg looked at her hands. "It was hard that day he looked to see if I was still a virgin, but I needed to know right then and there. He did so much for me that you and Lisa don't know."

Meg looked at her watch. "So, back to my story. It's almost time to pump again."

"Are you getting much?"

"Just colostrum, still only drops, but the nurses keep telling me it's *liquid gold.*"

"I'm sure it is, especially for a preemie. Okay, go ahead."

"Before Frog was born I wasn't enjoying being pregnant and I didn't do all the motherly things like read to her or dream of her growing up. Stuff like that. That's when I told Aubrey that I didn't want to be a mother. So, we started talking about adoption."

Holly felt a chill and didn't want to hear about not getting to watch her precious granddaughter grow up. She tried not to show emotion. She knew she could let it all out later on Charlie or Brody and Lisa.

"We researched adoption agencies until I found one that I liked, one that finds people who don't already have kids. I had to wait to sign up until I turned eighteen. Aubrey and I pooled our money. That's why I haven't bought the GPS. Anyway, I didn't sign the baby away. I just shopped for parents."

"Mike's doctors told Brody that if the baby is Mike's there's a potential that she would die before she was born because they expected her chromosomes to be all mixed up because of the leukemia and the chemo." Meg brushed her bangs away from her eyes. "In a way, I expected that she'd die before she was born. Maybe I wished it as well."

"No wonder you didn't bond, honey."

"Yeah, well, all that was in the back of my mind. I was angry at Mike's doctor too. When Brody told him that the fetus was alive and healthy, he doubted that the baby could be Mike's. I can't wait to show him the results. I'm going to march right in and throw the evidence in his face. Frog is Mike's baby. Sometimes I think I'm the only one who believes that."

"I believe you, Meg, and I'll go beat the door down with you."

Meg burst into tears and so did Holly.

"I still haven't decided what to do." Meg blew her nose. "You raised me, Mama, to be responsible. I listened to you when you told me it didn't matter what I did, but it did matter that I took responsibility for my actions. You helped me focus on my heart, but my brain kept getting in the way. I'm trying to do the right thing, but right now I don't know what the right thing is."

"Just talking about it will help you decide. It's a big decision. We all have our opinions and we'll support you whichever way you choose. But, you have to choose what's best for you and what's best for Frog." Holly swallowed hard.

"I got mad at Sarah Without an H one day. She dropped a bomb I didn't expect from her. She asked if I was taking responsibility or trying to get rid of the evidence." Meg bit her thumbnail. We didn't talk again for a couple of days. Was I trying to get rid of the evidence? Yeah. That's exactly what I was doing. If I could get rid of the baby, my life and yours could go back to the way it had been. I couldn't stop dreaming of how happy and full of hope and expectations we were last Christmas and how I had ruined everything between you and Charlie."

"Then I thought about the possibility of Mike's sperm being damaged. What if the baby ends up brain-damaged? I don't know if I could handle a baby who's not normal and will need a lifetime of special care. I felt selfish and that made me feel guiltier. And, what about you? I didn't want to keep the frog if it was going to hurt you or prevent either of us from having a normal life, and on the other hand, I didn't want to abandon a baby because it was damaged. I wanted to die. I didn't want to kill myself, I just wanted to pack a bag and walk away to a place you'd never find me so you could have the life you want with Charlie."

"I'm glad you didn't walk away. I need you, Meg. You know that I love you, but I don't think you realize what my life would be without you."

Meg leaned toward Holly for a hug.

"Mama, yesterday afternoon, the whole world looked bleak. Seeing Frog today makes it easier to, to feel responsible for her."

"Are you having second thoughts about adoption?"

"No. I picked out a couple, but they haven't been contacted yet. The agency thought it would be best to wait for the chromosome report so they'd know what they'd get. I picked this couple because in their initial questionnaire they said they'd accept a baby or child with disabilities." Meg shrugged. "So, we'll just have to wait and see. I think they'll love Frog just the way she is—even if her chromosomes are all mixed up."

Holly sat stiffly. She wondered how differently things would've been if she'd pressed Meg for answers or gotten her to counseling early on. She felt guilty that Meg had been living in fear right under her nose. She was disappointed that she hadn't recognized Meg's pain, but Meg had put on such a convincing act.

"What do you want to do now?" Holly asked.

Meg stood next to the bed. "Apologize to you. I'm sorry I had sex without protection. I'm sorry I kept all this from you. I cheated you. I won't cheat you anymore. Honest, Mama."

Meg sat back on the edge of the bed. "I don't know what to do with Frog. I look at her and she looks cute. I like that she has blond hair like Mike did when he was a baby. I miss Mike so much that my heart is full of aches and there's no room in there for Frog."

A knock on the door interrupted the conversation. Before opening the door Holly held Meg's face in her hands. "I love you."

Holly felt relieved to see Aubrey. Perfect timing.

"I'm sorry I couldn't get here sooner. I wanted to skip school so bad, but I had a stupid test in sixth period. How are you, Meg? How's the baby?"

"I'm good. So's Frog."

"A little girl frog." Aubrey sat on the bed next to Meg.

"Mom knows everything, so it's okay to speak freely."

"Mrs. Gaynor, I'm so glad that Meg finally told you about our conspiracy." Aubrey grimaced.

Holly smiled. "Thanks for sticking by her. You're a wonderful friend. What about Tia? Was she privy to all of this?"

Aubrey and Meg exchanged glances.

"She knows some of it," Aubrey said. "She's just a little naïve if you know what I mean."

"Wasn't she upset that you didn't include her more?"

"Tia didn't realize what all we did." Meg squinted. "Sometimes, well, she's in her little fantasy world."

"She certainly supported you, stuck by you."

"And did most of the worrying for us." Aubrey forked her fingers through her hair.

Meg looked at the door as it cracked open. "Sara Without

an H, I'm so glad to see you. Aubrey just got here too."

"Hello everyone. Dr. Adams let me out of work a couple of hours early. He knew how badly I wanted to see you."

"I'm glad you and Aubrey are here." Meg brightened a bit. "I just told Mom everything, so we can say what we want."

Sara looked at Holly. "So you know about Ruth."

"Yes, Mike's sister in Miami." Holly took a deep breath.

"Well, you'll never guess what happened." Sara smiled and looked at Meg. "Ruth called and left a message on my voice mail last night. Weird, huh? Like she knew the frog was born. She said she'd like to adopt the baby if that's what you want to do, but only if it's Mike's."

Meg sighed.

"There's more," Sara said. "When I called her back, I didn't tell her that the baby had been born. Ruth told me that Kelly wasn't liked by Mike's family. She wasn't Catholic and she told Mike she was pregnant so he would marry her. Mike's family has money and they think she was after her share. Guess she got it too."

"Was she pregnant?" Meg's eyes opened wide.

"No. She tricked him. Ruth said that she wasn't a very nice person. She didn't fit into the family. They even blame Mike's leukemia on her."

"They'd probably hate me then. Wouldn't they?"

"Honey," Holly said, "don't worry about them until the paternity test comes back. And until you decide what you're going to do."

"I agree with your mom." Aubrey stood up and walked to the window. "I don't think we need to tell Ruth that Frog is born. She's not expecting to hear from us until the end of June or early July."

Meg looked at the clock on the wall. "I need to pump and go visit Frog. Do you guys want to meet her?"

"Yes, of course." Sara cocked her head. "But they have

strict visiting rules. Will we be allowed to see the baby?"

"Family only. I'll tell them you're my sisters."

Frog looked much the same as she had all day. The receptionist let Aubrey and Sara in, and the day shift nurse allowed only two at the bedside at a time. She didn't seem to buy the story that Aubrey and Sara were Meg's sisters and made them leave after just a few minutes.

They returned to Meg's room just after a dinner tray had been delivered. Meg lifted the lid. "Yucky. Mystery meat and greasy gravy." She looked to Holly. "I think I'll wait until we get home to eat."

When Aubrey and Sara said their goodbyes, Meg rang for the nurse. "Time we blow this joint, Mama."

By the time the nurse finished Meg's discharge instructions, it was almost eight o'clock. On their way out, they stopped by the NICU for one last visit before driving home.

Carolyn greeted them with a smile that set everyone at ease. When Meg approached the bed pictures of Frog that Carolyn had taken with the Pod's digital camera greeted her. One of the pictures had been taped to a green card along with a cartoon picture of a baby frog, dressed in a pink tutu, dancing on a lily pad. Draped around the bed were more cartoon figures of frogs, all pasted on pink construction paper.

Meg flashed a toothy smile. "You did this, didn't you Carolyn?"

"I couldn't resist. I've never seen a baby named Frog."

Meg reached out to Carolyn with arms wide. "Thank you."

"You're welcome. Now, come and sit and let me tell you about Frog and the progress she's making."

On the way home Meg stared at the picture of Frog while Holly prayed that Meg would make a choice she could live with and not regret for the rest of her life. She remembered the tears Meg shed when she turned from Carolyn's hug. Were they hormones, bonding, what?

"There's one thing that worries me, Mama."

"What's that?"

"The grans. Should I call them or did you already call them?"

"I called them while you were in the recovery room. They've called me several times since, but they're waiting to hear from you, to tell them what they should do."

Meg blew air into her cheeks. "Is there no end to the complications of this ordeal? What should I say? If they see her, they'll pressure me to keep her, won't they?"

Holly shrugged.

"I'll call them when we get home." Meg stared blankly at Holly.

"I'm afraid to see my room," Meg said when she and Holly walked in from the garage.

"Don't be afraid. Go look. You'll love it."

Meg shrieked when she opened the door. "It looks like Lisa's been here, again. Am I right?"

"Absolutely."

"It's gorgeous. She must've shopped until midnight and worked all day on this. What would we do without Lisa and Brody, Mama?"

Holly smiled. "I don't know. They certainly make life easier...and more fun."

"Will you call Lisa and thank her for me and tell her that I'll call her tomorrow? I want to call the grans now then take a nap before I have to pump again."

"Aren't you hungry?"

"I'm too exhausted to eat. Maybe I'll have a grilled cheese when I wake up."

"Of course."

Meg changed into a nightgown, climbed between the crisp, new sheets, and picked up her cell phone. "Nana…"

Holly smiled and closed the door. She felt numb and cold and confused. She realized that she'd begun to hope that Meg would keep Frog. The numbness turned to sharp pain when she thought of Meg handing her baby to strangers. She wondered if she should share this with Meg, but thought better of it. Maybe when Frog grew stronger and shed all the tubes and wires and looked more like a baby than an alien Meg would bond with her. Meg had been diligent at pumping so she could provide the best nourishment for Frog. Holly looked at that as a positive sign. If Meg were completely unattached, why would she want to pump?

Before Meg settled in for her nap she looked for Holly and found her reading in bed. "Get prepared. Nana and Bug already had their bags packed and they're on their way. Grandma and Grandpa are going to meet us at the hospital tomorrow morning."

"Did you tell them about giving Frog up?"

"Yeah. I told them just about everything."

"And what did they say?"

Meg flashed a grim expression that didn't surprise Holly. "What do you think?"

17

The grans weren't nearly as dreadful as Meg and Holly had expected. Nana cried when she saw Frog. She kissed her tiny foot and told Meg what a beautiful baby she and Mike had made. Bug stood back in fear shaking his head. He thanked the nurses for all they'd done. Grandma wanted Meg to give the baby a name and have her baptized. To Holly's surprise, Meg called the hospital chaplain who sent a priest to perform the ceremony that very afternoon. Much to Grandma's distress Frog didn't get a name, but she was baptized. Grandpa ventured a little closer to Frog, even bent to look her in the eye and gently brush a finger across her toes, which he swore looked exactly like Holly's did when she was born. They all knew better than to express their desires for their great-granddaughter, but Holly felt the vibes.

The nurse on duty took pictures of each of them standing next to Frog and a close-up of Frog with her eyes open and made copies for everyone.

When they left with their pictures in hand, Meg's emotions were in shambles. She went into the bathroom in the hall and wailed. She didn't care if the whole world heard her, there was nothing she could do to stop the flood gates from bursting open anyway, and after a while, she started to feel better. That's when the tears turned to torrents and a moan erupted so loudly that it brought Holly to the door.

"Meg? What is it? Please let me in." Holly felt weak and

Meg's cries frightened her.

"Mama..." Meg could barely speak. The crying softened and when Meg tore off a length of toilet paper to dry her face she caught a glimpse of herself in the mirror and began to laugh. She opened the door and held her soaked sweatshirt away from her leaking breasts. "Looks like my milk came in."

Holly walked with Meg to the pumping room and watched her pump two ounces from one breast and almost three from the other while her tears and giggles mingled.

Every morning for the next week Holly dropped Meg off at the hospital on her way to work and picked her up on her way home. Frog continued to improve and pretty much stuck to a predictable course. While some things improved in Holly's court, the news wasn't good from Charlie's. Jordan's condition remained staid. Holly and Charlie stole kisses in the hospital's lobbies and coffee shops. The only thing Charlie knew to do was stand by and that's what he did.

On Monday morning Brody called with the results of the paternity test. Mike was the father, no doubt about it. The test also revealed there were no genetic defects in Frog. Instead of visiting Frog that morning, Meg stayed home and baked a fancy cake to celebrate Frog's paternity. She made a cake that Holly had often baked for her when she was growing up—a rainbow cake with swirling layers of pink, yellow, blue, and green. She decorated the cake with fluffy pink marshmallow icing and a green candle. Next to the candle, she propped the picture of Mike.

By now, Frog had several nurses who rotated taking care of her. Sandy, an older nurse who was counting down the days until her retirement, met Meg at the door and took the cake from her. Meg looked past her to see several doctors and nurses surrounding Frog's bed. She looked at the blaring heart monitor and saw a slow heart rate and low oxygen saturation.

"What's wrong?" Meg cried out.

"She's stopped breathing a few times and dropped her heart rate. It's pretty normal for preemies to have what we call apnea and bradycardia. But she didn't respond well and we think she just tired out."

"Tired out? What does that mean?"

"She didn't have enough energy to breathe. The doctors did a septic workup—drew blood and spinal fluid and checked her urine for an infection. They're intubating her now."

"Like, putting her on a breathing machine?" Meg grabbed a chair for balance.

"I'm sorry, Meg. Her CBC came back just before you walked in. She has an infection. We've already started antibiotics."

"Can I see her?"

"In a few minutes. Look, her heart rate is normal now and her sats are in the nineties. Come with me and I'll get one of the doctors to talk with you."

"I called Carolyn early this morning and she said Frog looked great."

"The infection came on fast and lowered her tolerance. I wish it weren't this way, but things can change quickly in the NICU. It's just part of the—"

"Roller coaster ride. I know."

The doctor didn't have much more to say than what Sandy had. Neither adequately prepared Meg for what she saw when she stepped to the foot of Frog's bed. Her skin had paled to gray and she was so still she looked dead. Tape to secure the tube to the ventilator spread across her upper lip and cheeks. One end of the tape covered an ear and pulled it into a grotesque shape. Dried blood clung in clots to both wrists and an IV held one foot cockeyed to a tiny board.

Meg called Holly and asked her to come to the hospital. "Mama, Frog's gonna die. She already looks dead."

Over the next two days Frog's condition teetered like a crystal vase on a narrow shelf in an earthquake. Carolyn let Meg sleep in one of the rooms for parents since Frog hadn't shown any signs of recovery. On the third night, Carolyn knocked on Meg's door at three-thirty. "Your frog is croaking. Come see."

Meg sprang from the bed and opened the door. Carolyn's smile reassured her.

"Come on," Carolyn said. "Bring your bathrobe."

Meg followed Carolyn into the pod and gasped when she saw Frog.

"She's pink...and..." Meg covered her open mouth with her hand.

Carolyn smiled and put her arm around Meg. "And active. Look. She opened her eyes."

Meg leaned down to look into Frog's eyes. "Her eyes are blue. She's looking right at me."

"A little miracle frog."

Meg offered her pinky to Frog's tiny hand. "She grabbed my finger. Look. What a grip."

"Meg. Look at me." Carolyn took Meg's free hand in hers. "I think it's time you held her."

"But, the ventilator—"

"No excuses this time. The vent settings are as low as they can go. The doctors want to take her off of the ventilator in a few hours anyway. If she extubates, if the tube should slip out, while you're holding her, that's okay. She's on very little support and no oxygen. The antibiotics have done their job. Now, it's time for you to do yours."

Meg bit her bottom lip. "Okay, but I don't know what to do."

Carolyn told Meg to put her robe on, unbutton her PJ top, and sit in the reclining chair next to the bed. When Meg was settled, Carolyn lowered the back of the chair as far as it would go. She gathered Frog and her tubing and wires, and placed her belly down between Meg's breasts and then pulled Meg's thick, chenille robe over the baby.

Meg closed her eyes and brushed her lips across the top of Frog's flaxen head.

At six-thirty Holly called in a panic. She'd called Meg's room several times and when there wasn't an answer there or on Meg's cell, she was sure something was wrong.

Carolyn reassured her. "Little Miss Frog has been out of bed for almost three hours…Yes, Meg's holding her. You'd better get over here with your camera."

Fifteen minutes later Holly stormed into the Pod. When Carolyn pulled back the privacy screen, Meg smiled her old pre-Mike smile.

"Oh, Meg." Tears streamed down Holly's smiling face.

"Mama, you said she was a miracle and today she proved it."

Holly stooped beside the recliner. "I don't know who to kiss first—you or Frog. You're both so beautiful."

"Carolyn, will you hand my mom Frog's name card and your black Sharpie?"

Carolyn took the green card with the baby frog dancing on a lily pad from the top of the warming bed and handed it to Holly along with the felt-tipped pen.

"Mama, will you cross out baby girl and write Lily Michael Gaynor?" Meg handed the card back to Holly. "Lily belongs to me…I'm keeping her."

As soon as Meg could pull herself away from her baby, she called the adoption agency to inform them of Lily's early arrival and her decision to keep her. Meg began to sob when she hung up the phone.

"What is it, honey?" Holly asked.

"They were waiting to hear from me and waiting for me to sign the final papers before they contacted the family I'd

251

picked out. I can't believe it. I was afraid that I'd offered them the thing they wanted most in life and then snatched it back just when they got their hopes up. I'm so happy I don't have to feel guilty for deciding to keep Lily."

On the way home from the hospital that night, Holly asked Meg what she was going to do about Mike's sister.

"This is something I can't pawn off on Aubrey or Sara Without an H. I'll call her tonight and tell her what is, is, and that she has a beautiful little niece who is Mike's gift to me. I'll leave it up to her whether or not to share the news with the rest of the family."

"I think that's best."

"You know, I kind of feel bad that I told her about Lily. As much as I tried to convince myself otherwise, I told her for selfish reasons."

"Yes, but you proved to Mike's doctors that she's a real miracle. Now, they can submit a research paper on how sperm isn't always killed by cancer and chemo. They may become famous because of you."

"Didn't I tell you that Mike was a stud?"

"Megan Marie!"

"Well, it's true, isn't it?"

Holly lifted her shoulders. "Guess so."

"Hey, what do you want Lily to call you?"

"Grandma," Holly said, thrilling to the sound of the word.

Meg looked at her mother. "You're happy about her, aren't you?"

"Yes. I've been happy about her since the first moment I saw her."

"That's good to hear. So, that means you'll let me share Lily with you?"

"Like in babysit?" Holly looked at Meg and smiled.

"Yeah. And like in, spoil her."

"You don't have to worry about that."

"I'm worried about something else."

Holly stopped at a red light and looked at Meg. "What's that?"

"I want to be able to date and party while I'm young. How can I do that and be a responsible mother?"

"That worries me also. But you've got me, and Charlie and Jessica, two sets of doting grandparents then there's Lisa and Brody and Aubrey and Tia. Most single mothers don't have a support system like yours."

"I don't want to live with you even though I know you'd let me. I'm not going to be a burden on my support system." Meg bit her bottom lip and looked out the side window. "I want and need an education. Aubrey and Tia are off to different colleges in the fall. They're going to live in dorms and pledge sororities and go to parties. I can't grow up if I have to live at home or with my grandparents. I just can't figure out how it will all work."

"Maybe you should start looking at the smaller picture, like the next three months."

Neither spoke until Holly pulled into the garage.

"You're right. It's strange, but I already feel like a mother and I know I want and need an education. It's just going to take a little time for all of this to sink in."

After a week of silence, Jordan spoke—first to Jessica by phone and then to Angie on one of her daily visits. She wanted to know if Charlie hired Angie to visit and seemed pleased when Angie told her she was there out of friendship and concern. That afternoon Jordan showered and washed her hair. While it was still wet Angie styled it into a series of French braids. She dressed in a pair of denim capris and a purple dip-dyed top that Jessica had left for her.

When Charlie arrived that evening she looked at him but didn't smile or stand up. "Hi, Daddy," she said softly while she twisted her hands in her lap.

Charlie opened his arms to her. "Jordie. You look like an angel sitting there."

"Angie fixed my hair. Do you like it?"

"I like it and I love you." Charlie pulled up a chair next to her. "Is it alright if I sit with you a while?"

"Sure. When can I come home?"

"Whenever the doctors give the word."

"I'm ready to start studying with Angie again."

"That's great, honey. I'll call your doctor tonight."

Jordan rocked in her chair and looked away. "Okay," she said. "I want to go home soon."

Charlie talked to her in his usual way and although she didn't speak again that night, she kept her eyes open and glanced at him when she thought he wasn't looking her way. She let him kiss her forehead when he got ready to leave and kept her eyes glued to him as he walked away.

He spoke briefly with the nurse on duty then hurried to the elevator. Once in the lobby, he called Holly.

Jordan's hospitalization lasted two weeks. Charlie drove her home on the same day Meg decided to keep Lily.

Over the next couple of weeks, Lily and Meg thrived. Meg graduated, with honors, from high school and when she visited the NICU that afternoon, Lily had a diploma of her own—she'd graduated to an open crib. Graduation day had also been the first day Lily nursed well enough that she didn't need to be supplemented with a bottle. Lily's doctor told Meg that if Lily continued to gain weight, her last NICU hurdle, she could come home in three or four days. She weighed four pounds, fifteen ounces, and it was just the middle of June.

When Charlie heard the news that Lily was about to come home, he brought Meg a replica of an antique cherry cradle and a matching rocking chair.

"Meg will adore this. But you didn't have to…"

"I want to do more, but my hands are tied." Charlie sat on the recliner.

Holly ran her hands over the smooth wood and rocked the cradle. "What do you mean?" She looked to Charlie then walked over and sat on his lap.

He pulled her to him and she nestled her head in the crook of his neck.

"I'd like to buy us a new house."

"What?" Holly looked up at him.

"When you marry me, we could sell both our houses and buy a new one…with a mother-in-law apartment attached, for Meg and Lily. The apartment would have a separate entrance and a separate garden with a deck. Maybe it could have a second apartment for Jordan as well."

"Charlie. Are you out of your mind?" A slow and sexy smile crept across Holly's face. "If that happens I won't be able to meet you on the deck in my birthday suit. We won't be able to make love under the oak tree."

"You amaze me." Charlie curled his arm around her waist, pulling her closer to him.

"I thought I was going to get to live in your Pittsboro mansion…"

"Just dreaming. I can't live without you. I love you and I need you. My divorce will be final next week. You said you'd marry me. Marry me on the fourth Saturday in June."

"Charlie. What about Jordan? We can't get married before she meets me."

"She's not ready for that. Not yet." Charlie rubbed his forehead. "She may never be ready."

"I'm sorry that Jordan's taken a back seat to Meg and Lily lately."

"We've both been busy. You know that light at the end of the tunnel?"

"Yes."

"I can't see it anymore."

"My God, Charlie. Why didn't you tell me?"

"Holly, you had so much to worry about. I didn't want to add to—"

"Why is everyone trying to protect me? First, my only child spends weeks trying to dispose of her transgressions to protect me, and now you're doing the same thing." She sat up straight. "When I marry you, I marry Jessica and Jordan the same way I expect you to marry Meg and Lily. Either we're going to be a complete family or we're going to be nothing."

"That's why I love you, Holly."

"We need to put all our energy into Jordan now."

"I don't know what more to do. She knows the truth about us. If she'd just stop sulking, then maybe, just maybe..."

"Is she studying with Angie?"

"Yes. Thank God. Angie has been so good for us. They're not quite the pals they were before, but Jordan keeps her nose in the books."

"Then do all you can to be happy and accepting. But, never let her feel abandoned or unloved. And don't let her think I'm taking the place of Jill." Holly threw her hands up. "I'm sorry. I know you're already doing that."

"Sometimes it's difficult. She turns her back when I try to talk about you or Meg and Lily. She talks to Jessica a couple of times a day. It's all very confidential."

"What do the doctors think?"

"They think the progress she's made is remarkable. I'm a little impatient—I want her to snap out of it, but I don't know how to help her do that."

"I know something I can do to help her." Holly ran the tip of her tongue over her top lip.

"You do?"

"Yes, I do," she said and planted a juicy kiss on his lips. "Keep your spirits up. Help you keep a positive frame of mind."

"You don't know just how much you're already doing in that respect."

"Well, I have an idea to improve things, especially since I don't have to pick Meg up for another two hours," Holly said, her smile teetering on seduction.

Charlie brightened. "What's that?"

"Have you ever made love in a recliner?"

18

The green-gray boughs of the great oak bobbed in the warm breeze, casting mottled shade over Jordan and Angie as they studied on the deck. Daylilies, calla lilies, black-eyed Susan, Shasta daisies, foxglove, purple coneflowers, and zinnia spread so brightly across Charlie's gardens that the likes of Georgia O'Keeffe would be inspired to put a brush to canvas. Jordan had been home for two-and-a-half weeks and she'd spent the majority of that time with Angie. Their rapport improved by the day until their relationship was just about back to what it had been before Jordan's hospitalization. Today they were deep into calculus when Jessica drove up the twisting drive, honking her horn to announce her arrival.

"It's Jessica," Jordan said and looked to Angie. "She's home for the summer, but I didn't think she would be here until next week."

Jessica bounced up the stairs dressed in sandals, white shorts, and a neon-green racer-back tank. "Hey, girlies. Surprise."

"You're early." Jordan stood, showing off her new skinny jeans.

"Wow, Jordie," Jessica said, "you look great. How much weight have you lost?"

Jordan smiled. "Not that much, eight or nine pounds, but I'm two inches taller all of a sudden."

"And your boobs...holy cow. My little sister finally has

boobs. Turn around, let me see your butt."

"Jess..." Jordan said protesting but turned around anyway.

"Woo-hoo. That's going to get you some wolf whistles."

"It's my same butt. You've only seen me in baggy clothes."

Angie remained seated, smiling at the animated chat. "Welcome home, Jessica. It's good to see you again." Angie wrapped her ponytail into a bun and secured it with the same band that held her now purple and green striped hair. "We're drinking cranberry-pomegranate lemonade. Want some?"

Jessica screwed up her nose. "Is there any Diet Coke?"

"There's some in the refrigerator. It's what you left the last time you were here." Jordan sat down and picked up her calculator.

"We're almost done here," Angie said. "Is it okay to finish up?"

"Sure. I'll just be inside." Jessica smiled then sashayed into the house like a movie star.

Angie shrugged and picked up the calculus book.

When they'd finished the lesson, Jordan and Angie joined Jessica at the dining room table. The remnants of a peanut butter and strawberry jam sandwich sat on a paper towel in front of Jessica and she held a second Diet Coke.

"So, Jordie, how's life treating you?" Jessica asked in her bubbly voice. "Or should I ask how are you treating life?"

Jordan looked at Angie before answering. "The same as when we talked yesterday. I thought you were going to Daytona."

"No. I decided that I wanted to be here for the divorce next week. I wanted to be here for Daddy and Holly and I wanted to be here when Meg gets to bring Lily home."

"I can't believe they're actually going to go through with it."

"What?" Jessica asked.

"The divorce."

"Jordan, We've been over that a hundred fucking times. What the hell's the matter with you? You're acting like a three-year-old friggin brat. When are you going to wake up? When are you going to stop feeling sorry for yourself? Give Daddy a break. He's certainly given you plenty. I could just spit on you."

"Spit all you want. I can spit back. And I can spit on Daddy too."

"You are out of your mind. I can't believe you. I thought you finally understood things. Daddy should have left you with Mom. He's not your real father. Mom doesn't even know who your real father is and she doesn't even care."

"He is too my real father." Jordan lunged at Jessica, pushed her out of the chair, and landed on top of her. "You're a liar."

Jessica pulled Jordan's hair and pulled her head away when she saw Jordan's open mouth and teeth heading for her neck. "Mom cheated on Daddy and got pregnant. She cheated on him all the time—just ask her." Jordan rolled to the side and Jessica rolled on top of her and began banging Jordan's head against the wood floor. Angie tried to referee, but she couldn't get near the kicking feet and jabbing elbows.

"When are you going to wake up?" Jessica screamed when Jordan boxed her ears, but that just added more fuel and Jessica pinned Jordan's wrists to the floor. "Daddy could've left you at Mom's, but he loves you, you little bitch. When are you going to get it through your fucking skull that Mom kicked us out?"

Jordan wiggled until she got her foot on Jessica's pelvic bone and kicked until Jessica let go. When she did Jordan cried out and kicked violently with both feet. "You're a liar. You're a stupid liar." Jordan yelled.

Jessica lunged at Jordan again and Jordan fought until she could sit up and then she grabbed Jessica's hair, flipped her over, and began boxing her ears again. Jessica slammed her right fist into Jordan's jaw and then her left fist into the side of Jordan's face. "Stop fighting and accept the truth. Mom wants the divorce. She kicked us out. Why can't you see that Daddy is all we've got. Daddy has been mother and father to us all our lives. Mom will never be a mother to us."

When they'd exhausted every obscenity and move they knew they lay across each other totally exhausted and covered in grime, sweat, and blood.

Jordan gingerly stood and reached for her phone. "I'm calling Mom."

"Go right ahead. Confront Mom and she'll tell you the truth." Jessica sat up and leaned against the wall.

Jordan retrieved her phone and punched in her mother's number. "Mom...if I ask you a question will you tell me the truth?" Jordan glared at Jessica. "Jess says that Daddy isn't my real father. Is that true?" She listened for what seemed like an eternity then turned red-faced as tears welled and dripped down her face. She screamed, "I hate you," then hurled her phone against the dining room window causing the center pane to crackle completely from the center to the edges. She fell into a hysterical heap on the floor.

"I'm sorry, Jordie," Jessica said, still leaning against the wall.

Angie comforted Jordan until she relaxed. "Do you want me to call your father?"

"Why didn't somebody tell me...I mean when I was a little girl?"

"There wasn't a need. Mom told me after Granddad's funeral...when she knew it was safe to divorce Daddy."

"Why didn't she tell me?"

"Probably because she didn't want you to know that she'd been screwing around. Mom said she screwed so many guys that she doesn't even know who your father is."

Angie brought both girls warm wet washcloths.

Jordan covered her face with hers then looked at Jessica. "Mom just told me that. She doesn't even know who my father is. She doesn't care."

"I think I should call your father." Angie pulled her phone from her pocket.

"I'll call him. Everything's going to get blamed on me anyway," Jessica said.

"No, I need to do this." Jordan picked up her phone. "Please, Jess. This is between me and him." She looked at the shattered glass on her phone and huffed. "It's dead—just like my old life."

Jessica tossed her phone to Jordan.

"This is an emergency call," Jordan said. "I need to speak with Mr. Prince right away." She listened to elevator music until Charlie answered.

"This is Charles Prince."

"I want to go to court with you when Mom divorces us."

"Jordan? I thought it was Jess."

"It's her phone. She's here. She wants to go too. Will you take us, Daddy? Please."

"If that's what you want, sweetheart."

"That's what I want. I want Mom to see what she gave up."

Charlie swallowed hard. "Well, that's great."

"Will you be home soon? I have so much to tell you."

"I'll be there ASAP. It'll just take a few minutes to finish here. There's nothing more important to me than you right now."

"I know that now. I know everything."

"Everything?"

"Yeah, Daddy. Hurry home, okay?"

"Okay, my sweet girl. I love you."

"I...love you too, Daddy."

On the way to his car, Charlie dialed Holly. For the first

time ever, he got her voice mail. "Damn." He left a message.

When Charlie climbed the stairs up to the deck, Jordan and Jessica met him with their bruises, swollen eyes, bloody noses, bandages, ice packs, and wide smiles. They'd hobbled to greet him and just about knocked him over with their simultaneous hugs. "Look at you both. What the hell? Did World War III just happen?"

"We had a little knock-down-drag-out," Jessica said.

Jordan stepped back a pace, took in a long breath. "Daddy, I love you and I'm sorry about accusing you when I didn't know the facts."

"You don't have anything to be sorry for. I should have told you about Holly long before. I was trying to protect you, instead, I—"

"I should've been mad at Mom, not you. Jessica was right. Mom never loved any of us because she doesn't know how to love. I get that now. I get a lot of stuff now."

"Jordan, I'm proud of you and I love you more than I can say. We've survived and we're going to be alright, aren't we?"

"Yes, we are. Daddy?"

"What, honey?"

"Jessica said that I was being an absolute ass hole and she's right."

"No, Jordan—"

"Yes, Daddy. I was." She looked at her sister and smiled.

"And you're going to tell me about it right now, aren't you?"

"Yeah, but you'd better come in and sit down and promise not to get mad at us."

"That bad, huh?"

"I'm really sorry for blabbing," Jessica said with a pleading look. "But it honestly just came out. I was so angry at Jordan…"

Charlie set his briefcase at the bottom of the stairs then noticed the window. "What happened to that?"

"My phone," Jordan said. "I'll pay for it with my allowance. That is if I ever get one again."

"Hey, Mr. P. How's it going?" Angie asked.

"Great, I think."

"I tried to break it up, but it needed to happen. All of it. If it's okay, I'll leave early and be back in the morning."

"That's fine. Thank you, Angie."

"Kuel," she said as she let herself out.

Jessica sat across the table from Charlie while Jordan stood behind a chair at the head of the table. She hesitated and Jessica encouraged her with a nod and a slight smile.

Jordan spoke deliberately. "I know that you're not my real...my...biological father."

Charlie jerked.

"It's okay, Daddy." Jordan pulled out the chair and sat down. She placed her hands flat in front of her. "Jess told me first...then I called Mom. She told me the truth. I don't care to know who my biological father is...because you're my real father, the only father I want." Tears overcame her and she couldn't finish.

Charlie reached out and placed his hands on hers.

Jessica buried her face in the crook of her arm and sobbed.

"But, you know what, Daddy?" Jordan looked up.

"What?"

"I heard every word you said to me while I was in the hospital. Sometimes, I wanted to say something back but no words would come. I had mixed up feelings and I couldn't figure out how to say what I wanted to say. It wasn't until Jess shocked me with the truth. My biological father doesn't even know about me and my biological mother doesn't want me, but you do. Don't you, Daddy?"

"You bet, princess."

"That's the best thing Mom ever did." Jordan choked out the words with tears streaming from her bloodshot eyes. "She gave me to you."

Charlie pulled Jordan into a tight embrace and they wept together. When they regained their composure Jordan asked, "Will you do something for me?"

"I'll do anything."

Jordan took in a deep breath and let it out slowly without taking her eyes off Charlie's. "Will you take me to meet Holly?"

Holly and Meg exchanged nervous glances when they heard Charlie's car in the driveway. Charlie had called ahead to warn them of the impending visit and both Holly and Meg felt more than a little vulnerable.

"Mama." Meg reached for Holly's hand. They sat on the sofa and waited.

Charlie tapped lightly on the door. Hesitantly, Holly walked to the door, placed her hand on the knob, and let out a long, nervous breath. Meg stood beside her and nodded. Holly opened the door to see Charlie standing between his bloodied bandaged daughters.

Before Holly could speak, Jordan took a step forward. "I'm sorry, Mrs. Gaynor, that I jumped to conclusions. I'm sorry I hurt you and Meg."

As if by magnetic force, Jordan plunged into Holly's open arms and wept. Holly clung to her and kissed her hair. She felt Charlie's hand on her back and knew that the happily ever after part of her fortieth year had finally begun.

And what is, is.

A note from the author

If you've enjoyed reading *Baggage* please consider letting me and my publishers know by posting a review on the Amazon website.

Thank you from the bottom of my heart.

About the Author

Spurred by the gritty Miami sand in her shoes, Shelia Bolt Rudesill traveled the world in a complicated search for a simple life. For forty-five years as a pediatric nurse she dedicated her professional life to the wellbeing of children and acquired a tremendous empathy for those burdened with unreasonable hardships. Pieced together from her experiences, her stories are both gut-wrenching and triumphantly joyful.

Shelia admits to a weakness for dry martinis, evening gowns, and dancing with cats.

Also by Shelia Bolt Rudesill

Transmutare

Child of My Heart

Auspicious Dreams

All The Voices In My Head

Shelia Bolt Rudesill

www.ingramcontent.com/pod-product-compliance
Lightning Source LLC
Chambersburg PA
CBHW060733180626
46819CB00001B/14